Cosmigellan:
Shadowverse

The Sequel to
Cosmigellan: Universe Unfolding
by
Lily Splane

Anaphase Publishing
A Division & Imprint of Cyberlepsy Media

Cosmigellan: Shadowverse

The Sequel to *Cosmigellan: Universe Unfolding*

Copyright © 2003 Lily Splane

ISBN 10: 0-945962-17-7
ISBN 13: 978-0-945962-17-5

Also Available in Kindle Edition:
ISBN: 978-0-945962-42-7

Published in The United States of America
by
Anaphase Publishing
A Division & Imprint of Cyberlepsy Media
4669 Cherokee Avenue, Suite E
San Diego, CA 92113-3654

WWW.CYBERLEPSY.COM

Contents

CHAPTER 1

THE SYMMETRY OF CHAOS

Every exit is an entrance to someplace else.
—Qwiffian Handbook of Sapience

Just as I rise we see it in Cosmigellan's thoughts—a mere visual whisper—seconds before the blast from my weapon evaporates it into the infinite background of spacetime. All that remains is the hissing echo of its scream. The pulsing tube of energy fades. We can't believe what my eyes see.

What happened?

Phased out of here again.

Dammit! I missed? I didn't kill it? Charged with the mania of desperation, I rush to the control console. *Give me the sequence again! Quickly, before it comes back!*

It's not time, Rita.

What the fuck are you talking about? It's time! It's time!

You missed. You can't see zhan; I can. Wait for my cue, will you?

Not now with the lectures!

Zhe won't be back in this wherewhen until the next linear cycle. Zhe's out of phase.

Cos, dammit!

All right, all right. Don't get your tampon in a kink! We must wait twelve linear hours.

My god, why?

The generators are too weak. It could kill you to transport now. Besides, do you really want to leave now? The Hagion will be back; zhe will resume zhaz activities. Can you really leave now?

My blood ran cold, my skin becoming a sheet of goose-pimples. There is something predestined about everything that has happened since I've been guided here. All at once, it makes sense. There is a reason I've been left behind. A plan. And Cosmigellan, in his irritating wisdom, has arranged for me to play an integral part in its unfolding.

You bastard, I think-voice.

You misinterpret my intentions.

You knew.

It has to be this way. You are the solution.

The satisfaction of getting a good punch in at Cos will be denied me, now that he is safe inside my brain.

You need rest. You've been slipping into delta on occasion. If you don't stay alert, we could both dissolve into the substrate of The All That Is.

He's right. As long as I have to wait, I might as well try to rest some. I wince from the residual pain in my left upper arm as I lower myself to the cold hard floor of the ship. There will be no risk in sleeping out here in the open like this. There is only one Hagion left that believes me to still be alive—to the others, I had died days ago alongside my sister.

I know my sleep will be disturbed at best, filled with the replays of how I have come to be in this place, fighting this impossible war, a war I can tell no country's government about—a war I now fight on their behalf.

Hundreds, maybe thousands of the dissidents, two neohumans, and Stella have died since the Honorable Altruist discovered our plan. I'm trying not to let it get to me, the fighting, the waste of lives both Hagion and neohuman, the sick feeling of so much loss. I have to clear my mind of this grief; I need rest.

It is difficult to cuddle up here and close my eyes and not think about the surroundings, that floor, a floor I can't see, only feel. Ever since the visual molychine stopped functioning, it is like living in a ghost world. Though the phase shifters are still functioning, and I don't just pass through solid objects, I can see nothing around me but ethereal shadows and wisps of impressions—like afterimages that burn in the retina and the mind's eye after the lights go out.

My cheek presses against a floor that is invisible, transparent to all of space and the cold whiteness of Antarctica below me. I feel the stars stare at me from all around—I am vulnerable to them as I hover above Earth in this shadow of a ship.

In the last moments before sleep ensnares my weary brain, I wonder why I have come to care so deeply for the human race. I had not anticipated caring. Why should it matter to me what happened to them? They never cared what happened to me. Those fucking infrahumans, so eager to diminish each other, so convinced that they can't triumph unless someone else fails—why should I care about them? They'll just grab you by the ankles, hold you upside down and shake out the pockets of your soul until everything falls out like so much loose change.

But I do care. I don't want to. If I didn't I'd be home now: What was at stake for me personally has been recovered. As much as I've bitched about humanity, its stupidity and cruelty, I find myself reaching out to it when it disgusts me the most. What is society anyway, but controlled rivalry? Maybe I never really believed my own dismal evaluation of the human race—or Cos' either.

Cosmigellan started me on this species dissatisfaction I have internalized so completely. He took my alienation, my fear, and turned it into disappointment in my own kind. That damn alien showed me the truth. He did it just by being so different, by the way he and his kind cared for each other, cooperated without words, or laws, or tyranny. They may have taken human form, but the Phaedrans had not taken on human attitudes. That's what saved them.

They are so *conscious* of their own potentials, their belonging. The One. The quantum mind, each part a representation of the whole. This is what they have, and what humans have sought, fought for, killed each other for all of history; humans have never attained it.

The Phaedrans—neohumans—are what humans aspire to be. They are what every religion dictates humans must practice. They are everything humans are not.

What went wrong? What went wrong with the universal infection? The Phaedrans, originating in another wherewhen, an "otherverse," created this universe as their sanctuary, infusing intelligence into life throughout known spacetime, infecting life with awareness, connecting it to all other consciousnesses. Now that I am part of that, I cannot go back to living as humans do, honoring human values as they are practiced.

The contrast between humans and Phaedran neohumans has become so obvious to me that I scarcely have time for any other than Phaedran friendships. The neohumans have become my family.

Oh, I tried reaching out to humans every once in a while. The last time I sought human companionship—and the way things look for me right now, it really *could* be the last time—I had decided it was just time to howl within my own species. I had been so eager to start a relationship with a human male now that Cosmigellan was, well, noncorporeal.

Had I been able to carry a child to term, Cosmigellan would have become my daughter. When he lost his ability to consciously control his alien-human physiology, he would revert to his native amoeba-like form and die shortly thereafter. My only recourse was to accept his DNA within my brain, his consciousness cradled within me, his life ending, dissolving into the substrate of the All That Is when mine does.

As fine a friend as Cosmigellan is, the relationship is far from complete. My body has many fine memories of physical love with him and it hungered to return to erotic expression. But I had become very selective in my middle years. Cos was very understanding, even encouraged me to find a lover, promising not to interfere or make snide remarks while I enjoyed sex with another in his presence.

But the hope of connecting with a human ever again is a faint memory now. I may never again see the fascinating man I have come to love.

Nancy, formerly a human mate to one of the colony's neohumans, had invited Dr. Childress to the ranch for dinner one evening so that we might meet and start a friendship. I remember catching my breath when I first saw him—his long dark brown hair and green eyes sang a sensuous song so loud I nearly slid out of my chair. And he was an astrophysics professor, to top it off.

Though he seemed unusually nervous—smoothing his long hair, sipping brandy in timed installments, dabbing beads of sweat from his forehead—he impressed me with his unconventional demeanor. He carried himself like a dancer. When he moved he flowed, gently, deliberately, as if a path had already been etched through space for his body. He seemed to pass from one point to another without passing in between. This man not only understood the quantum world, I thought—he lived it. But his pale skin and soft middle betrayed an unathletic lifestyle. He was a man of the mind, a thinker who gave himself to the world, to the universe, not having time to indulge in California narcissism.

Nancy had not steered me wrong.

It was thrilling, just watching him stand there in the middle of the room, as if he owned it and everyone in it. He had everyone's attention as he spoke. I loved being next to him, captivated by his slight English accent, sharing his energy field.

"...star rests within its own gravity well that curves space in such a way that closer planets are obligated to maintain a higher orbital velocity just to keep from spiraling into the star. Those gravitational tides are also responsible for the fact that galaxies group into rotating clusters. Gravity waves are transferred between the galaxies, keeping them together.

"The most peculiar thing about galactic rotation is the speed at which galaxies rotate: There isn't enough visible mass to account for the observed rotational velocity of the outer stars. This, and other effects, compels us to postulate the existence of dark matter."

"And how does dark matter affect gravitational tidal forces? Are physicists still looking for gravitons, or can gravity waves be explained as a wave through a medium—much as sound in water?" I asked.

It took him a few seconds to think of an answer. "Ms. Grayson, I see you've been busy with the books I gave Nancy to lend to you. Have you read chapter thirty of *my* book? Spacetime *is* a medium. Also, you realize of course, that in order to complete the grand unified theory whereby all four forces of nature are one, gravity must be quantized. It's the only way a GUT will work."

"Yes, I agree. But trying to force nature to fit into a predetermined theory is not very satisfying when you have that nagging feeling that gravity is an effect—and *only* an effect, as is mass an effect of atomic velocity and expanding space, and time an effect of an expanding universe. Einstein himself stressed the concept of gravity as an effect. True?"

"Well, I cannot disagree...but quantizing gravity would put it all in a nutshell, now wouldn't it? The beauty is in its simplicity."

"Couldn't gravity be making waves through dark matter, matter that we can't see or detect in any way?"

"It's interesting that you think this," he remarked blithely, continuing his speech. *Aren't you going to answer me? Say anything?*

I looked around and saw approving faces as he continued to speak. I however, had completely changed my mind about him; I did not find him so attractive as I did unimaginative.

A glass of brandy later, the atmosphere of the living room had turned to something inexplicably odd. The tension among the neohumans was palpable. Even some of the outsider humans seemed disturbed by something. The children suddenly stopped their game on the sofa and sat quietly staring into space...waiting. For what? Listeners strayed from the gathering around Childress and looked out windows, at doorways. Someone turned off the stereo and the room was immersed in silence, except for the lone voice of Childress trailing off in mid-sentence. He seemed ill at ease now, though I don't think so much from the general change in mood as from the loss of his small audience.

The human mothers pulled their neohuman children, children that contained the entire personality and memories of each mother's former neohuman lover, close to them. A child's muffled sob escaped into the quiet room.

The changes had been imperceptible at first, but now there was no mistaking it: Alarm, danger clung to the air like blood clots on a silk scarf. I almost wretched, the feelings were so strong now. Something bad was about to happen. I had only seen it happen twice before in the preceding neohuman generation, but I knew it was inevitable: The neohuman children were about to spindle and there was nothing I or anyone else could do about it.

We heard loud thumps, like those of an amplified sage grouse, perhaps forty or fifty feet in the distance, approaching the entrance to the hospice. A jetliner at the local airport with engine trouble?

I looked from neohuman face to human face, all of them riveted on that kitchen door—the same kitchen door my psychotic father had burst through over six years ago, the same door that had allowed his entrance, had steadied his gait as he reached beneath the kitchen cabinet and pulled out a rifle, shooting into the crowd of neohumans, wounding Anthony, who died later. The same door that had allowed that bastard's escape into the night, and from prosecution for his deeds...the very same door I had re-entered to find Jim Grayson all but dead, skillfully poisoned at dinner by my own hand....

I reached into the neohuman minds, searching, finding nothing but unreconcilable terror, and...surrender. *Surrender?* What could be so horrible as to render an entire colony of neohumans completely passive and helpless? That was not the neohuman way—it was not *our* way, the Qwiffian way. I prodded their collective mind, insisted on an explanation. I felt them push at me, close down around me like two-dozen shutters before a storm. Much to my surprise, they had excluded me from their horror and I couldn't understand why.

Cos! Cos, tell me why...why are they...why are you— But Cosmigellan wasn't responding, either. He was part of me and he had deliberately sealed himself off from any contact. Without him, I was completely cut off from The One. Abandoned.

"No! No, don't shut me out! What is it? My God, tell me! What is it? We are Of The One, of The One Mind, The One—" Before I could get my last breath out, hell folded in around me and swallowed me whole.

The screams echoed piercingly throughout the hospice in a smear of frantic, running, climbing, clawing bodies. They were in spindle, and nothing, no one, could stop them. The thumping grew louder, closer. I heard a lamp, lots of glass, shattering over the screams, I spun around to face a frozen and horrified Professor Childress. He searched my face for an explanation, an idea of what to do, where to go. Before I could reach for him, a body crashed into me sending me to the floor hard. Someone stepped on my face, grinding my left cheek into my teeth, filling my mouth with the metallic taste of warm blood. I screamed in anger more than pain. Goddamned them and their uncontrollable spindle! Would they never be able to rid themselves of this one last ancient behavior? Through tear-veiled eyes I looked across the room and saw a pillar of struggling neohuman children, screaming, climbing across the furniture and each other, reaching for the ceiling, trying to *break through.*

The thumping sounds were in the living room now, all around us, coming from nowhere but everywhere. I rolled over to look for Childress, who stood stunned in the middle of the room. I still could see nothing, nothing to account for the neohuman spindle and the dull thudding shrouding us. A sharp pain ripped through my lower abdomen as I struggled to get up; it was so difficult, I felt so heavy. I couldn't move my legs—they were completely flaccid and without feeling. My God, the fall had done what I'd feared all these years:

paralyzed me from the waist down, the spinal cord finally severed by the arthritic growth in my spine.

And the thumping sounds continued. They became softer, nearer, down close to my head—so close, for a second I believed them to be my own heart, beating outside my body. I must be hallucinating—isn't that what happens just before death? Isn't that how the mind distracts itself when faced with its own end?

I rolled off my elbow onto my back, and listened with eyes closed, at the last sounds I believed I would ever hear. My own heavy breathing punctuated with gushing sobs dominated the background sounds of the thumping. Across the room where I knew the disgusting pile of neohumans to be, I heard only sniffles and soft whimpers: Spindle was over for them. Fleetingly I wondered how many had been injured or, Universe forbid, even killed this time. I couldn't be there to help them, ever again.

The thumping sounds surrounded my head at ear level as I lay on the floor. I listened to these strange rhythmic sounds, coming first from the left, then louder from above, then again from the left. A thumping rapport, it seemed. I knew then that I was not alone down on the floor. Something inside me now disassociated from me in my last breaths. A calmness was in control now, an acceptance. If this was how I was to die, then I wanted to be calm enough to *be there* for my last experience.

I needed to say goodbye to Cos, to tell him it was OK, that I was not afraid, but he simply was not there. When I dissolved into the substrate of the All That Is, I would take him with me, and there was no way for me to let him know: He would die with me.

I opened my eyes. The room looked crystal clear. Out of the corner of my left eye, Professor Childress sat hunched over on an ottoman with his head in his hands; it seemed like an inappropriate response. No matter. I would never even learn his first name. He was just a man, and my fascination, just lust.

Suddenly a stinging cold shot through my eyes. I slammed my face shut on the burning, the effort bringing to the forefront the chewed-up inside of my left cheek; my tongue found five deep half-moon cuts. The thumping grew tremendous and frantic...urgent. I had to see, I had to know the source of the deep throbbing sounds. It hurt like hell, but I flashed open my smarting eyes.

The ceiling was gone.

CHAPTER 2

F = g x Mm/r²
(GRAVITY INVERSE SQUARE LAW)

Particles = Energy = Forces
—Qwiffian Handbook of Sapience

Professor Jason Childress leapt the stairs to the university planetarium two at a time. He looked at his watch. It was 4:45 P.M.; he was forty-five minutes late for his class. Hesitantly, he weaved his way through the clogged entrance and down the aisle, taking a few deep breaths to ease the growing panic in his chest. The crowd was unexpected and it pressed in on him like a plastic bag in a sauna. There should have been only a few die-hard students to greet him. There were hundreds, most not his students.

"Professor Childress! Doctor!" a man yelled, waving his arms above the crowd.

Up at the front of the lecture theater, sweaty palms gripping the edge of his desk with all the strength that remained, Childress concentrated on his breathing, on calming a body nearly out of control. Just as he looked up, a young blond man oozed through the squirming mass of humanity.

He thrust a microphone at Childress' nose. "Dr. Childress. What do you know about what's happened with the ozone hole over Antarctica?"

His heart still beat too fast, his mouth too dry to answer. Finally, his English accent thickening, he croaked, "Would you please bring me some water? And, for God's sake, turn the audience lights down."

The young man dashed out the side door, just catching himself with one hand to pull himself back in and press the light buttons.

The theater dimmed except for Childress' desk area. The crowd vanished; only soft murmurs and the creaking of chairs remained to remind him he was not alone. Everything would be

OK now: He couldn't see them.

The events of two days prior, the confusion, the screaming and the voices still ricocheted like jagged stones off the inside of his skull. And Rita.

Rita: sassy, bright, striking long red hair. He had left her unmoving on the floor. Surely someone had seen her to her feet.

The young man returned with a paper cup full of water and instead of pursuing his taped interrogation, seated himself on the floor at the end of Childress' desk.

Childress downed the water and folded his hands in front of him on the desk. "A lousy forty-five minutes tardy and you gang up on me." Chuckles and titters escaped into the theater. He felt more relaxed now. "I've just come from WCPW. I suppose that's the reason for this unexpected reception. News sure does travel fast." He cleared his throat and pulled his elbow-length hair back behind his ears. "We've learned that the ozone hole over Antarctica, previously covering eight point nine million square miles, has increased in size by a phenomenal five hundred percent. That means that all of South America and upwards into Northern Mexico is affected. We don't know why or how this has happened. West Coast Planetary Watch labs will be monitoring the Antarctic from their five satellites for any changes. They've asked me to join them. That means no classes until further notice."

"Dr. Childress," a voice from the invisible audience said. "Can you speculate on how this could have happened and what the immediate effects on algae and phytoplankton growth in the Antarctic area might be?"

"Marion," he said with a smile, "marine biology is your major, not mine. We know of nothing natural or man-made that could account for such a dramatic change. This is an unprecedented occurrence. Though there are scattered and unsubstantiated reports of blind sheep and cattle in South America, there are no documented cases of human blindness or disability. We don't know what, if any, the immediate effects will be on other life—in the Antarctic Circle or elsewhere. I'm sorry, we just don't *know*."

"What does this mean for sports? Does this mean we have to put on SPF forty-five from now on?" another voice asked.

"It's best to stay indoors. I can't recommend any particular sun protection strategy other than that." *The world won't come to a standstill if you can't surf.*

"How long do you think you'll be at WCPW? I mean, like, how far behind will we get in this course? Will we have to take it over?"

"It's impossible to say. I don't know how long this thing will last, or how long they'll need me. It's unusual for them to request an astrophysicist as it is. As for having to take the course over... well, would it be so bad? I'm wounded."

Laughter broke out, interspersed with an occasional "we love you" and "you're the greatest."

With that, Childress rose and went to the lighting panel where he turned up the audience lights. "You'll be notified when the course resumes," he said quickly, facing the wall, hand still on the light controls. "I wish you the best in your other courses." He slipped out the side door onto a bright, empty sidewalk that led to a wide open lawn stretching two acres across the campus. At last, he felt welcome...and safe.

The bright February sun beating on his dark gray jacket brought back the reality of the new crisis, replacing the all too familiar battle with a new panic. This hole—this awful hole—had just swelled up out of proportion inside two days. And why the WCPW needed him, he had no idea. He was a deep space astrophysicist, his expertise extended off-planet, to places humans would never set foot. That last thought comforted him.

After all, humans seemed so adept at making places uninhabitable for so many—even themselves. For all Childress knew, one of the WCPW's own satellites could have blown up over Antarctica, destroying ozone on a massive scale, triggering the expansion of the hole. It would be so like humans, to dismiss and bury their own stupidity in search of mysterious outside influences—a cosmic scapegoat. Human stupidity, however, was more often than not responsible for the demise of other species, and that alone was what drove Jason Childress to accept the position with the West Coast Planetary Watch's Beta Team. He never even asked how much he would be paid.

Childress looped his hair back in a pony tail with a rubber band from his wrist, and vaulted over the door of his 1965 Mustang convertible, settling into the driver's seat. He smoothed his hands reverently over the steering wheel before reaching for the seat belts, fondling them indecisively yet again. Jerking his hands away, he started the engine; it purred like a panther in heat—a thirty-seven-year-old panther, but a panther nonetheless.

Before long Childress had found his way through the five parking lots and onto the narrow back road at the far east end of the campus. Hardly anyone took this road anymore, but for Childress it was the only route, out of three choices, that he'd taken home for the last nine years. It was the only road where he could be sure he'd never see another car, or even one of those new hovercrafts the rich bought their spoiled children to terrorize free airspace. These days all legal levels of airspace, every inch of ground, even a lot of underground, and the surface of every body of water was crawling with humanity. Except for this narrow road.

The sanctuary of his lone house up on the hill welcomed Childress with bright glinting windows and spacious gardens that unfolded back to an aviary behind the house. He had designed and built all of it himself; it was of his fantasies, of his dreams, of his mind.

A quiet Dalmatian pup frolicked up to his car, sniffing the tires, his pant leg, the attache he carried. Childress reached down to pet the dog, speaking softly. "Is it dinner time already, Phoebe? Not yet. It's still light. Come on."

Casually he glanced at his old digital watch. An odd uneasiness gripped then released him. He tapped the watch crystal.

His presence in the house aroused the birds in the aviary just outside the rear picture window, to noisy activity. "You too? A bit impatient, aren't we?" he mumbled. He snapped up the remote control, brought the large video screen on the central stone room divider to life, and flopped down on the big plush couch, struggling with removing his last shoe.

"...delay could affect the playoffs this spring. And the top stories at 6:00: Scientists at the West Coast Planetary Watch laboratories have confirmed through rigorous computer simulations that the ozone hole over Antarctica has stabilized and is not expected to expand further. There is still no data available as to the cause of the sudden inflation of the hole."

"Expectations for an unexpected event? Gimme a break," Childress muttered, absentmindedly folding the puppy's ears into little bundles atop her head.

The news continued. "President Benson spoke at a San Francisco Gay Rights Convention today, stating 'Your lifestyle is helping to fight overpopulation. If only more people were as—

"I've just been handed a bulletin. There is still no data available to explain the unusually bright evening we seem to be experiencing. Reports are coming in from around the globe that some kind of magnetic subspace fluctuation is affecting every clock on Earth. Here it is in the middle of February and it's still light at 6:00 P.M.! Researchers assure us that there's no reason to be alarmed and that the affects are limited strictly to electronics. There is no health hazard. Think of it as an especially powerful solar flare."

Childress clicked the volume down and checked his watch again. He jumped up to check the clock in the hall, then went on into the kitchen to look at the clock on the microwave. They all read approximately the same: 6:05 and 6:06 PM The puppy scrambling behind, skidding on the polished wood floors, Childress rushed on down the hall and into his bedroom where an antique grandfather clock sulked in the corner near his bed. He stared at it in disbelief: It too, read 6:06 PM.

"That explains your impatience with me," he said down at his puppy. "You're right. It's way past your dinner time."

After feeding Phoebe he sauntered out to the aviary where nearly fifty canaries, finches, and parakeets fussed and flitted. The birds were out of both food and water, and Childress worked calmly to fill their feeders.

It was in his yogic duty-trance that it all crashed in on him like a ceiling collapse: The grandfather clock too!

Finishing with the birds, he clamored back into the house and phoned the only person he knew he could ask a stupid question.

After he typed a one-key code, the modem dialed, squealed, and connected. A rotating silvery logo appeared on the screen. "Pacific Rim Quantics," a female voice cooed.

"Sidney Panadel, please. It's Dr. Jason Childress."

Seconds later the modem beeped and the smiling face of a seventy-year-old man drew itself on the screen. "Jason, how *are* you? We missed you at the game."

"I'm sorry. I've been selected by the WCPW and spent a hellish two days getting security clearance. Sidney, that's not why

I called. Nature's gone bloody nuts."

"That ozone hole thing? Damnedest happening."

"That's not why I called, either. Sidney, what's going on with the daylight? It isn't the clocks, it isn't magnetic interference, is it?"

"I...I'm not authorized to discuss that. But, no, it's not."

Childress lurched to a chair to sit down. "Then, what is it? Why is it still light? What is the media covering up?"

"This really isn't a good idea, Jason. It's outside your area of expertise."

"You know something, don't you? Tell me! We've been colleagues for years."

"I can't. It's classified. I'm sorry."

"Classi—" He stared at the screen, at Panadel's stoic expression. The old man's natural friendliness was cloaked. "It's me Sidney. Remember? I promise it won't go past this screen."

Panadel paused, eyes lowered. "Not like this. Go to code twenty-seven."

Childress pushed the keys. A blue line split Sidney's face and squeegeed it in opposite directions, leaving a blank cyan screen. Letters appeared, slow and white:

```
EARTH'S ROTATION RETARDED
DAY = 26.7 HOURS
CAUSE UNKNOWN
```

CHAPTER 3

RESPONSES

Universe = Possibility
—Qwiffian Handbook of Sapience

I choked to consciousness—blind, deaf, chest heaving for precious air I couldn't find. Inhaling a thick tasteless syrup through my mouth, swirls of the liquid curled over my tongue and through my lungs, expanding my chest in a huge wave of effort. I exhaled, pushing the fluid through with my abdominal muscles. This was going to take a lot of concentration. It didn't help that I felt numb, groggy, as if drugged.

I had no other body sensations. But, I sure as hell had lungs— my whole body felt like one big lung. Besides the tremendous exertion of transferring this viscous fluid in and out of me, all I was aware of was an extraordinary feeling of well-being. I was...*happy.* Was this death? This was not what the Phaedrans had told me death would be. There was no sense of expansion, of being the whole universe. In fact, there was a definite sensation of confinement, buoyancy.

Had I been reincarnated? Was I back in the womb? I listened for a distant maternal heartbeat. There was only silence, not even the sound of my own heart beating. Where the fuck was I? *Cos, Cos are you there? Do you hear me?*

Silence. Aloneness. Emptiness. And...I didn't give a shit.

The pressure was unbelievable—not exactly painful. I wasn't sure if I should open my eyes or not. It felt like goggles grew inside my skull and were trying to force their way out through my eye sockets. I knew if I opened my eyes, something I wanted to keep—like, my brains, for instance-- would jettison from my body into this thick medium.

I decided before I opened my eyes I'd try to move some body part. If I really *was* just a lung, then there was nothing left to do, not *even* open my eyes, which I wouldn't have anyway. I willed my fingers to move. They did—I thought they did. I lifted my arms, feeling the heavy fluid tug against them, and reached out in front of me, stretching my fingers, touching...something like glass. It tingled with weak electricity; it was not unpleasant. I felt my face smile then: I was more than a lung.

I spread my arms apart slowly, walking my fingers across the tingly surface, and determined that my container was cylindrical. Interesting. I was apparently in some kind of tube—alive, and not a bit concerned about my close quarters. I then kicked my legs, gently at first, then more vigorously. The fluid gushed upwards into my vagina. Woa, I won't try that again. Wherever I was, I had no intention of partaking in an involuntary Karo syrup douche.

Why was I here, and how did I get here? I didn't remember much happening before this. It was like *this* had always been; there was no before. But, intellectually, I knew differently. I had a whole past with the Phaedran colony. I just had no memory for the few moments before I came to be the contents of this tube.

I had to talk to Cos. He knew everything. *Cos? Cos, answer me. I need to talk to you.*

I felt his presence, at last, but still he would not communicate directly. I was aware of an impression of sorrow and defeat.

It was then I decided to defy the pressure in my eyes and, reaching up to press my fingers gently against the lids, I slowly opened them, ready for their escape.

My eyeballs shot out what felt like a quarter of an inch, into an azure sea. They stayed in their sockets though, and I strained to focus on what lay beyond the glass barrier of my cozy cylinder.

For the first time since I awoke, fear and worse, revulsion, gripped me like a tiger's caress. Bugs! Bugs standing upright on two legs! Huge exposed brains and chartreuse bulbous eyes! Dark roaches circled around my tube, glaring at me as if I were a lab specimen.

My lungs convulsed to keep up with the demands of a heart gone awry. Nausea overtook me as the cylinder seemed to spin while I remained stationary. Weakly, I pressed my hands against the glass, insanely trying to push myself as far back into the tube as I could—away from the leering, spinning spectators before me. I heard Cos' voice just before everything went sparkly, then black.

* * *

Rita? Rita wake up. Rita!

*Cos! Cos, I had the most horrible dream....*I took an easy breath of crisp room air.

It wasn't a dream. They have us, Rita. Rita, I'm so sorry. I have failed you in the worst possible way. It's all our fault—not just mine, but the whole colony's. We buried this threat deep within our minds, always believing we had escaped successfully. We denied to ourselves that the Hagions would ever find us, ever dare follow us. Our denial led them right to us, to you, to Earth.

Wha—? What the hell are you babbling— I opened my eyes and found myself staring up at an expansive clear dome that opened up the heavens as I lay on my back on a flat, hard table. The table was too short: My feet dangled off the end. "Where the fuck am I?" I said aloud. My voice echoed as in an empty room. Turning my head sideways, I saw the far walls of this circular room. It resembled a lounge with a beige leather-upholstered bench that went completely around the base of the wall, a bench that looked far too close to the floor to seat most people. The floor was gray, flecked with glitter or something. I pushed myself up and scooted to the end of the table; it too, was very low. As my feet just touched the floor it felt spongy, almost foam-like against my toes. I noticed I had on my dark blue caftan, but no shoes. "What is this place? A planetarium?"

A Hagion virtual-drive ship. We're several miles above Earth right now. Go to your right and put your hands on the wall, if you don't believe me.

I got up and walked to the wall. Before I arrived there, I realized that there was no pain in my back or legs, no limp. *Cos! Look! I'm not hurting, I'm—* I suddenly remembered the fall, the paralysis. I had been certain I would die. Now, I moved freely, and most remarkably, painlessly. It was the first time in twelve years I'd been pain-free; I'd almost forgotten what it was like. I jumped and ran in a circle. Still no pain—no arthritis at all, even in the hands I clenched tightly. I couldn't help it—I just laughed out loud. *Cos! How has this happened? It's incredible! I've never felt so good! Who did you say these geniuses were? Did they do this?*

Hagions—the Holy Ones. Rita, listen to me! Things are not

as they appear. It's all part of a grand deception, with you as the primary pawn. They've injected molecular machines into you. The machines have restored your broken spine, and will continue to clear out and dissolve any new arthritic growth. But, you must——

It's wonderful! I'm arthritis-free with nanotechnology! Forever!

No, Rita. Listen to me. The machines are wonderful, but the Hagions control the machines—

Somebody has to!

...and now, the Hagions control you.

Control me? What for? I haven't heard anyone ask me for a damn thing.

Yet. Know that the price will be quoted. Soon.

There's not even anyone around. Hey! Maybe I have the whole ship to myself!

I ran to the wall and slapped my palms on it just as Cos had instructed.

"Holy shit!" I staggered back a few steps as the whole wall faded to transparency. As far as I could see, there was nothing but black space and stars. I peered downward. There, white and beautiful below me, lay Antarctica, ignorant and peaceful as a swan. *My Earth. My beautiful Earth. I really am on a ship in space. Look at this ship! I'll bet this is just one room! This ship must be huge! These Holy Ones, as you call them, are obviously very advanced. What do I have that they could possibly want?*

They will take from you the most valuable thing you've ever had: the Phaedran colony. They will have us. And you will help them.

Oh, Cos! I laughed out loud again, this time at the absurdity of his fears. *What do they need with Phaedrans? Just look at this, Cos! Their technology is astounding! Molecular machines, that tube I was in, that shit I was breathing....* Then I remembered their faces, staring in at me as I thrashed in my liquid prison. *Well, maybe if I understand them more, their appearance won't be so disarming. They had to have had a good reason to put me in that tube—probably to repair my back and let it heal without pressure on it. And a fine job they've done! Molecular machines—my own personal army of surgeons. Imagine that! And what are the chances of an alien ship being of such a precise temperature for humans that the ambient air could be perceived as having no temperature at all? It's wonderful!*

Rita, I hope you realize that when whatever drug they've pumped you full of wears off, you'll have a whole different outlook on our situation here. At least, I hope the hell you will.

Drugs? Hell, I'm on a natural high! How wonderful to be out of pain. At last! Look Cos, look! And I had to show him how happy I was by running through the room and springing up like a dancer, legs apart, free, free like a gazelle!

Yes, drugs. Why do you think when you tried to contact me, that you didn't hear me respond? Your receptiveness was—in a way, still is—drugged out.

I'd know if I was drugged. I'm not, I tell you!

There was quite a pause before I heard more from him. Meanwhile, I was having a great time bending, stretching, kicking, moving in every way I hadn't been able to move in years.

Rita, he said in a low thought-voice. *I'm going to try and calm myself and wait out this chemical stupidity you seem to be enjoying so much. By the way, not that you'd ever think to ask in your condition, but no one in the hospice was hurt-- except for you. The children and the others are all right. When the reality of our situation hits you—and it will—call me. I'm going to my room.* I felt a twinge of remorse that quickly dissolved to relief that the neohumans were unharmed, then my mood mutated to mirth. I giggled. *Oh, Cos, you shilly sit! I mean...What room? My brain doesn't have rooms!*

That's what you think.

CHAPTER 4

SACRIFICES

Electrons maintain their own territorial energy levels
and can't collapse into each other.
—Qwiffian Handbook of Sapience

It felt like a miniature demented tree-surgeon with a chainsaw was inside my head hacking on every dendrite. It hurt to turn over, to blink, to breathe too deeply. My time-out from the euphoria that had seized me must have turned into a nap, and I had no idea for how long. God, I feel like shit. *Cos, are you there?*

Of course. Drug hangover? I told you so.

Don't start with me. I'm at a disadvantage with this headache. I sat up; unexpectedly, the throbbing in my head eased. The lighting in the lounge was soft; I hadn't noticed it before, but it didn't seem to have any definite source: It was just *there*. I damn near broke my ankle when I swung my legs to the floor from the cushioned bench where I sat: I forgot how close to the floor it was—not more than a foot.

How long was I asleep?

Twelve linear hours. Give or take five minutes.

Twelve! Jesus. Has anyone been here? Have we been alone all that time?

No, we haven't. We aren't now.

Huh? We're being watched? From where? I whipped my head around to look for two way-mirrors, cameras. Big mistake. It took several seconds for my brains to catch up with my skull—a serious case of the drunkard's stay-behinds. I heard myself moan.

I've been instructed to...to direct you to the panel on the wall behind you.

Instructed? By whom?

The...the Hagions. They—

My God, how could they know you're in here? How could

they?

They know. You told them. You have recently acquired the nasty habit of talking in your sleep. Now, will you do as I ask? We don't have much time, I'm afraid.

What did that mean? His thought-voice conveyed a restrained sadness. I felt my stomach fold in on itself. *OK,* I agreed, and went to the panel, bending down to reach it. It was an array of two dozen oddly marked keys. *Uh, what do I do now?*

Push in the half-circle key and hold.

I did. *Nothing's happening. What's supposed to—*

For an insane instant the whole lounge blinked out of existence and the only thing between me and infinity was my caftan. Before I could say another thing, I found myself standing in the center of a giant metallic parabola, perhaps thirty feet in diameter, sides so steep escape would be an impossibility. And escape was exactly the first thing to come to mind, but there were only a few inches of flatness in which to maintain a sure footing. The sides were too smooth, too curved to be scaled in bare feet. The metal's cold seared through my bare soles and rushed headlong to the core of my being.

A booming thud accosted me from somewhere up on the rim. The effect was like being inside an enormous speaker. The thunder seemed to bounce off the sides of the dish and reverberate back into my body. Startled, I clasped my hands over my ears and promptly slipped and fell on my ass from the sudden motion. The cold surface made my anus dive deep into my body, cramping me.

I suspect the words "anal retentive" have taken on a new meaning.

Shut up, Cos. Easing to my feet, I looked up into the blue-gray gloom, just to the rim of the dish about fifteen feet above my head. The air looked smoky and I could barely make out the muted figure of someone...some*thing* standing at the rim, peering down at me, booming and thumping.

Bite down, Cos thought-voiced.

What?

Bite down. The lingual decoder-transmitter has been implanted in your upper-right wisdom tooth.

I bit down so hard my head ached all over again. The thumping dissolved and was replaced by coherent, carefully enunciated English.

"...are not to consider yourself our prisoner. On the contrary, your role holds more importance than anything you have ever done. Vtekdao requests your assistance in implementing The Purpose. I humbly suggest your enthusiastic cooperation will result in glory beyond imagining, for you will return the universe to the natural order. And when this is done, you will be no less than worshipped. Idols will be erected in your honor for eternity. You will be known forever as the Savior of the Hagion race."

What kind of delusion is this? "I'm in the psychiatric ward, right? Are you a patient?"

"I am Vnoim, Second Flagellant to the Honorable Altruist."

Did he say "Flagellant"? Kinky. "Where am I ? Where is this place?"

"This place is Lolbah."

"Are we still on the ship or somewhere else?"

We're still on the ship, Rita. This wherewhen was phase-shifted to us when you pressed the button.

"What exactly, is *The Purpose?* And why, for chrissakes, do you think I know anything about it and can, or will help you?"

"It is no trivial undertaking, The Purpose. You, Ree-tah, have been chosen. You are solely responsible for its success. It is by the divine will of Hope that you have been sent to us."

"Sent to you! I was minding my own business at a party when I fell and was whisked away to this place! No one asked me if I wanted to go!"

"Vtekdao reveals the divine will of Hope. Hope has sent you to us."

"No one sent me! I was abducted! I can't help you! I don't fucking want to help you!"

Rita! Do not taunt him, he is only an instrument of the Honorable Altruist. He has been told who you are, and that's what he believes.

"Of course you will help us. You are weary from the conditioning and the surgery. And hungry, no doubt. Once you rest and take sustenance, you will remember your agreement...your important mission."

"What agreement? Goddamn it! What do you bastards think you're doing?" I hyperventilated a few seconds before going on. "I really appreciate the work you've done on my back and everything, but I don't have anything for you. Don't you understand that?" Right then I just lost it and began to cry, more out of frustration than anything else. "Goddamn you! Goddamn you!" I yelled through my tears.

Rita don't. You don't know what you're dealing with.

They're not going to hurt me! They think I'm their stinking messiah.

Look where they have you. Could you leave if you chose to? Would a savior be treated as such?

I had no chance to consider an answer before I found myself hovering in empty space for an instant and saw through eyes heavy with tears that they had sent me to a different room. Or, if it was true what Cos said, I stayed in one "place" while these rooms were brought *to* me; that would be a hard concept to digest.

There was a bed—long enough for me, I was relieved—and something resembling a round computer CRT imbedded in what I decided I would call the north wall. Below the computer was a metal bowl of...I looked closely...an attempt at lasagna. Not smart, putting hot food in a metal bowl. I leaned in to sniff it—no aroma at all. *Hmm, lasagna. They even know your favorite food. All of a sudden, I'm starved. Is this safe to eat?*

Yes. But you will be disappointed—as will I.

I picked up the utensil—a bizarre affair resembling a curling iron—and stabbed at the square of quasi-lasagna, then ensnared a corner of it with the clip on the utensil and shoved it in my mouth.

My brain must have frosted over.

Panicked, I swallowed. Right then, I knew I had just downed a bolus of hell frozen over. It sluggishly seared an icy path down my esophagus and crash-landed in my stomach like neptunium at critical mass—taking forever to fade to a reasonable temperature.

"Christ!"

I take it, that was not pleasant.

That, Cos, is one friggin' understatement. I think their messiah needs to command a warm meal. What do you think?

To summon a Hagion press the key that looks like a tornado.

Did you learn all this while I was being interrogated in my sleep? How do you know so much?

I remembered; I didn't want to. It's all come forth in a flood— like it happened yesterday. We Phaedrans have a long history with the Holy Ones, as you well know.

But, how can you know of their present technology? Things have to have changed in fifteen billion years.

For the Hagions, technology is arrested. They've spent fifteen billion years in life-suspension—until now. They have found their destination: That destination is us.

My God, why are they after you? Why won't you tell me why they're after you? I thought-voiced, pressing the tornado key on the wall console.

I don't think it's wise to—

"I am C'toikth. The reason for my presence?"

I caught myself on the edge of the desk as the figure materialized, almost subliminally *happened* before me from nothingness. Or had the room and myself materialized around *it?*

The first thing I noticed was that I towered over it but felt dwarfed by its bilious yellow-eyed stare. Those pupils-- they twirled like little propellers; I knew if I stared too long they'd own me. The second remarkable thing was its huge exposed oblong two-lobed brain. Its chest pulsed with the words it spoke. The teeth looked like little boulders, gray and uneven, and were exposed—lipless. The upper appendages-- six-digit hands, armless and helpless—jutted out from the torso. Those hands could not possibly be functional: They would never meet in any imaginable contortion. All of that, every bizarre feature, was set in a housing of dark blue chitinous shell, but I got the feeling if I touched it, it would "give," revealing a soft center.

"I, uh...The food's too cold. It's painful. Could you warm it up?"

"To what temperature?"

"Oh, I dunno. A hundred degrees?"

"It is done. I am honored you have summoned me. My function is actualized."

Accommodating creature, he was. I looked over at the bowl— its contents boiled furiously, dissolving into an orangish mush. "Fahrenheit, I meant."

"Please be hasty in taking your nutrition. You must be prepared for The Procedure. I will return in twenty human-minutes."

"Procedure? What pro—"

He had vanished.

Cos, do you know what he's talking about?

Eat, Rita. There's no sense in going over the details, since it's inevitable. You will not be harmed, nor will I.

What's inevitable? Little is inevitable. Isn't that what we Qwiffians believe? Dammit, tell me! I felt his refusal—an impression of arms crossing over a defiant chest, shutting me out. *I really hate it when you act like that.* I waited for the bowl to cool before picking up the utensil, dipping into the thick, unappetizing gruel; it looked like it had already been eaten. At least there was an aroma now, though not one that matched what I had believed was lasagna. I tasted it: The flavor was completely out of place, more like split-pea soup than cheese, tomatoes, and herbs. If I ate it with my eyes closed the visual signals wouldn't argue with the taste; I quickly devoured the whole bowlful before I had a chance to change my mind. A calmness enfolded me; it was hard to tell if it was just the leveling of blood sugar or the Hagions had drugged me again.

It wasn't important. It was time to explore this confining wedge-shaped space they'd put me in.

The bed was soft and appealing. Across the room the dumb stare of the computer screen beckoned further exploration. Reluctantly, I left the bed to study the two rows of twenty-four iconed keys; I could only guess their function. I didn't think it would be a good idea to start punching them at random. When Cos tired of his tantrum he'd clue me in.

The really bad thing about the room was that it had no windows, as well as no door that I could see; that was especially disconcerting. Remembering how the window was in the lounge, I walked the room patting the walls, looking for an opening of some kind. The "west" wall became suddenly transparent, revealing all of space, and below, the same scene of Antarctica as in the lounge. It was unnerving, but preferable to the claustrophobic feeling of before, so I left the wall transparent as I continued my discoveries.

Just at the foot of my bed in the "east" wall a seam appeared to my touch. It was apparently a door, but with no way I could figure, to open it. It reminded me of a police car—no handles on the inside. The effect was not reassuring.

Patting the south wall created an opening into what I assumed was the bathroom, though it was no bathroom I'd ever seen the likes of before. Again, the lighting had no specific source—the room just glowed when I went in. Behind me, the wall returned to solidity where the doorway had been. In a nervous impulse, I rushed back through again just to reassure myself that I could.

Back in the bathroom, I saw ahead of me a stall, dark and ominous. Standing at the edge of the darkness, I pushed my hand in: Nothing happened. I reached down, hoping I'd find a floor: I did. The stall came alive with light and five Ritas. I went in. All around me, on every wall, including behind, above, and below, my own reflection gawked back at me in six different views. Maybe the Hagions were a vain race, or so insecure as to require constant visual validation that they existed. I dubbed this place the *Ego Box*.

I bounced through the rear wall back into the bathroom. To my right stood a fountain set in the center of a circular grid where I presumed water drained. The whole affair was installed in a rectangular marble depression. This must be the shower.

Across from the shower, imbedded in the floor, grew a rather low golden funnel resembling a tuba. I tittered. Was I to shit in a tuba? I hoped I'd find out for sure before I went ahead and used it for that very purpose.

Satisfied with the facilities, I slipped back through the wall into my quarters. I came about three inches from crashing into a five-foot-tall roach.

"You're back. So soon," I sighed.

"It is time for The Procedure. Follow me." It turned on spindly many-jointed legs, click-clacking across the floor on hoofed four-toed zygodactyl feet.

"Wait a minute! What procedure? I'd really like some details here." I followed the Hagion through the wall, feeling it give around my body like warm bubble gum, into a tunnel-like corridor that had an obvious grade to it. "Where are we going? How come I have to walk this time? Can't you just zap our destination to us, like before?"

"This level is the Ignorant living quarters. We will be on the Society level soon, and then proceed on to the Procedure level. You will need to remember the ship's configuration, so please remain alert."

Cos, I don't feel good about this. Where are we going and what for?

There's nothing I or anyone can do. In spherical time, it's already happened. Neither of us will be—has been—harmed. Just remember: Whatever happens—has happened—I will always love you. You will always be with me.

Are...are you saying goodbye? Cos, please! Can the dramatics!

You will know, soon enough. No sense in getting upset in advance. You will need your wits about you.

But I *was* upset. I wanted to scream. I wanted to beat the creature ahead of me senseless. Something real unpleasant was going to happen to me against my will. But from the impression I got, it was going to be a lot worse for Cos than for me.

I stopped.

The roach kept going, clicking its way up the low-grade spiral. It then spun around—I didn't expect that it could move that fast. "Please quicken your pace. Vtekdao dislikes delays."

"I'm not going anywhere," I said, folding my arms under my breasts.

"You *are.*"

"I'm *not.*" I rocked back on one hip, standing fast. The tunnel flickered.

"You *have.*"

I stood beside the low table in the big beige and gray lounge, a hundred pairs of bulbous ochre eyes glaring at me, their flower pupils twirling. I had to look down, avoid the hideous spinning of those black pinwheels. For the first time, I realized that I was not in control.

"Ree-tah," a gentle low voice commanded from the group of Hagions seated on the bench against the curved wall. The large Hagion in the middle unfolded its many-jointed legs and rose. "I am Vtekdao. Hope has chosen you to implement The Purpose. Destiny will be fulfilled."

"Yeah, yeah. So I've heard. Just what *is* The Purpose?"

"To restore universal order."

Christ. "Your answer has no meaning for me. Would you mind terribly, expanding on that?"

"You will remind the Benefactors of their duties and rightful place, and bring them to us. In return, the Benefactor Cosmigellan—as you refer to zhan—will be returned to you unharmed."

About then, I could have sworn my brain spasmed.

This sounds ominous, Cos. What does he mean? "Who are these Benefactors? I don't know anyone by this name. Why do you think I can, or *will* convince anyone of anything? I'd just like to go home, if you don't mind."

"You refer to the Benefactors as Phaedrans. The Phaedrans must be restored to us. We cannot take them because of their self-destructive behavior when fear overcomes them...." He stopped speaking all of a sudden and froze. Wet membranes slid from the inner corners of his eyes and quivered at half-mast for maybe twenty seconds. Everyone just sat there, waiting. Was this roach epileptic or something?

"We do not wish them damaged," he continued. "You, Ree-tah, are greatly respected and trusted by your colony. They will do as you ask without quarrel, without incident. Your cooperation will fulfill The Purpose."

"Wait a minute. They don't *belong* to me. I don't govern them. I won't tell them what to do with their lives—I can't. From what I understand, they've been running from you since this universe began. They don't want anything to do with you. They hate you, don't you know that?"

Vtekdao's eyes expanded alarmingly, and his torso flushed a brilliant light blue. Was this anger? Fear? Amusement?

"The Purpose must be realized. It is the will of Hope."

I never got a chance to say another thing. Before I knew it, two Hagions had approached from behind with dangerously long tweezers—I felt a sharp sting on the back of my neck—and my whole body went rigid. I couldn't even move my eyeballs.

Instantly I was surrounded by a swarm of roaches; the ceiling rotated into view as I felt my body being placed on the table. Vtekdao twisted and leaned over me, unwadding his hand to place a small but alarmingly heavy silver sphere on my forehead.

A vacuuming sensation built to an agonizing suction, tearing at my brain, turning it inside out, pumping it dry of something I was sure I needed.

Cosmigellan's scream sheared through my head.

My God, what were they doing to him? I'd never heard him scream like that before. They were hurting him! Cos lied to me. Why would he do that?

Cos! Cos, what's happening? Are you OK? Say something!

There was silence now.

Mute tears ran down my face, pooling in my ears. I couldn't help him. I couldn't stop *them*. A feeling of emptiness possessed me, leaving me as hollow as a discarded egg shell—my very reason for being, ripped from my brain and taken...where?

CHAPTER 5

CONCESSIONS

In order for an electron to jump from one level to another,
it must "know" its own path as well as the paths not taken.
　　　　　　　　　—Qwiffian Handbook of Sapience

Out of frustration I slammed my fist into the wall with a wrist-wrenching thud. It was all my fault. If I hadn't been so tired and talkative in my sleep, the Hagions never would have known Cosmigellan was with me. I had serious doubts now that he wouldn't be harmed. My attempts to contact him through The One were fruitless—he simply would not answer. Cos had tried to warn me when we first came here, but I wouldn't listen. Now the whole colony was in danger.

I paced my small wedge, spending the adrenalin that gushed forth with my every regret.

So much for personal glory—all that spewage about being worshipped, idolized, was supposed to have been some kind of incentive to get my cooperation in turning over the colony to them. They expected me to be thrilled with my new role: I should have pretended I was thrilled. When I didn't respond appropriately, they took Cos as insurance.

No wonder Cos, all of the Phaedrans, had just surrendered to the Hagions. There was no resisting Hagion control when they could just zap you where they wanted you to be, paralyze you in mid-thought, take things from you without your permission. It was beginning to look pretty hopeless.

Hagion dominance explained Cos' obsession with freeing me of my abusive father so many years ago: It was born of his past relationship with Hagion oppression. He had delighted in psychologically tormenting Jim Grayson, had made it his reason for being. Now I understood why.

It was my turn, I decided, to repay the favor.

What I didn't comprehend was where Cosmigellan's strength had disappeared to. Where was it now that he needed it not only for himself, but for the colony, for me? Why was he so passive? It didn't make sense.

The Hagions called the Phaedrans "The Benefactors." I'd have to find out what exactly they were supposed to benefit: What *The Purpose* really was.

That's not all I'd have to find out. If in fact it was intended that I have free run of the ship, then I'd better start learning everything I could about my captors. Know your enemy; as far as I was concerned, the Hagions *had* graduated from unknowns to enemies.

Fortified with a growing confidence, I touched the east wall, felt the density change, and slipped through unimpaired. I hadn't taken five steps before I heard a rhythmic thumping from my right. Beside me calmly walked a Hagion, just thump-chattering away, hands gesturing in intriguing wadding and unwadding motions. I bit down hard to activate the lingual decoder; it must have got turned off when I went rigid during Cos' extraction.

"...level is Vtekdao's chambers and the very heart of Hagion governmental procedure."

"I'm sorry, my decoder was accidentally turned off. Would you mind repeating?"

"I merely enlightened you to the function of the levels of Lolbah. It is better I show you."

"Uh, I don't mean to offend, but you all look alike to me. Which one are you?"

"I am C'toikth, Obligant to the Honorable Altruist—whoever zhe may be."

Ah, yes. Of molten lasagna fame. "You mean Vtekdao."

"I will always be an Obligant to the Honorable Altruist; perhaps Vtekdao will not always be the Honorable Altruist. The upcoming election may prove otherwise."

Did I detect a certain sarcasm in its voice? "You don't like Vtekdao?"

"My feelings regarding Vtekdao are unimportant. The next election will decide all. The Ignorants will do the honorable thing for our society."

Obligants. Ignorants. Jesus, what kind of strange hierarchy did they have here? "Obligants don't vote? If you call it voting...."

"Only Ignorants may vote. We have arrived on level five. Enter here." C'toikth turned sideways and pointed a long first finger at a red dot on the wall, freezing in mid-action for about twenty seconds. Jesus, another petit mal sufferer. I was glad to rest my legs. The walk had been all uphill, and apparently in a spiral curling to the right. C'toikth recovered from his fugue and pressed the dot.

What I saw when I went through the wall with the blue roach had my whole attention now. My heart skipped several beats.

"Cos!" I gasped. He had been completely restored to his human body, a body he had been forced to give up that he might save himself from certain deterioration, reversion to his native amoeboid form, and ultimately, death. For six years he had existed as a DNA packet within my brain. For six years I had longed to look into those Hershey-syrup eyes, to wrap myself around his physique. And here he was, shrouded in one of *my* caftans, no less, recreated in every detail—I hoped.

But something important was missing from those dark eyes. The fire in them was gone, burned out by an oppressive resignation.

I rushed to hug him, but a Hagion quickly intercepted my embrace by stepping between us. If I'd had my boots on, I'd have stomped the roach into an unrecognizable goo right then and there.

"This Benefactor is not yours. You have not permission to handle zhan," Vtekdao said in his distinctive baritone voice.

His whole face smiled, filling me with joy. "Cos, are you OK? Have they hurt you?"

"I am well. And you, my beloved Rita?"

"Ak! The psychosis of *love!* Spare us!" Vtekdao bellowed, then said to a subordinate, "Take the Benefactor to Procedure. I have special plans for zhan." He returned his bile glare to me, pupils whirling.

"Honor your agreement and zhe will be returned to your custody. Violate it, we keep zhan."

"What agreement? I don't remember agreeing to anything."

"You will convince the Benefactors—the Phaedrans—to return with you to Lolbah. It is the will of Hope."

"You're sending me back down?" That came as a surprise. "I take it I'll be escorted."

"You will go alone, unimpeded. We do not wish to distress the Benefactors with our presence."

"How can you be sure that once I'm back on Earth, I'll do as you demand?"

"Do it, Rita!" Cos yelled over his shoulder as he faded through the wall with a Hagion at his heels.

"Your sickness for Cosmigellan nearly guarantees it. Nearly. To further ensure your loyalty, an Executioner has been implanted within your flesh that will kill you after a pre-determined time. You must return to the ship to have it removed.

"Gather the Benefactors and yourself in a closed circle; all must be touching to transport back here. Do not be so foolish as to attempt to bring anything back with you, especially weapons. Anything not of your flesh will be out of phase when you are put back in phase with Lolbah—and will simply pass through, falling back to your planet's surface. You do anything other than what you've agreed to do—you die. You have half a sextet—three human hours, starting...now."

I hung for a second in space, Antarctica below me, before I felt my bare feet touch solid ground again.

I stood, knees weak and shaking, in the kitchen of the hospice. I expected to be naked, but found my caftan intact. Maybe that phase thing worked in only one direction.

Two men sat at the dining room table sipping something steamy. In the living room an audience of human mothers embraced their neohuman children as if saying goodbye. No one spoke. I got the feeling they had been expecting me; Cos had probably told them through The One that I was coming back—and why. I wasn't really sure what to say.

I noted the time on the microwave clock; one twenty-five P.M. "I...I...uh, guess you know why I'm here."

"We know," Anne said, hugging her teenage daughter Jaynah close, a daughter born with the fully conscious personality of her former neohuman lover, Gilbert. Six-year-old Jaynah looked all of sixteen, developmental acceleration an unexpected consequence of Phaedran-human DNA conjugation.

"Stella's been looking for you," Anne continued, bitterness spiking her voice. "The children accept Stella; they're her friends. How will you explain this to her?"

Stella. I didn't have time to deal with Stella's neediness now. But once the colony was transported, where would Stella go? Who else could be there for her as we were there for her?

I hated my little sister just then—her alcoholism, her helplessness, the empty place in her that sapped the good out of everyone around her. I hated myself for not being able to help her, for not loving her as I loved the neohumans. I couldn't think about her now. Not now. Not ever again.

"I don't know how to say what I have to say..." My voice quavered and my face flushed hot.

One of the men at the table stood, pounding his empty cup on the table. He was Nancy's brother, Bob. "What makes you think you'll get away with this? Why should we listen to you? Who the hell do you think you are, little lady? No one's going nowhere. Got it?"

"Bob, you don't understand. They've got Cos, they've implanted a device in me that will kill me just after four this afternoon. I—we—have no choice."

He barked a short laugh. "Why should we believe you? You're a Goddamn traitor! You know what we do to traitors don't you? Same thing we do to anyone who breaks the codes!" He stepped closer to me, his voice lowered. "Hit the road, little lady. You're no longer wanted here."

"Bob!" Nancy broke in. "You know we've discussed this for two days. You promised to keep your mouth shut. Rita's doing the best she can. She...has to do it." Nancy shot me a quick glance; I barely caught it.

Bob mumbled something under his breath as he stared through his sister; I only caught the last part of it: "...women weren't in charge, it'd all be over. We could just storm the ship, catch 'em by surprise," he said, hitching up his pants and storming out the kitchen door.

I had the sick feeling Bob might be right. How could I tell the people I'd lived with and shared thoughts with through The One for six years, that I was about to betray them in the most horrifying way imaginable? How could I tell them that to save my own lover, my own skin, I was about to turn them over to a race of oppressors they managed to escape and remain hidden from for fifteen billion years? I should just reach into the drawer, pull out a knife and kill myself: I would be as good as dead inside without my neohuman family.

"The children will go with you, if that is what must be," Anne said coolly. "We don't like it, however, and we don't relinquish them willingly. It's just that...." Anne finally broke down in tears. "They insisted! They *want* to go! They said it's the Ancient Way! My God, I don't understand it! How can you all just give up like that?" she wailed, looking to each child's expressionless face, then back up at me. "And how can *you* cooperate with those monsters? What's wrong with you?"

I felt sick. Shame boiled up from the past: An image of my father sneering, pointing an accusing finger at his "bad seed."

Jaynah hugged her mother. "It's OK. We can't fight it. It's better if we just go."

"It may not be permanent," I offered. "I'm sure if we all work together, we can find a way to...." But I didn't believe it myself. There was a time-bomb ticking away somewhere inside me and if I didn't deliver, I'd be history. And knowing the Hagions as little as I did, I knew they'd find some other way to come harvest their Benefactors once I was dead. I managed to convince myself that my staying alive might be the only way to reverse this nasty turn of events. I just didn't have any good ideas right at this moment, but that didn't mean I wouldn't ever find a solution.

The neohumans, after all, seemed all too eager to submit to the destiny dictated by the Hagions. The neohumans believed that it was right somehow. The last words Cos said to me still rang in my ears: "Do it, Rita." It was completely against the Qwiffian codes: self-sacrifice for it's own sake was a crime in our isolated society on this southern California ranch. The only honorable action was to live to one's potential—not surrender one's values, everything one stood for, to the whims of another. The Ancient Way—submission to axioms, to fate—no longer held power. Or so I was led to believe.

Who was I to interfere? Still, how could I ever live with what I was about to do?

The Hagions had simply claimed the neohumans as their property. The Benefactors, they'd been called. How ugly. How utterly disgusting to possess another.

It *wasn't* going to happen! Not while I was still alive! "Where's Macro?"

"Painting. I'll call him," Anne said, closing her eyes.

Through the hall sauntered a tall, lean, dark-haired teenage boy: one of the masculinized females. When Abrazuver had transferred to Julianna, he chose to remain male.

"Macro, how are you?" I said, holding out my arms. Macro eased into them, returning the hug. "Have you had time to process our situation? Do you understand what's going to happen?"

He paused before speaking. "I th-think s-so. Tell me." His speech was improving. Julianna's death during delivery had left Macro with an unusual kind of brain damage that not only affected his speech, but had shut down the corpus callosum, so he had in effect two separate brains, and as a result, some remarkable information processing talents—the reason for his nickname "Macro." I held him, never able to forget the day he was born, a fully conscious being trapped in an infant's body, emerging from Julianna's fifty-one-year-old womb, giving him a second chance at life, only to result in her death. That day would be with us all forever.

"Macro, listen carefully. When you have the whole program, repeat it to me. It's important that I know you understand."

"Oh-k-k-kay. Go ahead."

"Hagions arrived. Hagions keep Cosmigellan. Hagions want Benefactors. Rita forced to help Hagions. Hagions return universe to previous order. If not, Rita dies. End program."

He looked up at me, a glimmer of something mysterious churning behind those crystal eyes framed by straight dark hair. I had to smile, seeing Julianna in his features, and knowing now that she had not been a natural blond.

Macro pushed away, a wild look in his eyes. "We m-*must* go. No choice."

He understood. No need to put him through the drill of repeating the statements. My heart sank. For a minute I hoped he wouldn't understand, would remain ignorant of his fate. "That's right." I pulled him in close. "I'm so sorry," I whispered. "When I promised to care for you, I never imagined I'd be up against the Hagions."

I still had time to try to talk some sense into these passive neohuman reborns. I called a meeting where I could have everyone's attention at the big dining room table. Bob came back in, sneaking to a chair at the far end of table.

"We have to fight the Hagions, don't you understand? I know there has to be a way. Now, I don't have much to work with yet, but

I've seen a few things that could help us—weaknesses."

"From what I can gather, the one called Vtekdao has absolute rule; the other Hagions defer to him without question. That is, I *think* they do. I'm not so sure about the one called C'toikth. I can't explain it, but I detect some animosity towards Vtekdao from that one. C'toikth told me there'd be an election soon and I got the feeling he and a class of Hagions called Ignorants—the only ones allowed to vote—would just as soon see Vtekdao out on his ass.

"Another thing: A couple of the Hagions suffer from some sort of absence epilepsy. Every once in a while they just stop and their eyes flutter. When they come out of it twenty or so seconds later, they continue speaking or doing whatever it was they were doing and don't acknowledge that anything odd happened. I don't know if any of the others have these seizures, but I'm hoping they do. Twenty seconds is a long time—enough time to do damage. I need to know more about their values—if individual lives matter to them, and if kidnapping or even death, if necessary, would be taken seriously. Do any of you know? Do you remember anything about them that could be useful to *our* purpose?"

The children shook their heads. "No one remembers," Darwinia said, more in defiance than apology.

"Important f-f-facts. Delay t-transport. I go w-with you. Others s-s-stay."

"You mean, call their bluff? Tell them the colony isn't ready or something? I don't see them as patient. It's my life and your freedom we're gambling with."

"I help you l-l-learn more. We m-must."

"You've got that right. Well, OK then! It's worth the chance. When it's time, you'll stand beside me.

"Oh, and that bullshit about my being their messiah—I'll flush that." I directed this specifically at Bob. "What being would set up their savior for destruction?"

Bob snorted, "Yeah, ask a Christian."

"Never mind. The bottom line is, I've been told one thing and am being treated exactly the opposite. I *am* their prisoner. If I don't return with at least some of you, I die sometime after four—if I can assume that transport from the ship was instantaneous.

"We're going to need a weapon of some...Damn! Vtekdao said anything that wasn't part of me couldn't be put back in phase with the ship." Yet, I had materialized with my caftan. "What does it mean—in phase, out of phase? Objects out of phase would fall through the ship, Vtekdao said."

"Phase refers to the resonances, the vibrations of energy/matter waves or knots. Essentially, the reason you can't walk through a wall is because you and the wall are out of phase—your waves are discordant and do not vibrate at similar frequencies," Jaynah said. "If you were in phase, you'd dissolve through the wall."

"But...that's the opposite of what Vtekdao—"

"It can't happen as he says."

I didn't believe Vtekdao would make such a mistake—not in his position, with all that advanced technology—not by accident. "Then, maybe we *can*...."

"I'll get right on it. Should have the calculations in a few minutes. The rest is easy." Jaynah sprang to her feet and trotted down the hall, long light-brown curls bouncing around her shoulders.

At last, some effort from the neohumans on their own behalf. It was going to take a lot of encouragement on my part, but if I kept up this strategy of enlisting their help for my sake, they'd eventually be involved in saving themselves from a fate they were far too willing to accept.

"Jaynah's a bright girl. She'll be just as adept at electronics and math as Gilbert was," Anne said. She laughed softly. "I keep forgetting Jaynah *is* Gilbert."

"Do you really think we have a chance against the Hagions? Is it crazy to think the colony can survive? I understood it was hopeless," Nancy said, stroking Doron's albino head. Doron still looked very feminine; the hormone treatments would have to be increased.

"I have no doubt we can do this—we have to. It's the *how* that has me stumped. Macro and I will gather more information...if, that is, Macro is allowed free run of the ship as I am. I never thought of that." Doubt threatened to rob me of my resolve just then; it would take everything I had in me to keep uncertainty at bay.

I got up from the table and seated myself in the overstuffed chair that faced out the picture window to the east pasture. By some miracle and a lot of ingenuity, this would not be our last day on this ranch—our sanctuary, our sovereign society where no one uninvited intrudes.

The neohumans and their human companions had built this place together. Following my father's planned demise, they all pitched in and bought the ranch, erecting seven new houses soon afterward. We lived together in peace, subject only to our own values and codes while rejecting most outside influences. No one even owned a TV or read newspapers. The U.S. was a foreign country to us; we would no more be influenced by the media from it than we would India. Whatever the government did to its citizens was their problem, not ours. We chose to live separate from society and its woes—the pollution, the traffic jams, the waiting in line, the stealing, drugs, killing, and the obscene roster of new restricting laws put on the books daily—all manner of obsession and oppression.

For all those years we had been nearly self-supporting, raising our own food, making our own clothes and most of our tools, repairing our own equipment from cars to computers. Yes, we still had to go to the cities occasionally for supplies—we called it our monthly excursion into hell—but in essence we had just dropped out of society. No neohuman was even registered with the Social Security or the school system. And much to our surprise, no bureaucrats bothered us. Civilization barely knew we existed.

We who lived here were truly free, accountable only to ourselves. Individuals excelled in their own chosen fields of expertise, from mechanic to medical technician. We were a truly integrated village society, and it all happened without greed, without bribes, threats, force, fighting, punishment, or killing—without laws. It would never happen again in the history of this planet.

And the Hagions thought they could end that? Invalidate it with their *need*? Not in *my* lifetime, they wouldn't.

"It's all here!" Jaynah said, bounding back into the living room, a trail of computer fanfold flying behind her from her left hand. She went directly to Macro, who folded the sheets into a neat stack as he read them.

"It'll w-work. L-look, Rita."

The first page was cluttered with row upon row of mathematical equations. I understood nothing. "I'll have to take your word for it. What does it mean?"

"It's the complete formulas and diagrams for a compact laser pistol," Jaynah explained. "One power setting only, I'm afraid, due to its small size. But it will stun a human for an hour, maybe more."

I sighed. Didn't she—didn't Gilbert—remember that the Hagions had an exoskeleton? Didn't any of them remember *anything* of their feared enemy? "Stun, Jaynah? I need something that'll kill." The look on her face was that of utter horror. "I know, I know. Except for food and self-defense, it's against the codes. But this *is* self-defense. I have every intention of exhausting every other option before I resort to killing, believe me. But, killing is sometimes necessary."

"I will not build a weapon to kill. I will *not*."

Oh boy. I hadn't anticipated this snag. "Jaynah, please. For the colony, for me. What if I am cornered, what if I have no choice but to kill or die? Wouldn't you want me to choose myself over a Hagion?"

"But, you're on their ship. It is not self-defense if you go to them."

"They force me to go to them. Remember? The Executioner? I must fight them on their own turf—that is the arena *they* have chosen, not I."

"I...I don't have any experience with such a situation. I don't know...."

"That's right: You *don't* know. But I do. I was raised in a human society. I know very well. Make the weapon, Jaynah. It must kill."

Saying nothing, she turned and left with the stack of print-out. I followed her.

"Wait. There isn't time to build it the conventional way. Are you able to visualize the device?"

"Yes, I can see it clearly."

"Then, quickly. Go eat something rich. You'll need the calories."

"There's something I need to tell you about—"

"Now! Time's short." I felt a twinge of remorse, snapping at her like that.

She returned with a saucer piled high with cream cheese. It wouldn't be digested quickly enough to contribute to the heavy energy output about to take place, but it would eventually replace her own reserves that were likely to be depleted.

"What are you going to use for your material?" I asked.

She swallowed hard, a grimace contorting her smooth young face. "A 'C' battery, I think."

"That's enough mass?"

"Sure. How many do you want me to make?"

"I hadn't thought about it. How big will it be?"

"About the size of a Bic lighter. That's what I wanted to explain. The design calls for a special hiding place. A body cavity."

I gasped with delight. "Of course! How brilliant of you! Inserted, it'll be put into phase when *I* am. Good thinking, Jaynah!"

I rummaged through a drawer below the aquarium and handed her four batteries. "This many...for now."

Jaynah moved to the center of the spacious living room. She took a few deep breaths as she tilted her head back and closed her eyes, right hand hovering over a battery in her left hand.

A dull infrasonic hum consumed the large house as everyone watched, riveted on her hands. Liquid lavender webs oozed from her fingertips, wrapping around the battery, making it pulse in a hot purple glow. Long strands of fluid electricity pulled in concentric rings around and through the battery, stretching it, reshaping it from the inside out. The sub-bass hum reached a chest-thudding peak and suddenly died, evaporating with the lavender filaments.

In her hand, Jaynah held a solid silver cylinder about the size of a lipstick. She smiled and held it up for all to see. Her stomach growled.

"That's it? How's it work?" I asked.

She pointed it at an apple perched atop a bowl of fruit on the dining room table. Her thumb slid up the cylinder and a sharp pop split the air. A faint cider odor laced the room.

The apple had vanished.

"Shit. Will it do that to a whole Hagion?" I said.

"Any part of it about the same size and mass."

I warded off a vague wave of nausea. That thing could be messy in unskilled hands. "Well, you've sure as hell come through for us. Nice work. Now, how'd you like to explain to me how you turned it on? I don't see any switch." She handed it to me. It was totally smooth—no buttons, no seams, no opening on either end.

"Use your thumbnail. The friction sets up a chaotic vibration that builds and is released from the end as amplified light."

I turned the device in my hand. "Christ, I can't tell which end is which."

"It doesn't matter. It fires in the direction scratched."

"Terrific. As long as no one's scratching from the other end, huh?" I aimed at a banana in the bowl and scraped my thumbnail forward on the cylinder. A pop and the room was filled with acetone-like banana vapor. Wouldn't the pentagon love to get a hold of this? Self-contained, portable, no moving parts. "What's the energy source? How long will it last?"

"It's recharged with light. It should last a long time--I'm not really sure."

Great. I knew there had to be a catch. I sat at the table while Jaynah transmuted the other three batteries. She collapsed on the sofa shortly after finishing the last one. Anne brought her a quart of orange juice fortified with a cupful of honey; Jaynah guzzled it. As fantastic as it was, the neohumans seldom converted objects. It just took too much out of them.

It was three-thirty. I had to decide if I had the courage to attempt deceiving the Hagions. Macro would go back to the ship with me, but who else? Macro would be invaluable with his ability to derive correlations from dozens of apparently unrelated observations.

I considered each of the neohuman's individual talents. It would be difficult to anticipate what skills would be needed aboard the Hagion ship. Jaynah was an electronics genius, but she had probably done all she could do for now. Darwinia—formerly Tobey—and her background in evolution could be useful in many ways, but perhaps not immediately; she was a bit testy today. Doron—of Alabaster's DNA packet, though skilled in empathic psychology, was physically delicate and could be at risk in an emergency. Bohrelia (Alexander) could help with understanding the physics, especially the ship's drive and transport system. But Bohrelia was blind. Not a good choice, unless I had no choice.

It looked like Macro and I would be going up alone. I inserted one of Jaynah's devices into my vagina; Macro put his in his anus. I insisted that Macro hold my hand from then on-- transport could occur at any minute. I hadn't even given serious consideration to what kind of bullshit story I would feed the Hagions when they found me with only one Benefactor. How would I convince them that only one neohuman would return willingly? Surely the Hagions knew of their Benefactors' passivity. They would be suspicious of this sudden surge of defiance. Maybe I'd try to convince them—

A sudden whiff of something familiar, but not exactly welcome registered in my nasal cavities. Turning my head in many directions, sniffing for the source, it hit me: The smell did not waft from any direction; it came from within my own head. Almonds. Now I tasted it: sickening bittersweet almonds.

Oh God! Why didn't they come for me? Were they just going to let me die? "No! It's killing me! I don't want to die!"

Marco gripped my hand tighter, then let go to hold me by the shoulders. I felt drained, like the life-force was oozing out of me. My knees gave out; I stumbled into the kitchen counter, dizzy, gasping. I saw my pink face in the chrome toaster, a swimming reflection of a dead woman. My eyes. Something was wrong with my eyes—the pupils. *Not the same size! Not the same!* Macro hugged me tightly. Voices crowded in around me, speaking words I didn't understand. I thought I heard a plaintive meow, felt a warmth curl around my leg.

A roar devoured the inside of my head as the hand of eternity closed down on my throat, hurling me into a black wall.

LILY SPLANE

CHAPTER 6

INFINITY QUANTIZED

The only static thing in the universe is change.
—Qwiffian Handbook of Sapience

The guard at the front desk of the West Coast Planetary Watch labs turned from the monitor and greeted Jason Childress with a moustached grin. "Afternoon, Doc. They're all waiting for you." He handed Childress a plastic magnetic pass.

"How many?"

"Just the Beta Team. Five. The Alpha Team won't be in till tomorrow."

That was good news. Tomorrow was his day off; he'd never meet the twenty-member Alpha Team. He walked briskly down the long white hall to the last door on the left, inserted his plastic card in a slot where the door handle should be, and waited. A buzzer sounded in unison with a flashing red light above the door. The door swung open automatically and he slipped into the dimmed room.

None of the white-coated team members turned to acknowledge him. They stood riveted on the thirty monitors arrayed on the back wall, each monitor revealing a different view of Earth—from satellites, balloons, stationary and r cameras.

"Bring up monitor nine," a voice called out. Instantly all thirty monitors reverted to a patchwork of the view from monitor nine: Antarctica from satellite. "Now, whaddaya make of that, people?"

Childress stepped between the rows of computer consoles and plotters to join the source of the voice. "Dr. Aames."

"Jason, glad you could join us. Take a look at this. We just picked it up off the network a few minutes ago. McMurdo Station sent this up after it hopped the nodes from Palmer Station to Leningradskaya to Dumont d'Urville. Practically everyone on that continent has seen it, and no one knows what the hell it is. They shunted it to us in hopes our astrophysicist could give us a clue."

The view of Antarctica filled the screens, washing the dark lab in a frigid white glow. New imaging techniques had rendered the perpetual cloud cover invisible, and the full outline of the mysterious continent was etched out in cold crystal clarity...except for the dead center at the U.S. South Pole Station. The resolution there was markedly diminished, as if filmed through a Vaseline-smeared lens. Periodically, ripples moved across this indistinct area, like waves on wind-blown water.

"How big an area does it cover?" Childress asked.

"That's just it. It seems to be getting bigger. Three hundred miles across now."

"Christ. Do you think it's connected to the sudden ozone depletion in the area?"

"Jason, old boy," Aames said, gripping Childress' shoulder. "They told us we were crazy for inviting a space cadet in for this. I wouldn't want to prove them right. This is *your* baby, now. What do *you* think?"

Helmut Aames was not a stupid man. Weaseling out from under Aames' grip, Childress asked the obvious question. "This isn't an artifact? A lens distortion?"

"Nope. If you compare this with the level-seven air-barge flybys, you'll see the same thing."

"So, do you think it's something atmospheric? Or...off planet?"

"Atmospheric's been ruled out. Has to be in space. And the most interesting thing of all, is Dr. Marx at McMurdo reports seeing this same rippling distortion from the ground. Breaks out a pair of binoculars, there it is."

Childress pointed at the monitor array. "I thought this was a satellite shot, sans cloud cover. It can be seen *below* the clouds as well?"

"Yep."

Childress stared at Aames' snowy face. "You *do* think this has something to do with the expanding ozone hole, don't you?"

"Not only that," Aames added, "but, haven't you noticed the weather lately?"

"Not the weather—the day length. Sure I've noticed. How could I miss it?" He didn't tell him he'd contacted Panadel.

"And the tides—higher than have ever been recorded.

Whatever's up there, it's creating drag. Slowing the planet." He sighed a ghostly sigh. "We're in big trouble here, Jason."

Childress chuckled. "If I didn't know better, I'd say Earth had just acquired another moon...Helmut, I don't know what you think I can do." He brought his hands to his chest. "What do you want from me? The anomaly's been observed from space and from the ground. What else is there?"

"You know damn well your skills with computer image scaling would be invaluable here. You could pinpoint exactly where the effect begins and ends. Not only that, you have priority observation time at Palomar Observatory. If all else fails, you might have to look farther out. I don't know, that's your area. You'll have to decide what happens next."

Childress stared down at a box of computer printout on the floor, tapping the edge of a desk with his fingers. "I'll need to know everything you've found out from the beginning. How long has it been now?"

"Three days. We discovered the phenomenon three days ago. It could have been there a lot longer, we don't know. It's when the ozone ratings took a dive that panic set in." He snorted a laugh. "Hell, no one even seems to be upset about the extra long days, or the ferocious tides."

"The media's pretty much got the panic quotient covered with some kind of bullshit about magnetic waves affecting the electronics. People don't give it much thought. TV is more real to them than their own experiences."

An uneasiness crept into Childress' soul. For the first time since grad school, he felt he might be in over his head. "I'll have assistants, won't I?"

"Lenny and Dr. Handelman will get you anything you need."

Lenny Wontok, yes—a helluva programmer. But Inga Handelman, that was a different story. He had no enthusiasm to work next to her. But how could he pass up the best optics technician on the west coast?

"One Dog, get over here," Childress barked into the dim corners of the lab.

A bear's shadow emerged from the obscurity and lumbered around to the front of the lab, eclipsing a third of Antarctica. The big man's planetary face beamed from between two gray-streaked black braids trailing down the front of his white lab coat. "Dr. Jason. One Dog at your service."

"It's Childress. Jason *Childress*. Ok, parallel man, grab a box, grab your bum, let's get rolling."

Lenny Wontok bent over like a collapsing skyscraper, stacked one box atop another, and hoisted them both up with a grunt, following Childress through a side door into a well-lit conference room.

Childress stood with his hands on his hips, staring ominously at the boxes set on the long conference table. "How much time does this represent?"

"About five hours. Since about eight this morning."

"Christ. Well, we've got to start somewhere. What I need are comparisons—ground observation to satellite data. I'll need upper and lower altitudes, oh-three density at one millimeter increments—"

"The measurements don't go that fine. They're at ten millimeter increments."

"Ah, that's why *you're here*. Program the analysis to extrapolate measurements at one millimeter. I don't want *wags*—I want averages at every millimeter clear through the anomaly. No fudging. We need to know if it has a cycle, if it fluctuates. That'll give us an idea of what to do next."

"We'll be here all night for sure. There are six more boxes."

"No problem. We can send out for pizza or something. You got better things to do?"

"Nah. But we'll need Handelman to rework the lenses. She might not like it if we stay late."

"Yeah. Uh, would you mind being a liaison between us? I really don't have time for any messy situations. She doesn't give you any trouble, does she?"

"Losing your nerve with women, Doc?" Wontok's whole face chuckled.

"Just *that* woman. Never mind. Tell her we'll need to dispatch a platoon of air-barges at levels two through eight, equipped with graduated lenses and microfine filters with UV and infrared readout. Oh, and a sensor for x- and gamma-ray radiation. She knows what the score is. She did nearly the same thing for the Great Lakes fires of '98."

"Sure 'nuf, Doc. And while I'm distracting the lady with lusty words of super-technology, you can go over those printouts and mark what you want in which channels. Keep in mind we only have time for 115 channels of the 28,000 available, so don't get crazy."

"Why are we doing it by hand? Can't we just sort and collate the channels internally?"

"Unfortunately, those boxes of printout come from four different linear processors, and parallel computers aren't exactly user-friendly. I know it's primitive, but it's faster than starting all over. Besides, we'd need a monitor for each channel to see what's going on. And that would slow the process down terribly. Like an armless man using an abacus."

"One hundred-fifteen channels. No problem." That was a lie. It *was* a problem. He'd never done anything like it before. How Childress would keep all the channels straight in his head so he could mark them to be fed into the computer for simultaneous processing, he had no idea. The effort promised to be worth it, though. In the end they'd have a one-page printout that defined something no one had ever seen before.

About halfway through the second box of fanfold paper, Childress noticed the sheets were numbered, so got the idea that it might be easier to handle so many channels by separating the sheets and making piles for each channel. And if he labeled the piles, he wouldn't have to remember anything his already tired brain threatened to skip over.

When Lenny Wontok saw what Childress had done, he furthered the cause by fetching pushpins and paper clamps so they could clip the piles up on the cork bulletin board that ran the full length of one wall.

"With this system, we'll be done in no time. What pisses me off is that I never thought of it before," Wontok said.

Childress hesitated clipping his last sheet for channel forty-one. "What happens if there isn't the same amount of data in each channel? Won't it screw up the correlations?"

"Nah. The smaller channels rest and wait till the large ones are done. Then the knitting begins."

"Knitting?"

"Yep. For instance, node one in channel one connects to node two in channels one and two, node three in channel three, node four

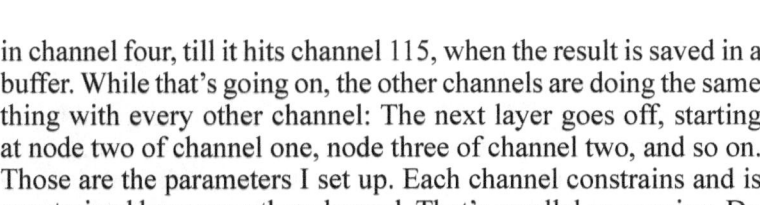

in channel four, till it hits channel 115, when the result is saved in a buffer. While that's going on, the other channels are doing the same thing with every other channel: The next layer goes off, starting at node two of channel one, node three of channel two, and so on. Those are the parameters I set up. Each channel constrains and is constrained by every other channel. That's parallel processing, Dr. Jason. It's awesome."

"If you say so. How long will all this knitting take?"

"It varies. This should take about ten minutes or so. Somewhat slower than the human mind, but far more accurate. This machine may have been modeled on the human brain, but it doesn't make guesses, isn't influenced by impressions. And it doesn't change history, rewrite scripts, like humans tend to do. It's always right. If you feed this data into the channels the same way, you'll get the same answer; if you don't, you won't."

There was a possessed look in Wontok's eyes. "That's the most fascinating thing of all. If you shuffle the data around to different channels—even though it's the same exact data—you'll get a different answer. That's chaos theory stepping in to tweak reality for you. Ha! I love that!"

Wontok must have been the only person in the universe thrilled by uncertainty. "What use would that be? You could get, say, twenty different solutions to a problem depending on how you arranged the data. Why do that when you need a definitive answer to a problem?"

"Ah, that's the beauty of it. In real life, there are no definitive solutions to problems. That's because of chaos—sensitive dependence on initial conditions. Change one tiny variable, the whole movie changes. Then you've got a different solution, eh? It's good to have an array of alternatives. The big `if' looms like a man-eating beast, ready to change your life."

"That's just what I need: a philosophizing programmer. Let's get this going here. Inga—er, Dr. Handelman is still out?"

"Yep. Probably won't be back till eleven, maybe later. Had to air-barge it to Los Angeles for the crystals for grinding the special lenses you ordered."

"Good," Childress said going back into the empty lab where the view of Antarctica still stared coldly from the array of monitors. "This feed is still live off the comsat from UARS, right?" Wontok nodded. "Then I'll do some image shifting over here on the Cray."

"Aw, more data, Doc? Tonight?"

"Just a sample—nothing major. This machine's too old to be of much use, anyway." Childress sat at the computer and dumped the cloudless image of Antarctica from the network feeds into the Cray's memory. He brought the image into focus, the strange central shimmer even more pronounced on this small black and white screen. Leaning closer to the screen, Childress pulled his hair back and knotted it into a self-tying lump at his neck. "What are you?" he mumbled to himself, pressing his own special sequence of keys on the keyboard, bringing the ripples closer, scanning from left to right and back, scanning for *something*—he wasn't sure just what.

He zoomed in as close as he could, filling the screen with the anomaly, then pulled away until the ripples took up only a fraction of the view. Something wasn't quite right about what he saw; he couldn't put his finger on it. Maybe he was just tired, his eyes fatigued from poring over thousands of pages of data. Again, he pressed keys, zooming to within three miles of Antarctica's frozen surface, then quickly pulled away to twenty thousand miles into space. The ripples remained: the same, in close or far out. It hit him in the head like a rubber mallet.

The ripples remained!

"Wontok! Look at this!"

Lenny bound over from the parallel console. He stared. "Yeah?"

"Don't you see anything weird here? Watch. I zoom in to about five kilometers, then pull back to thirty-two thousand kilometers. What do you see?"

"Not a damn thing. What am I supposed to see?"

"I don't see anything either. That's the point—those ripples. They stay the same size no matter how close or far out we look. They should get smaller or larger, or change somehow. They don't Lenny. They *don't.*"

"Shit."

They stared at the static ripples as the image repeatedly zoomed in and pulled back. In his mind, Childress visualized the lens on the tenth-generation modified Upper Atmosphere Research Satellite obeying his frenzied demands. "Whatever it is, it's *thousands* of kilometers thick. Thousands!"

Three beeps sounded from across the room. "Soup's on!" Wontok yelped. "This'll be the final word. If this can't tell us what the hell that thing is, nothing can." He lumbered back to the far side of the lab, Childress following. A two-sheet printout waited, flapping like a tongue, mocking him. He glared at it and kicked the bottom of the metal box that housed this electronic brain. "It's out of it's friggin' mind," Wontok whimpered. "It's deranged."

Childress tore the sheets from the tractor feed and read the first page:

```
 - - - - - REPORT 97842 - - - - -


ALTITUDE RANGE 5-10,000 KM


SUMMARY OF 1 MM INCREMENTAL REPORT:


AVERAGES:
PARAMETER    AMOUNT              LEVELS        NORMAL RANGE
O²           00.15%              0-13 KM       20.9%
*O³          12 DOBSON UNITS     12-30 KM      110-235 DU
CL⁻          00.00%              ALL
*N           3.24%               0-13 KM       79.1%
S            0.00%               ALL
C¹⁴          0.00%               ALL


*ATM PRESSURE:50 MILLIBARS       ALL           940-1050 MB
WIND VELOCITY:0 KNOTS            ALL           10-200 KN
RADIATION:
COSMIC       0
GAMMA        0
X-RAYS       0
UV           0
IR           0
MW           0


ATMOSPHERIC TEMPERATURE (CENTIGRADE):
ALT KM       TEMP                LAYER         NORMAL


                  [EXOSPHERE]
```

10000	350	G LAYER	1230.0
		[IONOSPHERE]	
550	34.9	F LAYER	1150.0
450	33.2	E LAYER	160-620.0
200	27.9	DUST BELT	-96.0
		[MESOSPHERE]	
80	30.4	D LAYER	-2.0
		[STRATOSPHERE]	
30	28.9	OZONE LAYER	-46
		TROPOPAUSE	-57
13		[TROPOSPHERE]	-18
8		[ECOSPHERE]	15

1 MM INCREMENTAL REPORT:
UNPROCESSED ***** NOT SAVED TO CRYSTAL RAM

ANALYSIS
NON-ATMOSPHERIC AREA
CYLINDER APPROX. *499 KM (312 MI) DIAM
X *10,000 KM (6,000 MI) HIGH
* VALUES NON-CONSTANT

VACUUM DOMAIN
POSITIVE FOR GRAVITATIONAL EFFECTS
PROPOSE:
SMALL MOON

ALTERNATE:
MINI BLAcK HOLE:;#M,M0(VVV@9999
303030

DETAILED 1 MM INCREMENT REPORT TO FOLL##(VV-
SYSTEM SHUTDOWN
SYSTEM SHUTDOWN
SYSTEM SHUTDOWN

CHAPTER 7

DIVERSIONS

The formation of everything we see
is governed by that which we cannot see.
—Qwiffian Handbook of Sapience

The unwelcome taste of living human flesh brought me to the border of consciousness. I awoke to Cosmigellan working over me with the detachment of a mortician, his probing fingers pressing a hard bead beneath my tongue. I didn't have time to scream: My scalp exploded into throbbing liquid fire, cooling almost as suddenly.

"I'm really getting tired of this shit," I mumbled as he withdrew his fingers. "What happened? Why did they wait so—"

Just then the ceiling, Cos, everything, winked out of existence. There were only stars against the void; my eyes pulled from my head out to them. I felt fingers I couldn't see push my eyelids down, welding them shut.

"Hey, what's going on?"

"It's all right, Rita. Just a few seconds. Be still, I have to recalibrate the phase-shift modulator and synchronize your vision."

"The *what*? Cos, what is this? Where are you?"

"I'm here, right here. You just can't see me, yet. Hold on."

The surface I was on tilted slightly to the left and I felt a cold pressure at the base of my skull. Cos still pressed my eyes shut as I was tilted back to lay flat.

"Now, open your eyes, slowly. Tell me how things look, how you feel."

The first thing I saw was Cos' smiling face, accented with a crease between his brows.

"I'm surprised to be back here. They damn near killed me, Cos," I whimpered, remembering the horror of realizing the Executioner had been activated.

"Not damn near—*did.* You were clinically dead."

"I...*died?*" The news didn't surprise me so much as being revived, yet again. I hoped I could improve on my future consciousness ratio.

"Yes. Your well-being is now my responsibility...since I've been replaced in Application by Macro."

"Macro! How is he? What have the Hagions done with him? Are they pissed there's only one Benefactor?"

"Pissed, yes. But they were mostly, I think, confused. You see, they can't decide whether you've honored your agreement or not—they don't understand partial compliance. And they are quite taken with your little surprise, so for the time being, are distracted. What made you think to do it?"

"Well, I just gambled they wouldn't kill me when I brought only one Benefactor, because they'd need me to get the others."

"No, I don't mean that. I mean, bringing Shana."

My heart crept up into my throat and fluttered there. "Shana?" Shit, it *hadn't* been my imagination. My cat *had* been winding around my ankles when..."No! She got transferred? Where is she? What have they done to her?" I sat up quickly. The room swayed, everything shifted and separated into a thousand poorly stacked frames. "Cos," I moaned, looking up at his blurred face, a face surrounded by a multi-colored aura. "Something's wrong. It looks all...funny." A prismed arm reached behind me and I felt a thump on the back of my head. The room, Cos, flowed into focus.

"Thanks for the adjustment, Tony. You do valve work?" Cos' laugh sprinkled me with delight; I hadn't heard it in years. "So, where's Shana? Where's Macro?"

"Shana is with Vtekdao. She intrigues zhan."

His voice faded to the distance; I didn't hear the rest of what he said. My mind was flooded with images I didn't want to think: my beloved half-Siamese cat skinned and splayed on a platter, a well-done hindquarter parting under the pressure of one of those curling-iron eating utensils.

"Rita, she's OK. They won't harm her," Cos said quickly, holding my shoulders.

"You read me? I didn't think we were—"

"We are of The One. We will always be of The One."

I'd have to ask him later why he had refused to answer me

when I mind-called him. "I want Shana and Macro here, in front of me, now. I have to see them. I have to know they're all right." About then I recalled what else I had arranged to be brought back on board with me. I squirmed, but felt nothing. Perhaps it had not converted, not been transferred. "Cos, I have to use the facilities. Where are they?"

"What you want is right here. I removed it." He held up the small silver cylinder, grinning. "Very clever. Surely you don't plan to use this on anyone."

That devious smile on his face was the first glimmer of the rebel I knew so well, the rebel who understood the price of submission. "When it's time and if I have to. They don't know, do they?"

"No, they don't. And I suppose Macro has one as well?"

"I hope he still has it. Cos, take me to him, to Shana."

"My orders are to bring you to the First Flagellant, Tmait. I dare not disobey." He winked, clutching the cylinder tightly, moving his hand behind his back.

Had I seen my rebel resurface? He confused me. I stood, stretching out my hand. "The device, please."

"I can't give it to you. It is a mistake to do what you're planning."

"Cos, *what* is the matter with you? Have they done something to you? Where's the fighter? The man who helped me get rid of my father, who rescued a whole colony of neohumans? It's not like you to be submissive and passive."

"There's too much at stake. Just...trust me. That's all I ask, Rita."

I thought about that quite a while, holding his eyes with my stare. Trust. What was it, anyway? A confidence in someone, that they'll do the right thing. It was obvious to me that we weren't in agreement as to what the right thing was. He had done a one-hundred-eighty-degree flip—not out of malice or allegiance to his captors, but out of a crippling fear. I hated to admit it, but I no longer had confidence in his judgement. I *didn't* trust him.

"Cos, dammit. You make me think and feel things I don't want to. I know you know what's going on. Of all the Phaedrans you may be the only one; everyone else seems to be afflicted with a convenient amnesia. How can I trust you when you won't level with me and you lock me out of your mind? Cos, I *need* you."

"You don't know what you're dealing with. I do. I've been through it before, and I remember." His voice quavered. "You just don't understand."

"Then make me understand! Don't shut me out, don't give in to them, telling me all the time that everything's going to be OK. Everything is not OK!" *Make me understand! Let me in!*

"Rita," he sobbed holding his hand over his eyes. "I'm so sorry."

It wasn't like I'd never seen him cry before, but this time was different. It tore me to shreds. "Cos," I said, hugging him, kissing a face I hadn't been able to see for so long. "Cos, you can start by explaining your reincarnation. How can you have this body when you were forced to give up the other one? How can you maintain it and not die?"

"I don't have to control this one. It exists without conscious influence, as yours does. The Hagions found the image within my memories and produced this body from their matter. It is—"

"Wait. *Their* matter? What does that mean?"

"Non-baryonic matter. The same as the Hagions, the ship... you."

"*Dark matter*? Matter without protons or electrons? Without *light*?"

"In a manner of speaking. The world of which we are now a part is out of phase with the baryonic matter world. We essentially exist superimposed on the other, without substance. Our only interaction with baryonic matter is gravitational."

"You mean, we're invisible? Ghosts?" My head reeled with astonishment.

"We may not even be present within standard dimensions. We may be enfolded within hyperdimensional spacetime—invisible to all but ourselves."

"May? You mean, you don't *know*?"

"They don't want us to know."

I released my embrace, sagging down to the low table in shock. "No protons, no neutrons. How is it I can feel, breathe, eat? How is it I can be?"

"The Hagions can be very accommodating with their illusions. Their nanotechnology is highly advanced. Implanted molychines—

molecular machines—put you in phase, make this world solid for you. Without implanted molychines, you would not even see this world. I was calibrating visual synthesis for you as you woke. And communication—remember the molychine in your tooth?"

I nodded slowly, dazed, staring at the sparkling gray floor. "Well, that explains a few things. I guess. And the Hagions control all this, I assume."

"Yes."

"But, if this world—I—can't be seen, how could everyone at the hospice, even the humans, see me?"

"Molychines deactivated. Reactivated when you were brought back here."

I had a growing feeling that my plan for escape just went up in vapor—laser-fire vapor. Even if I killed every last Hagion on the ship, not I or Cos or Macro or my cat would ever be able to leave this ghost world. We were trapped in a perfect prison: a prison that was real only for the prisoners and their captors and that no one but they would ever know existed.

I knew Cos was still concealing something—I felt it. But I decided not to press the issue—I was on reality overload and couldn't handle any more revelations right then. All I knew was I was invisible, forced to betray my best friends by epileptic roaches—also invisible—who put machines (invisible) in my head to release poison if I didn't cooperate. As a fringe benefit these blue bugs also had my lover and mentor by the balls (invisible?), and he had become so compliant I could have kicked his ass. OK, life sucked a little. All I could think of right now was my cat, Shana.

I didn't remember the description of the layout of the ship when I entered the spiral tunnel. If Shana was with Vtekdao it seemed natural to me that I could find her by walking up the spiral rather than down. She was my first concern. Macro, by no means stupid, was difficult to understand sometimes but he would be able to get what he needed by simply asking. Shana was another situation altogether. How would the Hagions know if she was hungry or thirsty or, Universe forbid, in pain? Would they have studied the feline species as thoroughly as they had apparently studied humans?

Dammit, I would have felt better with Jaynah's laser device with me. Even if it was stupid to use it, just knowing I had it would fortify me. Damn Cos and his interference. He had flagrantly acted against the codes, codes we had all had a hand in creating. There I was wallowing in my own remorse for distrusting him, and he obviously did not trust me with the weapon. He would be no help at all. The whole responsibility of getting out of this mess and preserving the colony had devolved onto me, and I didn't like it. I should be at my PC pounding out another spec-fic story, not saving my friends from their own inertia. And more importantly, I could be writing *this* whole experience down, but I didn't have a computer here—at least not one that I understood how to use.

I stopped at the red dot on the wall, catching my breath before pressing it. What I saw when a section of the wall dissolved could only be described as controlled chaos—a noisy industrial ballet.

The irregular-shaped room was huge. Everything in it, including the hundred or so Hagions gathered in a circle, was some shade of blue. Even the air, charged with a sourceless light, glowed a metallic blue. The domed ceiling loomed twenty or more feet overhead; that seemed especially strange: No structures, certainly not the five-foot-tall Hagions, extended upward to justify the height. It was like being in a place of worship—a kind of laborer's cathedral.

As I stood taking in the peculiar architecture, not one Hagion looked my way. They were immersed in a furious activity, standing side by side, wadding and unwadding their hands into their neighbors' hands, thumping and puffing garrulously, while a huge steel sheet rushed towards the group from behind.

I tensed in anticipation of a gory collision, that sheet came so fast. It must have been ten feet high and forty feet across, banging to a sudden halt what looked like inches from the circle of Hagions, then retreating just as swiftly to postage stamp size in the far distance. There it shimmered and quivered for a few seconds before returning, blowing up to nearly fill the entire length of the space in which it finally banged to a stop again. I closed one eye, finding it easier to accept the rapid change in size rather than comprehend the speed with which it moved. Unfuckingbelievable.

I crept closer, knowing this was not my intended destination, driven by an epistemic hunger that seized me and wouldn't let go. What, for chrissakes, *was* all this?

I was still too far away from the group to discern what they were doing with their hands in this mad trance-like finger-dance.

Before I could take another step, something jabbed me in the back. I turned to face two whirling black propellers set in yellow guavas. Three bass thumps rumbled my sternum. I remembered to bite down.

"...awaits. May I escort you to your destination?"

"Uh, sure. What is this place? What are they doing?" I looked past the Hagion's eyes.

Bang! The metal sheet slammed to a halt. I jerked.

"This is Assembly. Molychines are construct—"

It stopped dead. The pupils ceased their dizzying twirl, like the whole brain had shut down. I waved my hands past its eyes: no response. With some trepidation, I gripped the longest finger on the still outstretched hand: It felt cool and rubbery. What I really wanted to do was squeeze that big exposed brain, but decided that would be in poor taste. Realizing I had just another few seconds, I tapped the exposed boulder-like teeth with my fingernail; they did feel like rocks.

"...ed at this level. Now, if you will come with me."

I jerked my finger back, feeling a shot of fear skip through me. It hadn't noticed my probings; I was relieved. That meant these seizures made them totally unconscious. "Uh, what's your name again?"

"I am Tmait—First Flagellant to the Honorable Altruist and opposing candidate to Vtekdao."

Bang!

Interesting predicament, being at once a servant and an opposing candidate to the same individual. But not as interesting as the fact that Tmait was the third Hagion I'd seen with the absence disorder. "Isn't that a bit of a conflict of interest?"

"It is the way of our government. Now please, follow me."

"Wait. I want to see more of this—"

Bang!

"You have two human hour-fragments remaining."

Thank you, Ma Bell. "May I approach the circle?"

"Touch nothing. Distracting only one of the Obligants will result in dysrhythmia and disengage the entire assembly operation."

Amazing was a poor description for what the Hagions did. If they could do what they were doing with the constant chattering, the cyclical banging of that metal sheet just inches from some of them, nothing I could do would distract them.

Bang!

They manipulated glass slides and tiny electrical probes with such precision and speed, their fingers were a blur.

"They're assembling molychines? My god, how can they see them?" I whispered to Tmait.

"The will of Hope has given us a magnifying vision that we may prosper."

I understood now the reason for the circular configuration. Of course, it could be no other way: Their own hands did not meet. They solved this problem ingeniously, cooperatively: It took two Hagions to complete a task.

Each Hagion concentrated only on its right hand, while the left hand worked of its own accord in unison with the right hand of the Hagion to the left.

"But, how do they know what to do with their left hand? How can they 'see' their work?"

"Verbal instructions from the partner," Tmait answered.

"They work on microscopic machinery with their right hands while listening to instructions for moving their left hands? Simultaneously? Wow."

"That's correct. Ree-tah, Vtekdao waits."

"But, how?" I asked, turning to follow the impatient roach, my neck still craning to watch the wonderful coordinated activity.

"Parallel processing. We go, now."

Bang!

Just as I stepped away, the worker nearest me ceased its chatter and flurry of finger movements. The hands of the Hagions to the left and right also stopped, waiting, I assumed, to resume their work when Mr. Fugue snapped out of his stupor. God, I wanted to know what that was! I decided against asking. Yes, I assured myself, it would be best if I didn't show surprise at anything they did or said. That would be my strength, my secret weapon against them when the time to finally act was upon me.

We climbed along the spiral walkway, the roach leading the way. I had mixed feelings about seeing Vtekdao. I needed desperately to know that Shana was all right, but knew my being brought to Vtekdao didn't concern the cat. I was probably about to be reprimanded in classic Hagion style—whatever that turned out to be—for deceiving them and not bringing the whole colony to the ship. I wasn't looking forward to what I knew would be a confrontation.

There was no arguing with these roaches. Any protests from me would be pointless. The Hagions were not amenable to reason or even gratuitous emotionalism. And it would be a long time before I forgot about the Executioner.

Simply put, the only way I could get through this would be to grovel before His Highness, the Honorable Altruist Vtekdao. That idea really rubbed me the wrong way. Maybe Cos had been right in taking the weapon from me. He knew things about me I was slow to admit.

I'd have to exhume the Crystal Bitch once again, from wherever I'd buried her. I hadn't needed her since she kept Cos from finding out I was planning to kill my father. She had served me well then; she would again.

I had my strategy all planned: I'd apologize, grease Vtekdao with as much phoney remorse as I could dredge up. He'd never know I hated him, his whole fucking race for whatever they'd done to the Phaedrans in the past, were doing to me now. He'd never know I studied him and his kind like the disgusting bugs they were, just waiting for the opportunity to crush them and reverse the fate they'd thrust upon me and my people. And if he did anything to Shana, so much as harmed a flea on her, I'd—

The wall relinquished an opening and inside sat a Hagion, elevated on a platform overlooking a low, red, oval table, a cat perched on his folded many-jointed legs...purring.

"Shana!" I could have slapped her! She was *purring* for that... that *thing*! I suppressed a shout, forcing my breathing into a slow regular pattern.

"Ree-tah! You've honored me with a charming gift! The creature is splendid!" Vtekdao gurgled in bass tones.

My brain reeled in confusion. And alarm. "I...I didn't plan—"

"Zhe is an asset in the arduous life of the Honorable Altruist," Tmait said. "Your thoughtfulness does not, however, dismiss your transgression."

Vtekdao spoke. "We have conferenced and conclude that your partial cooperation is...You have not honored your agreement. You have brought only one Benefactor. We need them *all*. We know how many there are." He leaned forward, pupils spinning. His voice quieted. "You did not mean to deceive us, did you?"

I cowered before the ghost of my father that suddenly shimmered before me. "No. No, of course not. I—"

"Pity." Vtekdao leaned back in his seat, nearly enclosed in it like a cocoon. Shana looked up at the big yellow eyes and meowed, adjusting her footing on his knees.

I became mute. I knew then that he was looking for an excuse to kill me. Just one more stumble and it would all be over.

"There is also another matter of great concern. The Benefactor you brought to us is defective. Are the others also of zhaz caliber? Is the Benefactor Cosmigellan exceptional?"

"Well, Sir, Honorable Sir. I have no difficulty with Macro. He possesses extraordinary talent. He is an artist."

"Zhe is non-functional. Zhe is brain damaged. Zhe is incapable of following instructions. Is this true of the others?"

Didn't he know? Would it help the colony if I lied, or would I just be digging my grave with a backhoe instead of a trowel? "Yes. They are all like him. It's something that happens to them when they breed with humans." His eyes bulged. I'd hit a nerve, hopefully not a homicidal one. "Surely you were aware these Benefactors are not of pure stock, they are the result of human/Phaedran mating." I'd just reached the point of no return. I swallowed a dry gulp.

Vtekdao's pupils screamed to a standstill as he froze, hand in an awkward wad. I glanced to Tmait who waited patiently beside me, hands wadding and unwadding like nervous rehydrated maple leaves.

I wanted to reach up and pet Shana, to call her to me, but I didn't dare. She was Vtekdao's now.

Vtekdao nodded and resumed speaking. "An interesting confabulation. I'm impressed."

"I do not lie! They *are* half human—at least the physical half."

"Are the others defective in communications?"

There was no point in lying any longer. He'd just keep drilling me until I buckled. The truth would have to suffice. "No. They are not. They have different defects. One is blind. Another is albino and very sensitive to—"

"Untrue! Benefactor Cosmigellan tells the same lies! Why

did you not bring them? You have dishonored The Purpose and the will of Hope. It is most shameful for us who did not anticipate your deceptions."

Welcome to Casa Grovel. First up on the menu: a smidgen of crow. "I'm sorry, but they...they were so upset! I was afraid they would harm each other, go into spindle, if I pressured them. Macro, the defective one, agreed to come with me if I left the others. He, of course, is not in full possession of his faculties, and well, let's face it, he just doesn't understand the situation."

"The Benefactors have always submitted to us readily! They know of their importance, and of our great concern for them!" His chest heaved in and out and his whole body blanched light blue.

I was sure I'd pushed him over the edge, angered him beyond hope. And there Shana was, teetering on his bony knees as he rocked back and forth, puffing and wheezing in his wrap-around chair. The cat hopped down onto the table, then back up into his lap, meowing. *Run Shana!* I screamed in my head. She should have run—she would have had it been me quaking furiously beneath her.

"They would not—" he huffed in a bellow. "Would not refuse!"

I knew I was in deep shit now. "Please, I just wanted to make sure no one got hurt. I beg forgiveness. Give me another chance. I'll bring them. I'll bring them," I whined. Horrified I'd just offered up my friends to him, afraid beyond reason he'd hurt Shana out of his fury, I dropped to my knees and cried. I had failed miserably. It was all over. I was his, Shana was his, Cos was his, everything that meant anything to me was his. Cos was right. It was inevitable.

"Ree-tah! You amuse me! You are a genius. No one has made me laugh like that in thousands of stellar cycles! Get up, get up! This is no way for the Savior to behave!"

Laugh? The son-of-a-bitch was laughing? When I finally composed myself and looked up, I met Shana's eyes staring at me from her seat at the edge of the red table. I reached for her, to welcome her, reassure her, let her know I'd missed her. Her fur was soft as always, her purr vibrating to the surface of her skull, as always. In revulsion, I snapped back my hand. "What have you done?" I gasped, afraid to look Vtekdao square in those hideous orbs. "What is this?" Carefully turning the cat's head sideways, I saw imbedded in the back of her skull a small white ceramic square with a plug in it. "My god, what have you done? What's this for?" I cried.

"Observe. Tmait, if you will."

Tmait folded his many-jointed legs, leaned down and sideways and inserted what looked like a silicon chip into the ceramic plug in Shana's head.

"No! No, don't hurt her!" I cried, but was afraid to stop him, to touch the rubbery fingers. But Shana was not distressed, she just sat there, her purr punctuated with an occasional meow. Then, in as clear a voice as I'd ever heard come from that feline throat, she hummed the first verse of "On The Good Ship Lollypop."

CHAPTER 8

MACHINATIONS

- *The particle/wave duality of matter is evidenced by interference patterns.*
- *Interference patterns are created by the unsynchronized meeting of crests and troughs of sine waves.*
- *Interference patterns in a spray of electrons occur even if electrons are forced to squeeze through a slit one at time.*

—Qwiffian Handbook of Sapience

I had straddled a bucking stegosaurus into hell.

After snatching up Shana without asking His Highness Vtekdao, I just ran—impulsively, blindly; I could think of nothing but getting away. I must have descended five, maybe six levels down the spiral into the bowels of the ship, squirming cat in my arms, before I realized no one followed me.

Shana still hummed broken verse all the way. Shut up, Shana. Just shut the hell up. I didn't think I could hack another five seconds of that damn song! "Good Ship Lollypop"—good god!

I was nearly winded. It was a lot harder going down the spiral than it was going up it. And it seemed much longer, somehow. I was sure I had to be near my own wedge on this level, but had no idea how to find it. I'd counted seven red dots—the entrances to various activity areas for each level-- but my quarters were unmarked. I'd always been escorted to and from my wedge and was now completely at a loss as to how to locate it.

I patted the wall until my hand disappeared into it, then jumped through, prepared to deal with wherever I found myself.

It was a small wedge, furnished strangely, what I could see of it. I stood there panting for several seconds, my eyes slowly adjusting to the obscure light. In the center of the wedge a Hagion lay like a broken puppet on something resembling a bean-bag chair, its eyes clouded with nictitating membranes, still, so very still.

It jerked.

Shana shot out of my arms, raking treads into my side. I stifled a grunt.

The Hagion's membranes slid to the inside corners of its eyes, revealing whirling black propellers in golden orbs.

"Uh, I'm sorry. Wrong room. Let me get my cat and I'll go."

"Please," it said, unfolding from its jumble. "Please don't go. Please stay." Its voice conveyed sorrow, a loneliness that pulsed like a toothache of the soul.

It would have been impossible at that moment for me to leave it. I sat on a low round toadstool-of-a-thing near where I'd come in. "Are you OK?"

"You are the human, Ree-tah!" it beamed. I felt the impression of a smile come from a face that had no ability of expression. "I'm honored to meet you," it said. "You don't know how long we've waited. Now, The Purpose will be realized. I will be freed!"

"Freed? You're a prisoner?" My god, that bastard Vtekdao never ceased to horrify me.

"Oh no! Not a prisoner. An Ignorant. My function will be fulfilled, my life will begin! You've brought the Benefactors, Ree-tah," it said, clicking up close, wrapping exquisitely slender fingers around my arm. "Thank you. We all thank you."

How much messiah crap could one take without wretching? "I'm afraid you have it all wrong. I don't belong here," I said, getting up and turning away from the roach. "And neither does my cat. Here Shana! Here, kitty, kitty!"

"You've taken Vtekdao's gift? Zhe will not be pleased."

"Tough totems. She doesn't belong to him. He misunderstands. She is mine." It wasn't going to be easy finding a gray cat in this poor light. "Here kitty. Shana, dammit!"

"The creature is in the hygiene area," it said, pointing a thin quivering finger at a blank wall.

When I dissolved through the wall I stopped dead. The tang of fresh cat shit permeated the air. Shana busied herself pawing at invisible litter on the fountain grate. "Shana, bad kitty!" I said, scooping her up, just escaping the downpour gushing from the center of the fountain. Holding the cat firmly, I leaned in towards the fountain, hoping to trigger the water again. It sprayed upward and out, wetting the sleeve of my caftan, melting and washing the cat turd through the grate. The only evidence of Shana's deed lingered in the air...along with the strained notes of that damn song as she hummed in my restraint.

Back through the wall I went, hoping like hell none of the odor followed. "Got her. Hey, would you do a favor for me? My fingers are too big. Would you remove this chip from my cat?"

The Hagion gently inserted two slim fingers into the hole of the ceramic plug in Shana's skull. Shana cut her humming in mid-note. At last, the "Good Ship Lollypop" had been mothballed.

"Thank you. I hate that song." I hated Vtekdao even more for modifying my pet like she was a Mattel toy. Shit, Vtekdao—he'd surely be after me. It would be foolish for me to go to my room, if I could ever find it. I needed asylum.

Hugging Shana close to me I settled down on the low stool. The cat purred and curled up in a squirrel-ball in my lap. "What's your name?" I asked of this mellow Hagion.

"Shalf—Ignorant to the Honorable Altruist."

I wondered if it knew what ignorant meant. "I need a place to hide. Vtekdao will be looking for me."

"Zhe knows not where you are until zhe is informed."

Uh-oh. "Are you planning to turn me in?"

Its eyes bulged. "I...I do not wish to. Your presence pleases me. But, if it is found that I've concealed your whereabouts from Vtekdao, I will be absorbed."

That last word sent icicles through me. I wasn't sure I really wanted to know what absorption entailed. I asked anyway. "What's absorption, Shalf?"

"To become one with the All That Is."

I nearly fell backwards off my tuffet. That was a Phaedran concept. Did the Hagions know of Phaedran beliefs, did they *live* by them? Cos hadn't mentioned *that.* "Are the Hagions of The One?" I had a hunch.

"The one what?"

What a relief. Had the Hagions been aware of the Phaedran mind-net, it would have changed everything. It meant they'd know our every thought, our plan. "Shalf, I need some—"

Shalf became rigid, the membranes quivering at the middle of each eye. I could do nothing but wait.

Shalf stirred and spoke softly. "Ree-tah, I am embarrassed to ask this of you, but I must. I must be in Application soon. It is too late to enlist a partner and it is forbidden for me to leave my quarters in my condition. I must be deodorized. Please, remove a deodorant pick from my brow and insert it into my cloaca."

"You want me to *what*?" So much intimacy so fast.

"I must not release pheromones. It is forbidden."

Just then I caught a whiff of what it meant: a curious blend of pine oil and wet charcoal. "Tell me more. What's in Application?"

"It is where the product of all Ignorants is placed in stasis, preserved for vivigenesis. It is the will of Hope."

"You mean eggs? You donate your eggs to a hatchery?"

"They are removed from us as dictated by the code of the elders. It is mandatory. It is the will of Hope as translated by the elders and implemented through the Honorable Altruist, Vtekdao."

Sounded like a script it had memorized. I shook off the desire to interrogate this roach further, and obliged its instructions. Rolling its brow skin, finding it unexpectedly soft and pliable as a puppy's coat, I found something like an incense cone and gingerly shoved it into its cloaca. It was not an experience I wanted to repeat any time soon. The odor instantly abated.

"So, you're not allowed to mate? That's what that thing's for?"

"The Purpose must be fulfilled. I would be honored if you would accompany me to Application, Ree-tah."

"What about Vtekdao?"

"Zhe will not consider your exploration a violation on my part. I will not come to harm."

"What about *me*? I don't want him to find me."

"Perhaps zhe will not." Shalf unwadded his hands in a follow-me gesture.

I needed to find Macro, to know he was well. With some anxiety I decided to risk discovery and go. I unrolled Shana and she followed us through the wall. It must be a crazy experience for her. She'd never adjust to Earth's solid barriers once we got back there. If we got back there.

The climb up the gently graded spiral turned into an expedition. The walk sure did seem longer than I remembered. To add to the discomfort, the thoughts of what Vtekdao would do to me for kidnapping his "gift" baked in my skull like a forty-pound souffle. "What level is Application on?"

"Four. Below Procedure."

I took that to mean the medical lounge. It felt like we had ascended six levels instead of three. Maybe I needed food, or rest. Even Shana meowed an occasional complaint in her effort to keep up.

The anticipation of Vtekdao's wrath still curdled my brain. Maybe he'd steal into my quarters while I slept—which would be soon, I felt—and just take Shana away and I'd never see her again. Maybe he'd kill her in an unimaginably horrible manner, just to get even with me. I'd made him laugh at me, my fear, my frustration. It probably fed him, like it fed my father so many years ago. And there was still the matter of the colony: another strike against me. For all I knew the cyanide-emitting molychine was still in place and Vtekdao's slimy finger hovered over the destruct button.

By the time we'd arrived at level four and stood in Application, all those fears had vanished. The darkness inhaled us like pigeons in a jet engine.

A red glow flickered at the corner of my eye, dilating from nothing to an expanse of harsh linear proportions—shelves, all labeled with severe black characters. Small pale ovals bobbed in murky glass cylinders. There must have been dozens of them, row upon row of what appeared to be pickled eggs, all arrested and classified in a huge chamber that was as warm as it was red. The effect was like standing inside a furnace on the verge of combustion. "What's all this?"

"The next generation," Shalf said, sadness tainting its voice. "I must meet with Benefactor Two now. Will you accompany me?"

"Uh, sure. Sure. Lead the way." A hollow meow echoed from the end of one of the red-washed rows. "Shana! Come'ere!" In seconds the cat was at my heels.

Shalf led us through another wall to our left, where the painful white light bleached the last of the red from my retinas. This room looked like another medical facility, though smaller and brighter than the beige lounge I had been operated on more times than I wanted to count. In the center of this room, from inside a textured-glass booth, a white-robed dark-haired figure shifted. A human.

The figure emerged from the enclosure, passing through the glass as if it were a sheet of stilled water. "Macro!" I chirped.

"R-Rita! I w-was worried ab-b-bout you."

He reached for me and I pulled him to me, ruffling his hair. "Macro, I'm so glad to see you. How have they been treating you? Are you all right?"

"I'm f-fine. I'm fine. I have an im-important job here. B-b-but, it is not p-pleasant."

"What do you do?"

Macro's mouth creaked open to speak, his eyes shimmering with tears. Before words could form, a Hagion shot through the far wall.

"Zhe extracts product from Ignorants. Zhe is quite skilled, my Savior Ree-tah."

I didn't think I'd ever get used to the way the Hagions just popped in when they pleased. It put me on edge. "And who might *you* be?" I said, crossing my arms beneath my breasts.

"I am Vnoim, Second Flagellant to the Honorable Altruist. I did not mean to offend you. My apologies, Savior Ree-tah."

That was more like it. "Only the *Second* Flagellant. Oh." I really didn't know what I was doing, but I went with it. "Why do you disturb my education? I have much to observe here." That felt good.

"Please forgive me. I only wish to obey the orders of Vtekdao, who humbly requests the return of zhaz gift. I am to escort you to zhaz chambers for a briefing. I do not wish to dishonor Vtekdao or insult you."

"Tell Vtekdao I'm busy. I'll drop by after I've eaten and rested. As for his gift...tell him that Shana has told me she wishes to remain with me. It is her choice."

Vnoim's eyes bulged and he flushed a brilliant blue. "I...did not know you spoke with the creature. This alters everything. Very well, I shall convey the information." He turned swiftly and dashed through the wall.

"Your courage is admirable," Shalf said, "but I fear, inappropriate."

How well I knew *that.* What the hell was the matter with me anyway? Just minutes ago I was wringing my hands in terror, and here I just went and tempted the ire of the Top Roach with my sudden insolence.

"V-Vtekdao will s-stop at n-nothing to as-assert his w-will."

Not what I needed to hear from my godchild. As bad as it might get for me though, I knew I had two allies right here in this room. I hadn't expected to think of Shalf in this way, but found his openness, his odd melancholy endearing. I knew Shalf genuinely liked me; it could be useful—if only I could solve the identification problem. I'd have to be sure who was who. "Shalf," I said, returning his previous arm caress gesture with one of my own, "I need you to teach me things. Like, how to tell you all apart. I don't mean to insult you or your kind, but you all look identical to me. You have names, that must mean you appreciate the idea of separate identities."

Shalf's body twitched, blushing light blue. "It's obvious!" he shrieked.

"What is?" I said, alarmed.

"The brow creases, of course. None are alike."

Jesus, I'd have to become a wrinkle counter? "The number, the size? What about them?"

"Yes. And more. The texture, the color, the depth."

I studied his four brow creases, the same creases I'd dug a deodorant cone out of earlier; I couldn't even remember from which furrow I'd gotten it. Was I supposed to recognize him, any of them, at a mere glance? It would be like identifying a person with a quick visual scan of his thumb. No way would I master this talent. "There's no other way?"

"Perhaps the voice. Possibly the lingual decoder adds some identifying nuance to our voices that we cannot hear."

"No. You all sound the same." Except for Vtekdao: There was no mistaking his baritone boom. "How about—"

"Ree-tah, please. There is no more time. I must enter Duty. It is my occupational function."

"Giving up your eggs is your *job*? You get paid for them?"

"I am not compensated for them, no. I have no need for compensation, to toil for my own support as the Obligants do. For the work of the Obligants is the work for all, that we who provide our product never experience the—"

Shalf then slipped into a long-overdue fugue, eye membranes aflutter. He had sounded so righteous, the melancholia lifting as he proudly described what I could only think of as a welfare state. This race disturbed me with every new thing I learned of it.

Shana, resting on a low table, began to hum in her sleep. "Dammit, I pulled that chip. How can she keep doing that? I'm so sick of 'The Good Ship Lollypop,' I could scream!"

"Anthem!" Macro cried.

"What?"

"Anthem of L-L-Lolbah!"

"Lolbah? The Good Ship *Lolbah*?" I hadn't even realized what I'd said until Macro nodded. The cat kept humming.

"—physical demands of the highest honor," Shalf continued his obviously memorized patriot's speech.

Macro grasped Shalf's armless right hand and led him into the glass booth. "I w-will be gentle...and q-quick."

I stepped towards them. "Wait, I want to—" But they had gone, obscured by the oscillation of textured glass.

Seconds later a shrill ear-liquifying scream-hiss tore from the booth through the empty white room, sending the cat zooming beneath the table.

CHAPTER 9

COLD FUSION

Anything that is not forbidden, happens
—Qwiffian Handbook of Sapience

The metallic drone of the C-130's engines shut down, turning silence inside out. A blade of light severed the rear hatch from the plane. The door fell away like a drawbridge, crashing to the ground in a puff of white crystals. Antarctic winds violated the fuselage with terrorists of light and cold that raged through, stealing the last image from dark-adapted eyes, the last warm breath from the lungs, the last calorie of heat from the skin. Jason Childress gasped.

"Put these on," the pilot said. "It's fifteen yards to Clothing Issue. These'll keep you from becoming a poster child for CryoGen Labs on the way there." Ernest Gage tossed Childress, Lenny Wontok, and six other researchers each a pair of Eskimo kamids—fur boots with hard soles—and an orange parka. "And take my advice, children—don't breathe. And don't smile—your teeth'll crack." He roared a sadistic laugh that must have carried clear to the foothills of McMurdo Station.

Childress lifted a small green plastic bag for Wontok's consideration. "What'll I do with this?"

"Ah, yes. The solid yawn. You know there was no turbulence, don't you? Gage was dicking with us." Wontok hurried into his gear. "If I thought I wouldn't need that bastard again, I'd hide it in the cockpit—for delayed discovery.

"Take a look outside, it's fairly calm. Might even get to see Mount Erebus."

"*This* is calm? It's a blizzard where I come from."

"Where you come from nobody even knows what this white stuff is."

Almost true. In Southern California, if Childress wanted to see snow he'd have to drive east for hours. But in this place, he was guaranteed to see not much else. His breath condensed in a wad that hung before him, blocking his vision as he dressed. He reluctantly left the protection of the cargo plane and ventured out onto the ramp. The frigid air burned his nostrils, growing to an ache that spread through his sinuses. His eyes throbbed, receding into the warm moisture of their sockets. Even in this transition month of March, it was unbelievably bright. In a month the sun would begin to set, shrouding the continent in darkness until September.

Wontok loped down the ramp to join Childress. They scampered through the snow and biting wind, following the other researchers along a suspended rope line leading to their first stop before the dorms.

Gage led the group of researchers into the clothing issue hut. A ghostly fog the size of a doorman formed in the space between the inner and outer doors as one door closed and another opened. Childress balked.

"Never mind Henrietta. She always shows up when warm air hits cold," Wontok said.

"Henrietta?" Childress said.

"They name everything here—trucks, tractors, even condensation. Wait'll you meet Darlene."

Clothing issue consisted of a desk, a dozen over-stuffed shelves, and very little floor space. Childress did not relish the thought of all nine people crammed into that small area, and crowded ahead to get his supplies and leave. He heard someone curse him in a not-so-low whisper. Though the building was a relatively warm forty-five or fifty degrees fahrenheit, Childress couldn't wait to grab his gear and get into the frigid space between the inner and outer doors. Henrietta was all the company he could handle about now.

Wontok soon joined Childress and they agreed that they would walk alone to the dorm. Opening the outer door, they left, Henrietta waving a misty farewell.

Childress felt the blood in his face retreat from beneath his balaclava to somewhere deep in his body as he strained to make out the buildings in the distance through the blowing snow. There were no guide ropes strung; he followed Wontok so closely his boot toes clipped the big man's heels. They traveled hurriedly. The weather could get bad, Wontok had warned. When you had things to do in Antarctica, you moved your ass. More likely, Jason imagined, Wontok smelled stew cooking through these fifty-mile-per-hour winds.

Entering the dormitory was like being slapped in the face with a hairbrush while kissing a full pin cushion. Childress' face stung with returning blood-warmth. The fifty degrees of the dorm felt like a hundred after dragging his face through negative-degree winds. As he removed the balaclava, his nose began to swell, capillaries filling like thirsty reservoirs.

"Ah-shit" Childress sneezed, shuddering. "It's not cold—it's beyond cold. When did we leave Earth?"

"It's late summer, Doc! Once the winds die down, it'll be a toasty twenty or so degrees. You outta try winter here," Wontok raved, removing his parka and gloves, wiping the snow crystals from his eyelashes.

"No thanks." Childress pulled the hood down to free his hair, burying his gloved hands in his armpits.

"You'd better undress. If you stay too warm inside, you'll suffer worse when we go out again. We only have ten days—you'd better acclimate as quickly as you can."

"I'm never going out there again and I'm removing *nothing*," Childress said, only half kidding.

Wontok rummaged through his gabardine bag, pulling out a lined flannel shirt. He held it up, scrutinizing the dimensions. "Hmmm. They never do make the arms long enough."

"That's because they're made for humans." Childress found his own smaller version of the shirt.

"Yeah, I told my mamma she shouldn't have humped a white-man. It does something to the kids. Monsters."

"Hybrid vigor."

Wontok's grin turned to a grimace as he eased into the shirt. Childress gasped and grunted when the cold lining of his shirt assaulted his skin.

"We've got rooms twelve and fourteen. The head's down the hall, chow's that way," Wontok pointed to the opening of a tunnel to their left. "Tunnels connect most of the buildings here. I'll bet you appreciate that. Just remember we're in the California Hotel. You'll see a sign over the tunnel entrances telling you where they lead."

"California Hotel? Trying to make us feel at home, are they?"

"Why not? Well, ready for the best food this side of oblivion?"

"Yeah sure. How many people you think will be in the mess now? Maybe we should wait for an off hour."

"Can't get more *off* than now. It's three-thirty in the morning, Doc!"

He trudged into the tunnel, Childress following. An endless string of clear fifteen-watt bulbs lit the way along the Granco arch tunnel. Rebirth at the other end of the tunnel greeted them with music, laughter, and curious cooking aromas Childress couldn't quite identify. It looked just like a bar, but somewhat better lit and furnished with metal military-issue tables and chairs. The other researchers with whom Childress had shared the flight, misery, and barf bags, huddled over a pool table and juke box in a far corner.

The pilot caught Childress' eye, pulled a toothpick from the log-jam of many imbedded in his tightly curled hair, jabbed it in the gap in his teeth, and swaggered over to meet him. "I was about to send out a search party for you children. You didn't wait for them to string the guide ropes."

Wontok took a step toward him. "I've been here enough times to know my way around. Don't worry yourself."

"Yeah, Tonto, give my regards to Nanook." Gage turned, spinning on one heel of his cowboy boots as the group behind him laughed.

"What a jerk. He always like that?" Childress said.

Wontok pulled out a chair and sat at the table Childress had claimed. "He wouldn't know how to be any other way."

"I heard that, Nikuma. Watch your step. I'm your only way outta here," the pilot barked from across the room. The group at the pool table laughed again.

"Let's get some tacos," Wontok said.

"Tacos? *Here*?"

"Yeah. Don't you smell it?" He inhaled liters of air, filling his large chest. "Ah, pemmican. They must have run out of fresh meat. I can smell the molasses and raisins in perfect balance with the Tobasco."

"Raisins? In tacos?" Childress' stomach gurgled.

"Pemmican's soaked in raisin syrup and molasses, then dried. Like beef jerky. You'll love it, Doc."

Somehow Childress would have to forget what he was

eating: Hot sauce and fruited meat was enough to convert him to vegetarianism. But, much to his surprise, pemmican tacos turned out be something he'd have to add to his list of exotic cuisine—especially when washed down with the New Zealand Beer sent over from Scott Base "next door." Childress was especially happy to discover he'd have to put away four thousand or more calories just to stay alive in Antarctica. He was pleasantly stuffed, mellowed and serene for the impending orientation speech he'd heard all new arrivals had to bear.

A thin darkly-bearded man of about forty stepped into the mess hall, clearing his throat. "Gentlemen. Listen up. Antarctica isn't a winter wonderland. You've been assigned a trainer and guide for a reason. Do what he says. You can't skate through your day on automatic pilot like you do in real life. This isn't real life—it's a living hell, made tolerable only by the knowledge that you'll ultimately get to leave.

"You don't get to make more than one mistake in Antarctica. One wrong step on a shallow snowbridge, you fall into a crevasse and die. No one will rescue you. Ask someone about Williams—he's still sitting in his bulldozer at the bottom of the sound.

"Forget your boot liners out on expedition, the moisture from your feet freezes, you get frostbite then gangrene—you lose body parts, maybe you die. Forget to zip up, forget your insulating undergarments, your core temperature drops—you die. Don't get your ass in at first sign of a blizzard or a white-out, you get disoriented, lost—you die. In Antarctica, you think about what you're doing, what you're going to do, all the time. Alertness and planning are your gods. Antarctica is like skydiving blindfolded: You have to be acutely aware of every clue in order to get out of it alive." He paused, letting the drama of his words soak in. All was quiet. "That is all."

That was it. Short and to the point. After a few hours rest Childress would get to see first hand if any of it was true.

Childress slept. Upon awakening he noticed only one thing: The wind that had sung him to sleep was now mute. He pulled out of his sleeping bag on the cot and climbed up on a desk to look out the high ceiling-flush window. Everything looked all white. The wind must have blown drifts clear up to cover the windows. He checked his watch: 10:05 AM. Feeling more in synch with the hour now, he was ready for his tour of the newly-built binocular observatories, a revolutionary achievement collectively known as The Cloud-Buster.

After the cold clothes warmed on his body, Childress went down the hall to roust Wontok...and nearly ran head-on into him coming towards his own room. "Hey, you're up. Have you called Marx yet to tell him we're coming?"

"Nope. No need. White-out."

"What? I thought you were going to set up some viewing time at the observatory. It's what we're here for. I'm dying to get my hands on that Cloud-Buster I've heard so much about."

"Even the Cloud-Buster can't deal with a white-out—if we could get to it, which we can't. We'll have to wait till the condition lifts. That's what happens sometimes when the winds die."

It hadn't dawned on Childress till now that had snowdrifts piled high enough to cover his window, it wouldn't have been so light in his room. "Damn. How long do these things last?"

"Who knows? An hour. Ten hours. A few days. Antarctica has crazy weather—fifteen different things can happen in one day, or it can be all the same for weeks on end. We just wait it out. That's why we're here for ten days for a six-hour project, Doc. Pray ten days is long enough."

Dejected, Childress followed Wontok down the hall and through the tunnel to the mess hall/bar, where a dozen other people were eating tall stories for breakfast. Childress chose a table in a deserted corner.

"Antisocial today, aren't we, Doc?"

"No, it's not that. I...I just don't like crowds."

"Ha!" Wontok laughed. "And you *teach*?"

"Yeah. Never mind that. They serve eggs here?"

"Oh sure. Eggs. We got lots of eggs."

"They're not...*penguin* eggs or anything like that, are they?"

"Nah. Chilean chickens'. Bawk, bawk, gringo!"

Childress smiled and ordered eight scrambled eggs with Canadian bacon and toast.

About halfway through their meal a shadow converged on their table. Childress looked up into a toothpicked grin. Gage the pilot was about to make a pest of himself again.

"You children sleep well? Hope you enjoy your boredom

during this white-out. Say, what *do* savages do when they're bored—twiddle their thumbs? Weave baskets? Jack off? Need a magnifying glass to find it, Running Bear?" A sprinkle of laughter came from the group.

Wontok chewed his eggs like they were jerky, keeping his eyes focused on his plate.

Childress spoke up. "Do you have a bloody problem? Why don't you leave him alone? What's he done to you?"

"Just trying to keep the world's women safe from his raping kind. I especially don't want him fucking my sister."

Childress glanced over at the group in the corner. He was certain there had been no women on the plane.

"Which one's your sister?" Wontok finally said.

The pilot slammed his fists down on the table, lifted it and pushed it over. Dishes crashed to the floor; Childress' fork flew up and hit him in the forehead.

"That did it, you red son-of-a-bitch! You're history—just like most of you savage bastards. We shoulda killed you all when we had the chance." Gage sprang forward, eyes wild, and swung hard at a towering Wontok, connecting solidly with his jaw. A sharp pop cracked the dry air.

Wontok flung his head back, red strands of bloody saliva slinging across his stunned face. For a few interminable seconds Wontok did nothing, then suddenly became a screaming confusion of flying hair and legs. A leg came between the pilot's ankles and jerked the man off his feet, sending him to the hard floor with a gasping grunt. With giant arms, Wontok reached down and lifted the pilot in the air over his head, and he strolled, as if in slow motion, towards the front entrance where he heaved the flailing pilot into and through the first of two doors to the outside, splintering it like a model airplane. Gage howled, scrambling to his feet, jerking back into the dining area, retreating, seemingly unable to choose between Wontok and the outer door.

With one decisive move Gage pushed down on the handle of the outer door. The room filled with blinding white. The pilot stumbled backwards into it and fell, the white abyss swallowing all but his angry screams.

Childress stared unbelieving into the absoluteness of it all, barely conscious of the applause Wontok's act had generated.

The white-out was everything he'd heard it was: a white blinding motionless null where all perspective ceased to exist. The division between land and sky vanished. Buildings shrank to toy-sized trinkets tossed in the snow. Reality warped to a flat two dimensions. It was like standing on the *inside* of a sheet of paper.

Snapping out of his awe, Childress ran to the edge of the white to find Gage. If Gage walked any distance he'd get completely disoriented and be unable to even guess which way was up. "Gage! Gage, where are you?"

A voice yipped in the distance. In seconds a shivering, bleeding man staggered through the doorway.

"Hey, we wouldn't want to have to send a search party out after you," Childress said, throwing his arm around the pilot's shoulders, leading him to an upright table. Someone slammed the door behind them. "Brandy!" Childress yelled at the bar, maneuvering Gage to a chair. He leaned down close to the pilot's ear. "Now you know what savages do when they're bored. Let me give you a bit of advice. Don't fuck with the Indian."

The pilot looked up squinty-eyed and exploded into a giggle. "No shit, English. No shit."

When the bartender delivered the brandy, Childress shot to the bar and pulled Wontok around, leading him by the elbow into the tunnel to the California Hotel. "How's your jaw?"

Wontok moaned, rubbing his face gingerly.

"Naughty boy, One Dog. Beating up on helpless brain-deficient red-necks. Nice touch, tossing him out in the white like that." Their laughter bounced off the curved tunnel walls all the way to the dorm.

* * *

Childress and Wontok were condemned to each other's company, playing poker, telling stories for two days during continued bad weather. On the third day their eyes met: The wind blew steadily but not fiercely, signaling the end of the white-out.

Veins full of glycopeptides to decrease oxygen demand and increase cold tolerance, wrapped in fifteen pounds of snow clothing, they ventured out into the desolation of Antarctica's frozen bowels. It would be a grueling mile walk to the observatory. Childress looked forward to it, meeting its challenge with something he had never found inside himself before.

The distant calving of ice, popping, crackling in the sound like far-off gunfire, reported over winds that howled in protest at human intrusion of emptiness and solitude. Though aloneness and the cold wind were constant companions, Childress drew not only his bearings, but his strength from them. This was a place where he could really know himself, be reminded of his frailty and his mission to carry on and triumph over his own inadequacies.

For most, aloneness was a way of life here, a specter that haunted the needy soul until resignation to its vastness consumed it; for Childress, it was a gift. When someone asked him later what Antarctica was like, he would answer: "It was what I could only describe as a religious experience, of being One with all that one surveyed, where no one should be at all."

Childress spent the first few minutes in the anteroom of the observatory probing through the balaclava covering his face, desperately chipping ice crystals from his nose hairs and eyelashes.

Wontok removed his heavy clothing. He peeled off his balaclava, offering a muffled introduction of Childress to Dr. Kevin Marx, the atmospheric phenomena specialist at McMurdo Observatory, home of one of the world's only binocular telescopes—and the only Cloud-Buster.

"Well, I'm glad they've finally sent in someone who knows what the hell they're doing," the gray-haired man said.

"Don't count on our finding out much," Childress said. "Our preliminary investigation turned up nothing. The data from UARS choked our infallible parallel computer. We still have no idea what we're dealing with here."

"Only one other researcher has used this telescope since installation. There's been no funding approved to send anyone down since."

"Well, you're in luck," Childress said, removing his snow clothes. "We're here on our own time and our own money. Haven't you used the telescope?"

"My field is auroras. We don't need a trillion-dollar telescope for that. Follow me. Darlene's through here." He waved his hand at the green door behind him.

"Darlene?" Childress whispered to Wontok as they ascended the cement stairwell.

"*This* is Darlene," Marx said, smiling.

To an eye unaccustomed to the astronomer's realm, it was nothing but a long tube coming up towards a crack in a domed roof, surrounded by a tangle of golden metal supports, levers, wheels, gears, all surrounded by banks of computers and laser technology. To Childress it was Christmas, and this was his first train set.

"Magnificent. It's nothing like I'd imagined it. Of course, I only have experience with the one at Mount Palomar in California. This...*this* is unearthly."

Passing through another door, the three men ascended the metal stairway to the top of the observatory, where red light, necessary to preserve dark adaptation during night viewing, washed over every surface in the small control room.

"It took Japanese microcircuitry to bring this dream to life. She's a grand experiment that worked on its first try. With fifteen terabytes of programmable ROM in that console, there's nothing she can't do—even filter out a cloud cover in Antarctica. And, she's the second binocular scope ever built, in perfect synchrony with the one next door. Everything you do here is duplicated in her twin. You have real 3-D imaging," Marx said.

"You'd have to be a programmer to use it," Childress said.

"Well, yes, to an extent. But she generally operates like a standard cadadioptic system—that's both refracting and reflecting, Wontok—with a focal ratio of three."

"Three? Christ. How do you handle chromatic aberration with a ratio that small?"

"Completely suppressed with the microcircuitry. And she is completely aplanatic—no spherical aberrations, either. You can actually change the concavity of the mirror, and add molecular filters to the lens for differential wavelength viewing, all with a few keystrokes. She also lends herself well to spectral analysis, interferometry, and infrared photography. No more messing with liquid nitrogen to cool the lens. Just let a little of the outside in with this key." He pointed at the control panel.

"Incredible," Childress said. "How do you keep snow out of the dome?"

"The slit's covered with a charged net. Snow can't get in or collect on it."

Childress stared upwards, mouth agape, through the white

slit at the top of the dome.

"And as you've no doubt noticed," Marx continued, "she's set in an altazimuth mounting. You can change altitude and azimuth at the touch of a key. With this reference chart," he handed Childress a laminated table of astronomical calculations and key sequences, "you can zero in and resolve any of the deep-sky objects listed. Anything not on the chart, I'm afraid, does take a programmer/ operator to find them."

"And through a bloody *cloud cover,*" Childress muttered. "I don't suppose it works in daylight as well," he joked.

"Not for deep space. But you can use her in daylight for other things—locating weather balloons and overdue aircraft, spying on Patagonians and Kiwis, and for the reason you're here: the phenomenon over the pole. Choose your magnification and lens conditions. Darlene does it all."

Yes, the anomaly was indeed the reason Childress had bribed Wontok into bringing him here. But, his work would be just a prelude to the real gifts of Darlene: objects in the southern sky. He could hardly wait for nightfall. Eleven p.m. seemed so far away.

"Thank you, Dr. Marx. Well, I guess we'd better get at it, One Dog."

Childress eased in the seat before the huge 3-D color monitor. Wontok wheeled up next to Childress in a big throne of an office chair, hands over one of four keyboards. There they both stayed— Childress observing and vomiting instructions to Wontok who madly tapped keys and saved Childress' comments on tape. Hot ham sandwiches from Marx's microwave provided a short break from the monotony. By ten p.m.—dusk—Childress elected to give up, disheartened. They had found nothing to add to the report from Wontok's not-so-crazy-after-all parallel processor in San Diego.

The only thing that kept Childress from screaming through the observatory like a psycho was his date with deep space, graciously provided through an occluded sky by the machine that had failed him in his research. It was time for a little recreation.

"I'm turning in," Wontok said, heaving his ursine body from the chair.

"Yeah, get some sleep. Don't wake me tomorrow; I'll be sleeping in."

"You'll only have about four hours of dark. Enjoy." And with that he pounded down the metal stairs. Voices. A door creaked shut at the bottom of the stairs and another set of footsteps, lighter, came up to the control platform.

"I heard the bad news. Coffee?" Marx said, setting a steaming cup on a bench.

Childress sighed, forgetting to thank him. "I guess we'll be pulling out of here in a couple of days. But before I go, I must take a look at deep space from this hemisphere. I've only seen photos of some of the nebulas and galaxies."

"All your key-in sequences are listed on the card. Be my guest," Marx said, turning to go. "I'll be in my office if you need me."

Childress nodded and pressed the appropriate keys. The round platform on which the telescope was mounted whirred and clunked beneath him, rotating slowly into place. The long tube tilted higher and locked into position. Childress leaned forward, peering into the big screen. The Milky Way sparkled in 3-D realism. He again punched in more instructions, asking for greater magnification. The Eta Carinae nebula glowed red and fiery, tiny blue and green flecks decorating it. Childress had never seen green wavelengths in any of his observations at Mount Palomar. He was in awe. He zoomed in to the keyhole in the center of the nebula, home of Carina II, the remnant of a twenty-five-thousand-year-old supernova.

He keyed in new coordinates again, sampling everything he knew to be in the sky. First the Horsehead Nebula in Orion, then the Orion Nebula itself. Lastly, he typed the sequence for Crux—the Southern Cross. His chances of getting a look at it again in his life were slim, and he savored the experience.

"There," he said softly. "There's the Jewel Box. I'd like to pluck one of you and take it to Rita." He chuckled to himself. What had possessed him to think of that poor woman? He made a mental note to call when he got back to find out how she was doing after her fall. He hadn't stayed to help her. He had run when the voices came, when the beating in his head took over.

Shaking off the disturbing memories of that horrible day, he zoomed to the stunning cluster of hot blue stars encircling the red giant, Kappa Crucis. He stared at that same spot for a full two minutes. He jerked back, rubbing his eyes, searching the drawers for anti-static cloth, finding only one. He rubbed the screen vigorously, again leaning into the monitor. "Where is it?" he squealed. "Where the hell is it?" He called up his last typed-in sequence: It matched the one listed for Kappa Crucis on the chart.

Something was wrong, terribly wrong with the sky. Bolting down the metal staircase, through the door and down the cement stairs, Childress dashed through the green door into the lounge. He shot a panicked look at the computer terminal, decided against using it without permission or supervision.

He went to a door marked "Lt. Commander K. Marx." *Shit, a military man.* He rushed in anyway, finding Marx sleeping soundly on a sofa, devoured by a sleeping bag. "Dr. Marx," Childress said softly. "Dr. Marx."

The man woke with a start. "Yeah?"

"I need your help. I have to talk with someone—anyone—at Las Campanas Observatory in Chile. I have to know if they've seen it too."

"Seen what? Australia's a better bet." Marx yawned and emerged from his cocoon.

"I don't know anyone in Australia. Just get on the net. It's *very* important or I wouldn't have awakened you. Ask for Buenovista. He knows me."

Marx waddled stiffly into the lounge, rounding the corner of the front desk. He clumsily typed in a code at the keyboard and waited. A red starburst flashed on the screen and the modem beeped. "Mac Eyes to Scamp. Marx code 899. Request patch-in to Dr. Buenovista," Marx said.

In seconds a young man with a dark droopy mustache appeared on the screen. "Dr. Marx. What brings you out at this hour?" he slurred through a thick Spanish accent.

"Sorry, Manuel. Dr. Childress says it's important."

Childress moved in front of Marx. "Sir, have you seen anything strange in the region of Kappa Crucis?"

"I don't know. I only handle the satellite data. Wait." Manuel's face eroded away in little red blocks, slowly painted over by the starburst. A full minute passed. To Childress it felt like an hour. Finally a familiar face appeared on the screen. "Dr. Buenovista here—Jason! How are you? It's been months. Maria enjoyed your jokes the last time we were—"

"Jorge, please. Have you seen anything strange in the region of Kappa Crucis? Have you looked over there recently?"

"We seem to have a malfunction in our large scope—artifacts of some sort. The mirror may be pitted, or maybe we need a new lens."

"It's not a malfunction. We've got the same thing down here. The Coalsack Nebula—it's supposed to be dark. It's all lit up with stars! The Coalsack Nebula is gone!"

CHAPTER 10

POLARITIES

Life rests on tiny coincidences.
—Qwiffian Handbook of Sapience

They came for me shortly after Macro had jettisoned Shalf's twisted lifeless body to Restructure down on level eight. Macro said that even in death, a Hagion was useful to The Purpose. Macro's lack of concern for the pain he had caused, for whatever he'd done to Shalf to kill him, disturbed me. How could this sequence of events just happen, and no one even remark of its tragedy?

Marching up the long spiral, a roach on each side of me, Shana trotting and complaining behind, I had time to reflect on *my* purpose. I was here to preserve the colony, I told myself, to free myself and my friends. I couldn't afford the luxury of grief for the windfall friend, Shalf. They lived and died as they chose. It was none of my business what the roaches did to each other, or how sick it was. Shalf had died during egg extraction. Its egg would be preserved and someday be fertilized. Simple. It had happened many times; it would happen many times more. The Purpose would still be fulfilled. The Hagions would not only survive, they would prosper. It was the will of Hope.

What I wanted to know was: Just who was this Hope bitch, anyway? She should be flogged.

My legs felt like sand had replaced my blood. I longed to lie down somewhere. Many hours of hunger had mutated into a nauseated fatigue. My body told me I'd been awake several days, and if I didn't get some rest my mind would start slipping into the dream state while I fought to stay conscious. In this nightmare of a place, I couldn't afford the hallucinations of sleep deprivation; there would be no way for me to separate reality from delusion. Already I had the ridiculous sensation that the ship was somehow getting bigger; it was my tired mind, my aching legs protesting their lack of rest. The spiral walkway just *seemed* longer than I remembered.

I balked at the entrance to Vtekdao's chambers, stealing a few seconds to catch my breath, let the blood ooze back into my legs as the two Hagions jabbed their nasty rubber fingers into my arms, urging me on.

"Vtekdao awaits," the roach on my right said.

I savored the little moment of defiance, resisting their tugs, reveling in the realization of how physically weak they were; if I tore away now and ran, there was nothing they could do about it. But I hadn't the energy, the strength for such bravery. I went limp in their grip, resigned to Vtekdao's impending anger.

Pungent smells of a wet burnt forest accosted my nostrils when we went through the wall. Someone was completely out of control here, releasing pheromone like a Tijuana whore. Vtekdao sat in his chrysalis of a chair, a roach at attention at each side of him. I couldn't tell from which of the Hagions the odor emanated, though remembering what Shalf had said about the taboo, I deduced it could only be Vtekdao who stank. Any one else would have been sent away, "absorbed."

"Ree-tah!" Vtekdao said. "Your delays in returning my gift to me do not please me. But I haven't much time to discuss it. I must be in Application soon. Before I go, I need you to understand how much it grieves me that you have witnessed Shalf's infirmity of faith. Shalf was weak, undisciplined, uncommitted to The Purpose, and so died. Shalf has dishonored me and the will of Hope."

I couldn't think of how to respond. The bastard saw Shalf as only a player in his maladjusted hierarchy, with no other value.

"Do you understand, Ree-tah?"

I nodded.

"I have many things to discuss with you. There remains the matter of the Benefactors. That will have to be delayed until after the election. The Benefactors will make the glory of my re-election even more profound, I dare say. And you, Ree-tah, will be responsible for the honor and reverence bestowed upon me by my Ignorants and Obligants."

The Hagion on my right shifted, clicking in place. I shot it a sideways glance: Its eyes bulged.

"Now for the matter of the creature. I've been told that you and zhe communicate. I have therefore decided to—" He slipped into a silent seizure. I didn't want to hear *what* he'd decided. My imagination ran amok in the twenty seconds of his absence.

"...remove zhan from your possession indefinitely. Zhe has witnessed the inner workings of the governmental chambers. Zhe has become a security risk." I gasped. "No harm will come to zhan. Zhe will stay with me." He uttered a fizzing noise from that quarry that passed for a mouth, and Shana darted between my legs, leapt up on the round red table, and padded into Vtekdao's lap.

I swallowed a mouthful of saliva, fighting off nausea and tears. He would never believe Shana didn't speak to me directly in some kind of secret language. It was too late to reverse my lie, but that didn't stop me from trying. "No, you don't understand. She can't speak—not words. She doesn't *tell* me anything. I just know how she *feels*."

Vtekdao rose. The oily pine-ash smell thickened.

"Please rest, Ree-tah. After I am reinstated as Honorable Altruist, we will arrange for you to honor your original agreement. I am due in Application this moment," he said, clicking towards me. "My product will be the first of the new generation to be placed in vivigenesis. Mine will be the first! My progeny will be heir to my throne, and re-election will be meaningless!" he raved. "It is the Ancient Way!"

I almost swallowed my tongue. That was a Phaedran phrase, long eliminated from neohuman speech along with the dogma it represented, and here it blossomed in all its hideous glory. How had Vtekdao learned it?

The Hagion to my right again stomped its hooves, gurgling a stifled whimper, an unmistakable cry of indignation and protest that would never be allowed to escape—not in Vtekdao's presence, but perhaps, with a little coaxing, in mine. I'd have to befriend this roach.

"Shana, come. Kitty, kitty," I pleaded with her, but she sat at the far edge of the red table blinking her grapefruit eyes, ignoring me. I knew Vtekdao would make her his goddamn music box again.

"Zhe is mine. You may not have contact until a way is devised to erase zhan memories of all zhe has heard and seen. Accept that." Erase? "No!" Fury and a surge of energy from deep inside gushed to the surface. I jerked my arms upward, freeing them from rubbery grasps, and rushed forward, slamming my palms into hard chitin, pushing Vtekdao over like an uprooted stump. He sagged backwards, hitting he floor in a controlled flail, hands wadding, legs kicking in the air. I heard a dull crack as he hit the floor, followed by a frail wheeze.

Oh god, I'd done it now—popped him open like a warm Eskimo Pie.

I imagined I'd see white creamy stuff oozing from cracks in his torso, but saw only a delicate rearranging of his spindly many-jointed legs as he pushed himself up with his long fingers and stood, chest heaving rhythmically.

"Stasis for the creature!" he boomed.

Two Hagions rushed towards Shana. She crouched, ears flattened, ready to bolt, but they were on her within seconds. She growled and hissed. Shana's forelegs and neck clamped between thin, rigid fingers, the Hagions carried her swiftly to a clear cylinder on a far bench, dropping her in and slamming the top shut. The jar filled with a viscous pink fluid.

I screamed in a struggling Hagion grip, watching my beloved pet thrash pitifully, chest surging for air, eyes bulging from their sockets, mouthing a fanged silent scream. Then, she went flaccid, eyes still open and staring vacantly.

I doubled over, screaming, "You killed her! You murdering bastards, you killed her!" I cried, wretching, trying to purge the deepest anger and hatred I had ever felt.

"Zhe is alive. Suspended. Zhe will be no longer be a cause of discord between us, Ree-tah," Vtekdao said.

Everything inside of me must have shown on my face when I finally looked up: Vtekdao stepped back. "You have *not* permission to touch me. *Ever.* You are the Savior, true, but the Savior *knows* zhaz place. Now, if you'll excuse me, I must depart."

Vtekdao's voice sounded humbled, somehow. Maybe I'd scared him. I couldn't take my eyes off of Shana, floating helplessly in the cylinder like an untethered astronaut, eternity in her eyes. I wanted to believe she was still alive, but found it impossible. Tears washed her from my vision.

I relaxed in the Hagions' grip and they released me. I wanted to die, right then and there. I couldn't bear the thought of the long trek back to my quarters.

"You wish to be escorted to your quarters?" the Hagion to

my right asked.

"Can't you just transport me back there? Why do I have to walk all that way when you can do that?"

"If you are able and willing to go, then we cannot. Energy must be preserved for Harvest."

Harvest. Great. What other wonder of Hagion propriety was I to witness? I looked down at this Hagion, the one who had reacted so strongly to Vtekdao's announcement of an heir. I had a hunch about this roach. Avoiding the twirling pupils, I studied his brow wrinkles, memorizing as best I could every blue crease. "You're Tmait. Am I correct?"

"I am honored you remember me."

My grief under control now, I planned carefully every word that would leave my mouth. "Ah, yes, Vtekdao's opponent in the election."

"And First Flagellant to the Honorable Altruist."

"Looks like Vtekdao wins either way. You'll still be First Flagellant, right?"

A rush of air escaped from its torso. "If a viable heir...The heir may choose anyone to serve beneath zhan."

"Perhaps he will choose you."

Tmait clicked to the wall. "Perhaps. Let us walk, shall we?"

I followed him down the spiral. "There's something I don't understand. If Vtekdao plans on putting an heir in his place, why have an election?"

"It...it is an unanticipated development. But the Ignorants must not be denied their duty of voting. The election will take place. True, in the event Vtekdao succeeds in producing a viable progeny, the election will be meaningless. The dissatisfaction the Ignorants may feel if that happens...."

The bitterness in his voice charged me. His suffering somehow made my pain and depression less. "*And* it is possible you will have neither title."

His silence betrayed his torment. What a subversive bitch I'd turned out to be. My delight in my own newly discovered talent was almost enough to extinguish the persistent internal image of my drowned cat. Almost. The horror of those protruding eyes, that crying throat, would be with me forever, even if by some miracle I did get her back alive. All the more reason to torture this roach with self-doubt: He had restrained me as Shana drowned.

The delirium of fatigue and hunger grew less. One thing would drive me: payback.

"What will you do, Tmait? How is this fair?"

He stopped, preempted by one of those seizures. I stared again at his brow creases, closing my eyes, testing my memory of minute detail. He would be indelibly imprinted in my mind, along with a catalog of other roaches that would become key to my plan. I could afford no misjudgments.

"I know not how to interpret Vtekdao's alteration of protocol. Zhe reinstates the Ancient Ways, long superseded by the election process," Tmait finally said.

I couldn't help feeling from his tone that he had betrayed a confidence, if not with Vtekdao, then with someone else. "Then, the election process is new to your civilization."

"It replaces the Ancient Way. Learned from humans through years of observing your activities."

And embraced. Along with silly songs. "Don't worry, I won't tell anyone you've told me this. You have the word of the Savior. Vtekdao dishonors every Hagion, the will of Hope, by what he does."

"Yes. Yes, Ree-tah, you *do* understand! Zhe must not procreate until The Purpose is fulfilled. It is the will of Hope."

"What *is* The Purpose?"

He stopped and glared at me. The question had been wrong for the Savior to ask.

"It is the will of Hope," he said.

I smiled and nodded in agreement. I would get nowhere with that kind of circular argument. I probably couldn't count on anyone telling me what The Purpose was. Except maybe Cos. Maybe.

The muscles in my legs quivered. It wouldn't be long before I collapsed from exhaustion. Again, that same impression of the walk to level seven being longer, *much* longer than before, nagged at my tired brain. The delusions of a weary mind took over, distorting perceptions. Flashes of Shana's submerged body stabbed behind my eyes, producing deepening waves of desolation. It was all I could do to keep upright.

We passed five red dots in silence. Tmait fugued twice. Some minutes later, passing the dot on level seven, I made a serious effort to count the paces from it to my quarters: twenty-seven steps. Just as Tmait stopped at my quarters he had another absence. I decided to get more courageous with my anatomy lessons. I reached up and delicately smoothed my fingers over the exposed brain, pressing a small indentation into the velvety cortex with my finger. The roach quaked in fine trembles, a soft gurgle crawling up from deep within its abdomen. The nictitating membranes slammed up over its eyes. At that moment I cursed myself for what I'd done.

"Forgive me! Forgive me!" Tmait squealed, suddenly running in tight circles.

I grabbed one of his hands, jerking him to a stop. "What happened?" I couldn't tell him I'd been feeling up his brain.

"I must go to Procedure. The Billboard has malfunctioned. The penalty is great if I do not have it corrected immediately!"

"Billboard? What are you talking about?"

"Billboard implant. The molychine of Worship!"

I stood, staring into Tmait's still eyes. The pupils no longer twirled. My grip on his wrist was so hard, I could feel his pulse—a peculiar two-phased one, so fast and rhythmic you could belly dance to it. "Tmait, it's OK. I won't tell. I promise." He panted.

Christ, what had he just told me? That messages, prayers played in his head? Was this the cause of the seizures? I had to get to the bottom of this. "Tmait, come to my quarters. I must speak with you." I tugged at his wrist, pulling him forward with me through the wall.

"I must remedy this. It is forbidden for me to proceed without—"

"Don't worry about it."

He relaxed visibly, fingers drooping. Inside my quarters I found myself looking around for traces of Shana and quickly buried the sudden recollection of her whereabouts. "What does the Billboard play?"

"They are different for each of us. Now I go." Before I could grab for him, he turned and dashed through the wall with the same terrible speed that had overcome my cat. Hagions could *move*.

I sat on the edge of my bed, ideas, questions, images spinning through my brain. I was vaguely aware I'd have to put some kind of food on top of the sadness that roosted in my guts like a ravenous vulture that waited to devour my soul when I finally slept. I leaned back on one elbow, pulling my aching legs up. Before long my only view was the ceiling and even it, in time, ceased to exist. I closed my eyes and imagined I was in the jar with my cat, staring out through the glass at the vulgar Vtekdao, willing his death, willing my own.

Cosmigellan. *Cos where are you*? I need you to know how bad I feel. I need you to hold me, show me you love me. I need you to sing me the song of The One, flood my mind with the Universe so that no images of woe can intrude upon my dreams, eroding my will to survive. I'll never make it without you. I'll never endure Shana's living death.

Rita, I am with you. Trust me. Know that Shana lives and is unharmed.

I can't believe that! It isn't possible. You didn't see what they did to her, the look on her face, the way she fought. I did. She is of The One. I experienced her fear. She knows you haven't abandoned her. Sleep now, Rita. Your strength will return with rest. His voice faded.

Stars explode in my head, shining brighter than any pain, filling me with awe and understanding. With quantum tentacles my mind reaches across the vastness of The All That Is, caressing it like a familiar friend. Galaxies dance a minuet about each other, tugging and being tugged in return, in a delicate balance of forces in perfect harmony. *That which is visible is governed by that which cannot be seen.* The galaxies rotate in their calculated manner due to something larger than them, something massive and unseen and dark, something that compresses them into form, giving their captured patterns meaning. *Without the darkness there is no light.* Ninety percent of everything is darkness, the light ignited because of it. Because of it, not in spite of it. Not at odds, in harmony. The way it is meant to be. The way of The All That Is.

My mind calmed, rested at peace among the galaxies, at One with all of nature. I slept.

My arm fell against something warm and smooth. I opened my eyes and found Cos' sleeping face next to mine, his dark eyes locked against his captivity. He slept as if we had never been brought to this ship, as if everything were as it should be. I wanted him inside me—his body, his mind, his love. I didn't remember much of what it was like to make love with him; it had been too long. All I could recall was that incredible sense of losing myself to an extraordinary power I could not-- did not want to—resist, as he entwined lavender electric filaments around and through my mind, seizing me, owning me as part of himself, erasing the boundaries until he and I were the same thing.

Watching him sleep so close to me, I realized it could happen again. I ran my fingers up the edge of his smooth jaw, through his thick black hair. He woke with a start, smiling as his eyes opened to my gaze.

"I'm surprised they let you come here," I said.

"Everyone is on Society for the election."

"I wanted to see that. But not as much as I want to stay here like this with you," I said, petting his face, rubbing his leg with my foot. "How will I ever thank you for trancing me last night? I never would have slept if you hadn't."

"I did nothing. Do I always have to remind you of your own skills?"

I smiled, feeling uneasy with the comment. Some part of me still didn't believe. "It was you, your voice, your caring that empowered me." My hand moved up his thigh.

"Rita, I can't."

"I thought the sex taboo applied to only Hagions. What business is it of theirs if we—"

"It is forbidden," he said, staring into me, grasping my hand and pulling it from his erection.

I wanted to cry. He desired me, but he allowed his fear to overpower his passion. Sitting up, I scooted off the end of the bed, leaving him to lie there with his excuse. "How will they know? How will they find out?" I shouted.

"They will know. They know everything you do."

"How in the hell do *you* know?"

He hesitated. A sheen of tears sparkled in his eyes. "I implanted the physiologic monitors and the transmitter. How else do you think they keep finding you, no matter where you are?"

I leaned against the bench below the computer console. It hadn't occurred to me how they always knew where I was. The fatigue had clouded my reason; perhaps that is what they wanted. Never again would this happen. Never. "Do they know my thoughts?"

"Of course not Rita, their technology is great, but not miraculous."

I felt better hearing that. At least I could have my secrets. "Take me to Procedure. I want the goddamn transmitter removed."

"Rita, no. If they don't find your pattern, it'll be a disaster. For both of us."

"I'll carry it with me. I don't want it inside me. Will you do it, or may I consider you a *defector*?" My coldness terrified me—it was so easy, so awfully easy. "Before we go, I need food. I haven't eaten in days."

"The pyramid key. Press it."

I did. A steaming metal bowl of quasi-lasagna materialized on the bench, a curling iron utensil beside it. "Hmm. Is this all they serve?"

"It is nutritious enough."

Quickly I stabbed into the warm square with the utensil, closing my eyes, preparing myself for the mismatched flavor of split-pea soup. I ate it quickly, without savoring it, then motioned to the wall. Cos nodded and we marched through it on our long walk to Procedure on level three. I counted thirty-nine paces from my room to level seven's red dot.

"How much sleep did I get, Cos?"

"Fourteen hours, with REM at every thirty-four minutes, lasting ten to fifteen minutes. The pattern was abnormal. You were very tired, Rita."

But I *had* slept. My brain probably wasn't playing tricks on me in a sleep-deprivation delusion. The distance was indeed longer between my quarters and the red dot, than it was fourteen hours ago when Tmait brought me here. I had no doubt now: The ship was growing.

Two levels up the spiral Cos stopped, gazing off in the distance.

"What's wrong? Are they on to us? Do they know what we're going to do?"

"No. It isn't the Hagions. It's Macro. He waits for us."

I understood. Cos was linked to the One at all times, and knew what befell any of the others, as he had with me. I was limited in my knowing, because Cos, for reasons known only to himself, restricted my access from day one on this ship. As much as it pained me, I had to respect his choice, as he respected my wishes when I had shut him out while planning my father's murder. If his reasons were at least as important, then I had no right to intrude. It was our way, the Qwiffian way.

When we entered Procedure we found Macro sitting slumped over on the low center table, his hands over his eyes, sobbing. I ran to him.

"Macro," I said, lifting his chin. "What happened?"

He looked up, his young face wet and flushed. "I lost another one. It w-was only zhaz th-third p-p-procedure. It...It sh-shouldn't have happened. It shouldn't have happened!" Holding him against my hip and stroking his hair, I rocked Macro, saying, "Shhh. It's OK. I know it hurts. I know."

"Th-they're coming here t-t-oo often, t-too m-many of them, t-t-too young! N-not one sh-should die! N-not one! Th-they say I'm b-b-blameless. How c-can that be?" Again, his hands went to his eyes, hiding his shame and guilt.

"Macro, listen to me. What happens if you refuse to engage in this activity?"

He stopped crying, looking up from wet hands. "Refuse?"

I felt Cos' hand smooth down my back. "It is forbidden, Rita. He cannot defy them."

"But what happens if he does? What have the Hagions told you they'd do to you if you disobeyed?"

I looked from Cos' to Macro's face, finding blankness in both. They glanced at each other several times before Cos spoke. "We can't remember."

I gasped in exasperation. "I don't believe it! You've turned yourself over to these roaches with no penalty spelled out for non-cooperation? Are you both fucking nuts?" I stomped around the lounge, my feet making no satisfying sounds on the spongy floor covering. Tramping and huffing, I went to the wall and pressed my hands against it, hissed at Antarctica bowing below me like a cowering dog, and stamped back to face two bewildered neohumans.

In a sudden surge of compliance, Cosmigellan produced a foot-long tweezers-like instrument from somewhere beneath the low table. "Sit down. It won't take long to remove the transmitter."

"I hate it when you de-rail me like that." I squatted down on the end of the table, still panting with frustration. An icy sting zipped through the back of my neck, making my ears ring momentarily.

Cos brought the tweezers before me, a tiny spiked thing resting in its small grip. "Your transmitter, Darling." He leaned down close as if to kiss me, but stopped. I stared at him. Lust danced in his eyes. I was afraid to kiss him, to violate the strange promise he had made to himself and to the Hagion ways.

Goddammit, I wanted him so badly I could have launched the QE2 in my underwear. To distract myself, I pinched the tiny transmitter from the tweezers, squeezing it painfully between the thumb and index finger of my left hand. "Macro, do me a favor. Take this and place it at the head of the bed in my quarters"

Macro smiled and carefully pinched the device from my fingers, bounding through the wall.

Cos spoke softly, seductively. "We've got about an hour before he returns. Now, what, my oh my, shall we do to occupy ourselves?" He pressed himself against my left shoulder. "No one will be in Application now."

I was puzzled as to what had changed his mind, but had no intention of quizzing him. He took me by the hand and led me to Application.

The redness of the lighting inflamed me, made me want him more than ever. I pulled him down to the floor, crawled on top of him, below the stare of the dozens of bobbing Hagion eggs. Beneath his caftan my hands wandered over every curve, dip, and rise of his musculature. He quivered and moaned as I straddled his hips, stabbed him inside me, rocked against him with the desperation of a whore's last fling before joining a convent. The heat wafted in waves from between us, flushing us in sympathy with the red of Application.

We climaxed together, stifling throaty cries. At that moment it occurred to me that something wasn't right. There had been no mental embrace, no dissolving into each other in an electric web of Oneness. It was just...sex, ordinary sex. We had both remained conscious of ourselves, the surroundings, the physicality of it. There had been no bonding.

"Cos."

"I know. It must be this matter into which we've been converted; it has no light."

"That's it. There's no light. It's all darkness, ordinariness." I rolled off of him and fell beside him, holding him as tight as I could, regretting what I'd said. How could I be so cold? I had rejected him and the way he dealt with the Hagions, wanted to punish him for his passivity, wanted to escape his spinelessness and impotence of character so badly I had chewed through a part of myself in order to sever him from me and free myself. And in this last effort to renew my love for him, regain what I had discarded, I was disappointed with the result. Someone should slap me.

"I understand," he answered my thoughts.

I was about to answer, to tell him how much he meant to me, when glass shattered somewhere up a row of beakered eggs. I sprang to my feet, straining to see in the ruddy dimness. A dark figure weaved at the head of the row, scrambled around a glistening puddle on the floor, and shot through the wall. I did not know if it knew we saw it.

Cos and I tiptoed to the site of the crash where we saw a pool of thick fluid, glass shards swirling within it. Something dark but semi-transparent squirmed in the center—a living, amorphous blob encrusted in small leaves of chitin. I leaned in close, watching its nostrils flare desperately. Reedy fingers drew from the ooze, small bulbous yellow eyes stared from the disorder, pleading with its last aspiration. The dead thing clutched an iconed medallion in its six-fingered hand.

"What is that? What's it holding?" I whispered.

"The symbol of Vtekdao."

CHAPTER 11

RESOURCES

Infinity is always one more than now.
—Qwiffian Handbook of Sapience

Cosmigellan and I discretely stalked the murdering roach down to Society on level five, maintaining a distance that placed us just around a curve, out of the range of the Hagion's view. It never turned around, clacking deliberately onward.

The desperation of its act haunted me. What could have possessed the Hagion to destroy a developing fetus so viciously? Did it single out Vtekdao's progeny or had it been a random act of cruelty, a protest of the loss of who knew how many lives through the mandatory extraction process? Did anyone on this ship care enough about the loss of life to protest its waste?

Our quarry stepped sideways up to the red dot, pressed it, and dissolved into the wall. We immediately rushed into Society, following the roach with our eyes as it seated itself on one of perhaps hundreds of tuffets around the huge auditorium that encompassed this entire level.

Hundreds of Hagions sat and stood in this theater, riveted on the words of Vtekdao, whose voice echoed forcefully from a podium at some distance from the gathering. I struggled to see past a huge central fountain that trickled a steady flow of water that was captured in a low scalloped bowl encircling it. At my urging, Cos and I moved closer to the fountain, able now to keep an eye both on our suspect and Vtekdao.

" ...destined to be our richest era yet. Soon the Benefactors will be returned to us and The Purpose fulfilled! It is I, and I alone who makes this possible! I have spoken with the Savior and our time is at hand!" Vtekdao bilged. "Witness! The Savior is among us!" He wadded out over the podium.

A thousand ochre eyes turned my way, their spinning flower

pupils pulling me into a whirling vortex. I buried my face in Cos' shoulder, disgusted and afraid. How dare Vtekdao speak of me as if he had invented me!

His arrogance would not go unchallenged. "I am *not* your Savior! I am an ordinary human, a prisoner, as the Ignorants are the prisoners of their life-threatening duty!"

Cos gripped my wrist hard. "Don't," he said low, jaw clenched, lips barely moving. "Do I have to explain to you yet again how things are?"

I dropped my gaze. "I'm sorry."

"The Savior still does not fully comprehend zhan important role. This will pass," Vtekdao apologized to the masses. "In conclusion, I wish to impress upon you once again the great responsibility we face in realizing our multi-cycle-long aspirations. Only under a skilled administration will The Purpose be viable. It is now within reach, good citizens! Don't discard it with a poor decision. Vtekdao is your future, your continued success!"

The hundreds of Hagions began to chant in unison, softly at first, then reaching a state of deafening fervor.

"I now release the podium to my worthy opponent and First Flagellant, Tmait." As Vtekdao clicked off stage, the figure we had followed rose and approached the stage.

"My god, Cos!" I gasped. "Do you know what this means?"

"Oh yes, Rita. Everything that happens is supposed to happen. This is truth."

I scowled at him. He'd slid back into that damn Phaedran dogma, again. A tiny smile curled a corner of his upper lip. He knew something.

Tmait spoke. "I have every confidence that the Ignorants will make the proper choice after what I have to say." He waited for the crowd to grow quiet and attentive.

"Your Honorable Altruist has deceived you. Zhe has placed zhan own product in vivigenesis in violation of the codes of the elders and the will of Hope." The crowd detonated into chaotic chatter. "Hear this!" Tmait continued over the babbling. "If Vtekdao triumphs in bringing to term a viable heir, there will be no election. Vtekdao's heir will succeed zhan and we will be condemned to Hope knows how many generations of zhaz questionable practices. And The Purpose will mean...*nothing*!"

My throat ached to finish his speech—reveal his shameless act of barbarity.

Cos' hand closed tightly around my wrist in warning. "Let it be, Rita."

Tmait finished. "As Vtekdao has said: Do not make a poor decision." And with that, he left the stage. He made no promises, revealed nothing of his own platform, only spoke to break down voter confidence in his opponent. No human politician could have done it dirtier.

I snickered. From my point of view it was indeed Tmait's election, in spite of—or maybe because of—his misdeed. I wondered how long it would take Vtekdao to discover his child's killer.

Hagions milled restlessly, many of them gravitating towards the big center fountain, and much to my astonishment, backing up to it, resting their upper legs in the depressions along the rim and defecating into the bowl. A public shitter, it was! I couldn't help gaping at them, dumping their bowels without a thought for privacy. I peered into the fountain where masses of odorless grayish-clear matter oozed to the fountain's center, disappearing through the opening ringing the central water-tower.

"Where does it all go?" I asked.

"To a lower level, I'd assume."

"Let's check out this place, Cos. How many levels does this ship have? I thought level seven was the bottom."

"No. You were transported to the bottom level once, remember?"

I thought hard. "You mean, that metal dish where they first informed me of my sainthood?" He nodded. "What level was that?"

"Level nine: Interrogation."

A sick wave undulated through my belly. A whole fucking level devoted strictly to interrogation? It smacked of Fascism of the highest order. "So ...what's on level eight?"

"Restructure. Where ship repairs are made. That's all I know."

"Then where does this sewage go?" From what I'd seen so far, it would be like them to dump it on Antarctica, where it would remain frozen and unchanged for eons.

Cos shrugged. "Let's find out. No one will stop us."

We met Macro on our way to Restructure. His eyes looked

dull, listless. "I've d-done it. L-left th-the t-t-transmitter."

I didn't have the heart to tell him it was probably for nothing, since Vtekdao had seen me in Society. "Thank you, Macro. We were just on our way to Restructure. Will you join us?"

His eyes darted in several directions. "N-no. I m-must eat."

"Come to my quarters, then. I'll feed you."

He nodded his acceptance and stepped beside Cos as we continued. When we reached the dot at level seven, I counted the paces—thirty-nine—along the spiral, and eased through the wall into what I thought would be my room: It was not. In the dimness I quickly turned and went back through to face a puzzled Cos and Macro. Cos put his hands on his hips and smiled smugly.

"Well, I *thought* I counted correctly. I was wrong, OK?"

"Your quarters are down here," Cos said, leading the way.

"I swear this ship is expanding," I muttered, counting again in my head. At step fifty-five Cos slipped through the wall; Macro and I followed. I couldn't have miscounted so seriously. One, two steps maybe, but a whole sixteen paces? "How do you know where it is? It's never in the same place twice!"

"The density of the wall changes at entrance points. I feel it."

"Something real weird's going on here." I punched the pyramid key and pushed the quasagna towards Macro. While he ate, I studied the odd keyboard, wishing there was some way I could write with it, keep a journal of my experiences and observations. Suddenly, I held my breath, afraid to say anything, afraid I'd imagined it. There, at the corner of the keyboard, etched in the wall in a shadow, stared three English-language characters. I ran my fingers over the scratches.

"Macro, did you do this?"

"No! N-no I d-did not!"

"I'm not angry, I just—Was anyone here when you came here? Did you see anyone leave?"

He shook his head. I glanced at Cos, who shrugged.

"Who else but us knows what this means?"

"I don't know, Rita," Cos said sarcastically. "Who did you tell?"

"No one! It is Qwiffian; it has no meaning for anyone else. Who could have done this?" I glared at it. *QWF.* It meant quantum wave function. We knew it as *qwiff,* the essence of freedom of personal choice, the foundation of our philosophy of the self's potential. When we popped qwiffs—collapsed quantum wave functions—we made choices, thereby creating our own reality—our own universe—from an infinite number of choices and universes. Only colony members knew the meaning of *QWF*.

A concept like *qwiff* would be completely meaningless to the tractable Hagions.

Cosmigellan jerked me away from my reverie, pulling me through the wall, Macro bounding through behind us.

Restructure appeared very much like Assembly: cold blue, spacious, clogged with laboring roaches. The Hagions grouped in circles of six here, around great vats being filled from orifices in the ceiling. A giant sheet of metal, identical to the one in Assembly, banged in the background, slamming to a halt just inches away from a group of roaches as they pulled levers, stirred the stuff in the vats, ladled the clear bluish ooze into funnels connected to long clear tubes. At the other ends of these tubes, Hagions wrestled with nozzles, jamming them into sockets in a wall covered in pipes and wires.

"What the hell *is* all this?" I said.

"R-refining. Sh-ship repair."

Suddenly, one worker crumpled to the floor. The others stopped and scooped him up and tossed him in the very vat he had been stirring. Then, a Hagion shot through the wall and took his place within the circle of six. They resumed stirring.

"Oh god," I couldn't help saying. It was their way. I shouldn't care. It was their way.

Bang! The metal sheet screamed to a halt, then sucked back along the expanse to its point of origin.

"Repair? But, what damage has the ship incurred, Macro?" I had a strange feeling about all this. "Macro, is this somehow connected to the expansion of the ship I've been seeing?"

His eyes fluttered, his jaw relaxed and hung as he thought. It would be a while before I got an answer. I watched lumps of gray-blue matter fall from twenty feet above, splash into the vats.

"W-waste. H-hagion waste. R-r-restructure. Yes."

Bang!

I held my breath, unbelieving. My mind returned to Society where dozens of Hagions had defecated into the fountain. Then my thoughts went to Shalf's quarters, where Shana had crapped in what I thought was the shower.

"You mean, this ship's made of ..."

Macro nodded enthusiastically.

I burst into laughter. "The Good *Shit* Lollypop?" Once I'd calmed down I realized what a splendid recycling program they had, and how very efficient it was. It made a lot more sense than what *we* did with *our* effluvium. But it brought to mind something I had never considered asking.

"Where do they get their food? Grow crops, raise animals, or—" A horrible image sliced through my brain. "My god, they eat their young, don't they? That's what extraction ...That's what The Purpose is, isn't it?"

Cos and Macro burst into a gale of laughter.

Bang!

"It isn't funny—it"s horrible!" I couldn't help it—I felt my own face crease up with mirth. It had been so long since I'd seen Cos in hysterics; it filled me with a ridiculously untimely happiness amidst the dark discovery.

"No, Rita," Cos cackled.

"They don't get it from Earth, do they? Is that what ...That word Tmait used, what was it ...Harvest?" I clamped down on the thought *humans for food* before I jumped to yet another conclusion.

"No. They make their food. From a raw material in—"

Bang!

"Damn that nerve-racking noise!" I ranted. Now that I had the opportunity, I'd have to see what the hell that metal sheet did. Skirting around to the left of the area, having estimated that there was indeed room for me, I hugged close to the wall, waiting for the approaching metal sheet. The sheet swelled from an apparent one-inch square to a looming monstrosity in a matter of seconds, the air cleaving me as the sheet scraped by at an alarming speed. The sensation was like being hit with the edge of a metal yardstick, parting even my pubic hair, I imagined.

I edged on down along the wall, the sheet whizzing by me many times before I reached the stationary plate. I stood at the edge of this plate and watched carefully as the moving plate rushed to it, arriving at breakneck speed only to slam to a halt less than a half-inch from the stationary plate. Sparkling confetti shot across the gap, charging the air. Every exposed inch of my face, hands, and feet tingled.

I weaseled along the wall, back up to Cos and Macro, the plate brushing by me again and again. "It's some kind of energy source," I puffed.

"Zero-point energy from the vacuum," Cos said, nodding. "Creates actual particles from virtual ones, literally stealing them from the vacuum. In direct violation of the laws of thermodynamics. There will be payback. The universe will see to that."

"It's too late. Payback's supposed to happen within nanoseconds. Instantons can't hang around like those things did. You see, I've been doing my homework."

"Oh Rita, have you forgotten so soon? It already *has* been paid back."

"Oh Jesus, are we going to exhume that spherical-time crap again? I told you not to do that to me. It's not that I don't believe it—I do. I've seen it with my own eyes. But my forty years of living with linear time just won't let go."

"I'm sorry. One can always hope that someday, you will—"

A deafening boom rolled through Restructure, followed by a thin, almost feminine voice. "Attention citizens. Dispatch to Society at once. The window has opened. Harvest occurs in point one sextets. Dispatch to Society at once. Those not in Society in point one five sextets risk chance absorption."

"What the hell's going on, now?" I complained. All of the Hagions working at the vats and pumps quit their work and filed wordlessly through the wall.

"We'd better get to level five quickly. The penalty is death if we don't." Cos grabbed my hand and Macro's arm and turned, following the vat workers into the spiral, merging with hundreds of roaches clicking their way upwards along the congested walkway. I had never seen so many Hagions. They bumped and squeezed by us, surrounding us, impelling us forward by their sheer numbers. Now and then we passed a roach caught in a fugue, captivated by its internal Billboard system. As we ascended the spiral, passing onto successive levels, roaches flowed out of the walls and blended in with the massive migration. Once, I saw a roach caught halfway in a wall, lodged there in an absence seizure, oblivious to its predicament.

By level five the pace quickened from a mince to a shuffle as Hagions streamed into Society at several points along the wall. Inside, roaches milled, distributing themselves subtly in what looked like a prearranged pattern, careful of the distances between them. By the time they had stopped moving around, the auditorium could have held twice as many with no discomfort to anyone. They became still and quiet, transfixed on the Hagion that overlooked the throng from the podium. I guessed it was the ever-visible Vtekdao. All the way around the auditorium and behind him the blackness of space bled in from the wall, made transparent by someone's touch.

"Welcome, citizens. Welcome to Harvest!" I was right, it was Vtekdao. "Once again in this universe, our kind will engage in this resplendent task, a task fraught with hazard not only for the chosen few who will engage directly in Harvest, but for the onlookers as well. Remain in Society. It is the only area of Lolbah in which you will survive the transition into phase-space. Phase-space will render all but Society non-existent for the duration of our flight. Enjoy, citizens! Enjoy the spectacle that awaits!"

My heart beat in my throat. "We're leaving Earth orbit?" I fought the terror inside me; tears ran down my face. "Cos . . . ."

"Easy, Rita," he said, rubbing my shoulders. "They need the Benefactors. We will return."

I sighed. Yes, we'd have to return if Vtekdao still planned to get the colony on board. I looked up, marveling at the clear domed ceiling. Space stared down at me, even though four levels spiraled above. Or...did they?

A barely perceptible tremor vibrated through the floor, buzzing up my legs and through my veins like rampaging ants. With a clunk the huge auditorium lurched sideways, sending several roaches scrambling for something to grab onto. I clung to Cos, mesmerized by the shifting starfield outside.

The long, dusty, diamond-sprinkled swath of lavender and blue Milky Way surged overhead, oscillating, warping from a banner to an oval, contracting to a disk. The starscape compressed inwards, stars squeezing in closer towards the brightening, bluer central disk. Stars exploded into existence and were pushed back, inwards by an encroaching cone of blackness along the periphery of the shrinking disk. Other stars sputtered, winked out. Through the rear window nothing whatsoever shone. With a spasm the disk shrank to the size of a bright tack held at arm's length, the entire universe contained within it.

"Holy shit," I mumbled, knowing well what I saw from my extensive readings in astrophysics.

"Once we exceed the speed of light, even that will disappear," Cos said. "What you see now is the microwave background radiation shifted upwards into the visible spectrum."

"I r-remember th-this," Macro said. "I remember this."

What could he mean by that? I wouldn't take my focus off the bright spot of light to ask him. The tiny disk of light shone for several minutes, then blinked out, taking the universe with it. Everywhere, all around, the sky was black and starless. The ship remained mired in phase-space for what I estimated to be an hour of subjective time. All the roaches stood like hideous statues in some artist's demented vision, silent, fixed on the void. Waiting.

Right then I noticed a peculiar thing. I thought it was my imagination at first, or some relativistic effect of warped spacetime. But the more I watched the Hagions, using them as a frame of reference, the more I was convinced I could also feel it.

"Macro, do you feel that? Do you see anything strange?"

Macro looked around the room, then down at his feet. "Y-yes. Everyth-th-thing's c-closer."

"This ship *is* shrinking, isn't it? Shit, why? And how far will it go before it stops?" I envisioned this ship, us, going the way of the tiny light disk. *Pop*!

"Sh-shit, yes. Restructure."

"What's Restructure got to do with anything?"

"Sh-ship feed. B-big. L-little."

Macro's own inimitable code. Sometimes he could be so obscure. I wouldn't drill him; it would just make him stutter worse. He said what he meant; it was up to me to decipher it. "Ship feed. Big. Little. Ship feed. B—huh? This ship consumes itself in flight? That's what Restructure is—like hogging out before hibernation, or Arctic migration?"

Macro nodded vigorously.

"Well I'll be damned." I reached out and patted his head, ruffling his hair.

We had to shift positions before the contraction pushed us on top of each other. The dwindling floor-space explained why the

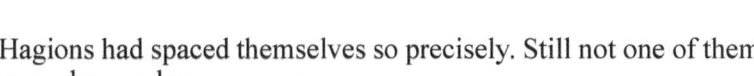

Hagions had spaced themselves so precisely. Still not one of them moved or spoke.

"Now if you could only explain Harvest," I said.

"D-don't know. W-we w-will see."

We did not have to wait. The auditorium shifted; I fell into Cos. His smile shone through the soft red blush of a dilating universe as spacetime unfolded like a fresh rose. I gasped, spellbound by the splendor before and extending around and above us. Towing Cos by the front of his caftan, I waded through the mass of still roaches, making for the window. I was wrapped inside of it: a stunning red nebula that stretched unimaginable miles across and above the ship.

My eyes devoured the vivid soul-rending colors, the intricate features hiding demurely within wisps of red hydrogen and green oxygen, the array of crystal stars so bright they burned into me. "Oh Cos! I've never seen anything so beautiful!" Then I laughed and cried at the same time. "No human has!"

I squinted through a stream of tears, shading my eyes from the painful brightness of the stars Sigma and Zeta Orionis. And there, at the bottom, diffused a bright blue reflection nebula. To the right, running along the bottom of the red gaseous clouds, sprawled the masterpiece of the cosmos like an encroaching oil slick, protruding into the red IC 434 emission nebula: the dark Horsehead Nebula, so thick and black no stars shone through from the other side. I knew the Horsehead Nebula itself to be nearly a light-year across. Though we still had to be many hundreds of thousands of miles from it, it filled the forward window and dome of Society.

I never wanted to leave. I wanted to stay here for the rest of my life enfolded within this magnificence.

"Citizens, please. Make yourselves comfortable. Enjoy Harvest," Vtekdao said from the podium above and beside me as I stood staring out at the nebula.

I heard roaches clicking behind me, crowding up to the window for an unobstructed view of whatever was about to happen. The floor shuddered and lurched. A silvery blob flashed by the left corner of my view, zipping past the ship. A small shuttle, I assumed. Again the floor shuddered; another silver shuttle blipped by, then another from the right, followed by a stream of them, heading straight for the dark horsehead. Soon the sky was asparkle with swift silvery motes, all heading for the black nebula, shrinking from sight, disappearing.

Slowly the sky brightened, blushing redder, filling Society with a rosy glow. Silver beads suddenly sparked from nowhere, arranged themselves in a loop, ringing the horsehead like a bejeweled crown.

I stretched up, standing straight, a tension building in me from an unknown place. Something was wrong.

In one choreographed movement, the beaded halo drew inwards, ensnaring the Horsehead Nebula in what I could only perceive as a choke-hold.

"No," I whispered to myself, my throat tightening, not understanding why. I watched the silvery ring for several minutes, an ugly foreboding spreading through me.

The auditorium flushed a rich flaming red. I could have sworn the horsehead moved, but quickly dismissed it. "What are they doing? Is this Harvest? What are they harvesting?" I asked Cos, studying his moist eyes, the paleness of his face even in this red glow. I looked back to the nebula. A little scream escaped my throat. "No! They can't do that! It's wrong!" I spun around. Macro slouched behind me, his head down, refusing to watch. I turned again to the horror before me, unable to take my eyes off of it.

As the dots of the silvery ring closed in, the dark nebula collapsed, slaughtered to a stump, exposing the red emission nebula of IC 434 in its entirety, flooding Society with a bloody gash of crimson light. The Horsehead Nebula was no more.

Behind us, thousands of Hagion voices rejoiced.

CHAPTER 12

BELIEF SYSTEMS

The unperceived supports and validates the perceived.
—Qwiffian Handbook of Sapience

The floor of the lab at the WCPW lurched sideways. The stool on which Jason Childress sat, rolled across the floor, sending him flailing, grabbing for the computer bench as boxes, printers, and monitors crashed all around him.

"California wrecking crew, people!" Dr. Aames yelled over the commotion of falling equipment. "Take cover!"

Childress dove beneath the computer bench as a keyboard slid off it, smashing to the floor behind him. He wedged himself tightly within the small dark space, bracing himself against the sides with his elbows, the room tilting in an effort to pull him from his shelter. Someone yelled over a crash of exploding glass.

As quickly as the emergency had begun, it ended.

The only sounds were residual rumbles and creaks coursing through the shaken building.

Childress emerged from under the bench, standing slowly, crunching through the broken glass and plastic keys popped from the keyboards when they hit the hard floor.

"Holy shit," Wontok said, wading through the destruction to the wall of monitors at the front of the lab. Two monitors lay smashed on the floor, another was dead, but the others dutifully displayed astounding activity from all over the globe.

Childress trudged through the debris to share in Wontok's astonishment. In every working monitor some disaster was unfolding or had just finished. Volcanoes spewed on nearly every island along the Pacific Rim. Tsunamis flattened the coasts of Japan, The Philippines, and the Hawaiian Islands. Typhoons tore through India, the East China Sea; hurricanes through Louisiana, Florida, and the Carolinas. Gobs of pillow lava billowed up along the Mariana Trench and the Mid-Atlantic Ridge. Everywhere he looked, nature convulsed in a sudden wild fury.

"My god," Childress said.

"Armageddon," Inga Handelman said, easing up beside Childress, brushing his shoulder.

Childress inched away, focusing on each monitor, letting the details of each disaster sink in. Maybe Handelman was right; maybe this *was* the end. The floor still rumbled slightly through the soles of his sneakers.

Then he noticed it.

He turned towards Wontok, who stared, slowly shaking his head. "Is there enough equipment intact to bring up a mosaic of monitor nine?" Childress asked.

"I dunno."

"Snap out of it, Lenny. Something's not right. Don't you see it?"

"No shit, Doc. Nothing at all's right about this."

"No, I mean monitor nine. Look at it."

Wontok stepped closer, the white glow of Antarctica bleaching his copper face. "No activity of any kind."

"Exactly. See what you can do. I need the Big Picture."

Wontok picked through the electronic rubble, salvaging what he could. Within an hour a somewhat wounded patchwork of Antarctica sprawled across the array of monitors.

"Christ, it's gone!" Aames said, stepping up beside Childress. Two other technicians joined him.

"Where is it? Where did it go?" one technician said.

"How could an anomaly we've been watching for weeks just up and disappear?" the other technician said.

"Probably the same way it appeared in the first place," Childress said. "We still have Comsat access?" Aames nodded. "Good. One Dog! Get a network conference between JPL, Kitt Peak, Wilson...any other observatory you can think of within two hours' hovercraft flight of here." He checked his watch: 4:10 p.m. "Tell anyone who'll listen to meet me at Palomar Observatory at seven this evening."

"You can't leave now, Jason," Aames protested. "The roads will be jammed with emergency vehicles. There's likely to be an aftershock. Perhaps many."

"I'm willing to bet my left nut there won't be aftershocks. This was no ordinary earthquake." He threw on his jacket and dashed out the lab door and down the hall, hopping over a long fissure in the floor tile as the guard waved goodbye. Childress rushed past him, pushing through the empty metal frames of the front entrance, crunching out onto the glass into the darkest afternoon any human had ever seen.

Uh-huh," he said.

* * *

At the peak of San Diego's isolated Mount Palomar, Jason Childress felt humanity crush in around him. Clammy hands and a racing heart could not deter him from finishing addressing this noisy assembly of the world's top astronomers. "Please, please," he said, voice cracking, accent becoming more pronounced. "My fellows and colleagues, I know you have many questions." The room quieted. "I've told you everything I know. The source of the phenomenon is now our riddle to solve. The data from observatories all over the world reveals dissolution of dark nebulas in at least three different areas of the sky. I believe the atmospheric, seismic, and deep space phenomena are somehow related."

"Dr. Childress, forgive me for this," a young man in the front row said, "but your correlations seem absurd. Surely someone with your background realizes that what happens in deep space— however bizarre and unexplained—cannot possibly affect Earth's atmosphere or rotation to the degree that you suggest."

A young woman stepped beside Childress at the front of the room and handed him a sheet of paper, disappearing out a side door.

He gawked at the figures, drop-jawed. It was all falling apart before their very eyes and they wouldn't acknowledge it. "I have the new reports from the Hoyle Telescope at L5. Fellows, this is unprecedented. Significant aberrations in rotational velocity of galaxy clusters has been detected and...it has become apparent that something beyond our experience is...I can't believe it," he finally mumbled, clearing his throat. "M 51—the Whirlpool galaxy— has completely unraveled! People, if this doesn't convince you something crazy is going on in the universe, then I don't know what will."

Someone from the back of the room spoke up over the sudden

murmurs of the audience. "That there are indeed peculiar things going on in deep space is irrefutable. Correlating them with Earth's climactic and seismic fluctuations is no better than accepting planetary motion as influencing human fate. What you propose is no more sophisticated than the pseudoscience of astrology."

The small auditorium erupted into laughter and conversation. Haunted by a gnawing feeling that had been with him since he left McMurdo, Childress stared down at his notes. The figures burned into his brain like a raw ulcer.

Nothing Childress thought to himself, no amount of pouring over the data or recalling the shocking images from the Cloud-Buster could shake him from his suspicions. He looked up and into the audience. His heart still raced, adrenalin coursed through him, more from resentment than nervousness. "I take offense at your narrow views," he announced. He laughed to himself. He remembered displaying that same attitude to Rita just weeks before; it was a part of that insular scientific posturing he wasn't all that sure he wanted to embrace anymore. "Thank you for your valuable time." Childress snapped his briefcase closed and left the auditorium.

Childress removed his jacket as he strode to his car. The breeze cooled damp patches on his shirt, sending shocks of cold through his skin, and comforting flashes of the desolate and unpeopled expanses of Antarctica through his mind. He should have stayed. He knew someday he would return.

Starting the engine of his car, he turned on the CD player and caught the beginning of "Fortuna" from Carl Orff's *Carmina Burana.* He took in a deep lungful of pine-scented spring air and sang at the top of his voice, pulling out of the small parking lot of the Mount Palomar Observatory and heading down the long winding mountain road, dodging rock slides and cracks in the pavement, to highway 76. The music, the aloneness, the movement down into the darkness filled him with overwhelming joy. *This* was what life was all about. This *here.* This *now.* Not back up on the peak where dogma and unyielding certitude thundered down on imagination and freedom of speculation like an arrogant Norse god. Childress stopped singing and laughed heartily, reprogramming the CD player to repeat the music five more times, turning the volume up. He did not understand why, but once he caught 15-South, he would not be turning off onto 8-East for home this evening. He would keep driving south. He had to.

* * *

In the distance, a little square of yellow bit into the night as Childress drove by the unlit dwellings along the gravel road entering the ranch. Echoes of that terrible day, the chaos, the voices, could not deter him from his mission.

Before his knuckles met wood, the porch light came on, the back door to the main house opened and Nancy greeted him with a smile.

"Jason. What brings you out here so late?"

"I'm sorry to bother you at this hour, but I just had to—"

"Come in, please. Twelve-thirty isn't late for us. You look...I don't know...upset about something."

"Oh, my work, Nancy." He stepped into the kitchen and hung his jacket on the back of a chair. "Do you ever get the feeling that life is a lot stupider than it's meant to be?" Nancy smiled. "No one will listen to me. There's got to be a correlation between the planet-wide disasters, the sudden expansion of the ozone hole, the aberrations in deep space. I can't get anyone to listen to me."

Nancy's forehead wrinkled. "What disasters?"

"It's been all over the news, Nancy. Didn't you feel the earthquake today?"

She blinked stupidly.

"Doesn't it bother you that it got dark at four today, after so many unusually long days?"

"Oh. Yes. Strange," she said, a vacant look in her eyes.

What's wrong with her? This wasn't the Nancy he knew, full of curiosity and lust for knowledge. There was a coldness in her voice. "Nancy, I know you probably still haven't forgiven me for leaving you, but we've been through all that. How many times do I have to apologize to you for not wanting children?"

"Oh Jason. Why bring that up? That's over. I have what I want. Doron is everything to me. Besides, why would I set you up with Rita if I still felt anything more than friendly affection for you?"

"Then what is it? Is it my running out on you that day you introduced me to Rita? I couldn't stay, not with the children misbehaving like that. I know you understand my problem. Are you going to hold *that* against me?"

"No, Jason. I'd never do that."

He searched her expressionless face. Then it came to him. "Ah, it's Rita. I should have called earlier. How is she? I'm sorry I didn't get a chance to say goodbye."

"She is well."

"Then, she wasn't hurt seriously?"

"No."

"May I see her? Is she awake?"

"She isn't here."

Childress sighed. Nancy volunteered nothing. "Nancy, I need to see Rita. I'd like to apologize for my hasty exit that day, and I'd like to talk to her about something. She said something—I can't remember exactly what it was—I think is important."

"I'll be happy to relay a message."

Childress ran his fingers through his hair, pulling strands roughly from the rubber band that held it. "Just tell me when she'll be back. I want to talk to her in person," he growled.

"I don't know when she'll return."

He glared at her. "Is it bigger than a bread box? Goddammit Nancy! I'm tired of playing twenty questions with you." Nancy jerked to attention. Breathing heavy, Childress removed his jacket, paced through the dining room from one end of the table to the other. "I'm sorry, but can't you surrender a few clues here?"

"She's been abducted by a UFO," a husky voice grated from the hallway.

Nancy spun around to face the man, fists clenched. "Bob," she said. "I don't think Jason is in the mood for jokes."

"Aw, Nance, you *know* I ain't joking. It's the gosh-darn truth," he said, looking past her into Childress' eyes.

An apologetic smile creased Childress' face as Nancy turned to meet his gaze. "I'm sorry. I've obviously stepped into the middle of something...I should leave," he said, grabbing his jacket from the back of a chair and making for the kitchen door.

Bob rushed in front of him, blocking his exit. "The only argument is whether anybody should tell the truth around here. It's *true*." He looked up at the ceiling while pointing a meaty finger upwards. "Rita's way, way up in the sky."

Childress would have been convinced the man was drunk if

it were not for Nancy's instant assault.

"You son-of-a-bitch!" she screamed, running to her brother, pummeling him with her fists. "We told you not to say anything! You don't belong here, you ignoble, traitorous bastard! We told you not to tell! Why do I let you stay here?" She cried, curling her hands up on Bob's chest, sobbing into the front of his shirt.

"Because you love your little brother," he said, patting her tenderly on the back as she hid her face in his chest.

Childress spoke softly, "I...I have to go. I hope you both feel better soon."

"Not until you know," Bob said, his eyes moist.

Nancy pulled away from her brother's embrace, shaking her head, pleading with her eyes for Bob to change his mind.

"If Jason Childress don't believe us, who will? Don't you think we can trust him? Of all people?"

Nancy sniffled. "We agreed, Bob. We agreed."

Childress crossed his arms over his chest. "What is this? I knew something was wrong with you, Nancy, when I first walked in that door."

Bob reached to his right, opened a cupboard above him, and pulled out a bottle of cognac and three glasses. "You gotta sit for this, Jason," he said, lumbering to the dining room table.

Two teenagers padded in from the hall, hair mussed, eyes sleepy and squinting in the bright light. "What's all the noise?" Darwinia said.

"We're telling a non-member, Sweetheart. Sit down. You too, Doron," Nancy said. "Professor Childress needs to hear your story."

Soon, three other children wandered in and sat on the sofa in the living room, across from the big dining room table. Childress straightened in his chair, nervously sipping his cognac.

"The children will tell their story as only they can, but first you should know this: Everything you are about to hear is true. Bob and I, as well as all the other adults here on the ranch, are not of their origins."

Childress suppressed a laugh. What had he got himself into? What excuse would he have to sit and listen to a bunch of adolescents tell some group fantasy to him at one o'clock in the morning?

Bob said, "My sister here, met them first. They're not from

here...not from Earth. And they're being pursued by another race; Rita's on their ship. This other race is using her to bring the colony to them, because if it isn't done just right, these kids will spindle."

Childress felt his jaw fall away from his face. "Spindle? The colony?"

"Remember when you were here last time, and you had to leave? The kids all panicked? That was spindle," Bob said.

"The tantrum, you mean?"

"*Spindle,*" Nancy said. "An ancient survival behavior they've been unable to abandon since coming to Earth and taking human form. You have to understand. These children—the members of this colony—are not completely human. Oh, they have human bodies, but their intelligence, their personalities, are alien."

Childress remained calm, detached from the hilarity of her words. "And where do they come from? Where is their ship?"

Nancy continued. "They were ejected from Phaedra—the fourth planet of Epsilon Eridani—which was destroyed by a dark comet. They knew to come here because Cosmigellan had come here first. Rita found him in the garden and rescued him."

"There's no such thing as a *dark* comet. And who's this Cosmi character?"

"Cosmigellan. He became Rita's lover, spending some time in human form before injecting his DNA packet into her brain. She carries him within her."

In her warped imagination. What else would one expect of a writer? "And now this other race has Rita on their ship and they're coming after you."

"Not all of us," Nancy said. "Just the children."

"Hmmm. I see. And where *is* this ship?"

"Hovering over Antarctica."

A sharp jolt darted through Childress' stomach. "I just came from Antarctica. There is no ship. Trust me."

"Listen that you may know your internal truth," the African girl, Darwinia, said. "We of The One know without knowing how we know. The One understands the workings of the All that Is. We understand your reluctance to accept."

He was to believe *this* was an alien? Her features spoke of the origins of all of humanity. "The one what?"

The children recited their story:

Darwinia: "We ran. We could do nothing else. Born of our desperation, our fear: this place—our haven, our sanctuary."

Doron: "We spark meaning from nothingness, from chaos, create form and structure, infuse knowing into the life that springs throughout the cosmos."

Jaynah: "For millennia we roam the void, unrooted, free, free at last to design and live our lives on a new world. New corporeal forms materialize from the prebiotic fallout of comets that shake our new world. We send the comets away and our world cools, congeals, incubates our new race."

Bohrelia: "With the stars we dance, with the galaxies we sleep. Of the One Mind. Of The All That Is."

Pascalia: "In our exhilaration, the memories fade. The horrors of enslavement and servitude lose power in the One Mind. Fear has no home in our hearts."

Doron: "We of The One Mind spend millennia experiencing, learning, sharing the wonders of our creation. Sharing the knowing is our life."

Darwinia: "But residual fear can take us, drive us to spindle, to give ourselves to the internal drive, to reach upward into the void. Many survive at he expense of many others. It is the Ancient Way. It is who we are, who we have become."

Pascalia: "When the dark comet comes, tearing the new world to fragments, many discontinue. Those of us who survive encapsulate and come to where one of our kind finds us. We adopt his form that we may live. The new humans are us."

Bohrelia: "In our short time as neohumans, we devise a method of maintaining our new corporeal form and undergo rebirth as DNA infused into human female haploid cells. We are the neohumans. We are Homo Novus."

Childress gulped cognac and gladly accepted a refill as Bob poured. He did not like what he felt. He didn't want to hear anymore; he couldn't stop listening.

Jaynah: "But the Hagions know where we are. They follow. For centuries, eons, since the First Spark, they follow."

Together, the children chanted:

"And still they come. Relentlessly. Determined, unhurried. Confident and proud, they come. From another wherewhen.

"Another universe.

"And they pursue we who fail to submit to the destiny prescribed by their eons of control and dominance.

"Unseen.

"Undetected.

"Dark and heavy. Dark and ubiquitous.

"Justice will be theirs. But, it is a perverted justice.

"And the future shall emulate the past, for time is spherical.

"Baryonic imperialism will be our downfall! This is their solemn promise to the Betrayers."

Childress rested his forehead in his hands, elbows propped up on the table, as if trying to prevent a cranial implosion. "You really don't expect me to *believe* all of this, do you?" he said, watching his lips move in the reflection of the polished table surface.

"I think there's something inside you that wants you to," Nancy said.

Childress exploded into hysterical laughter. "Either I'm the victim of a most elaborate practical joke, or you're all daft." He pushed his chair back from the table and stood. "I thank you all for a lovely performance." He bowed, sweeping his hand before him. "And now, I bid you good morning."

"I'll tell Rita you asked about her," Nancy said just as he closed the door behind him. He shuffled to his car mumbling about the peculiar vanities of theater folk, stabbed a key at his car door, scratching at the lock area until he felt the key sink into the slot. He took a deep breath of the cool country air and started his car, listening to the satisfying smoothness of its engine. Fumbling for the headlight knob, he eased the car through the halo of light ahead, down the dark driveway.

Just as he pulled out onto the pavement, the inside of his head unfolded.

The voices came. "No. Not again. No, I don't hear this," he said to himself, beating the side of his head with his left hand as he steered with his right. The voices swelled, enveloped his mind. *Of The One. We are of The One. Jason, hear us. Be with us. We are all of The One. You know. You know truth.*

"I don't hear this! I don't! I'm not crazy!" He reached up with both hands and slammed his palms over his ears. "No! I don't hear this!" In his headlights a pole bound from the right and slammed into the grill of his car. The last thing he saw was the steering wheel surge into his face as an acute pain tore through his head. The monotone of a car horn blared out over the voices, fading, growing distant and muffled.

Jason Childress dreamt of the dark.

CHAPTER 13

SUBTERFUGE

Electrons can tunnel because they are both a particle and a wave.
Electrons can pass from one quantum level to another without passing
between the levels. Electrons, therefore, can potentially exist in two
places at once.
—Qwiffian Handbook of Sapience

On my knees in my quarters, I watched my vomit slip through the fountain's grate, destined to become some part of the ship. None of Cos' warnings could have prepared me for the wanton plunder, the unconscionable slaughter of the Horsehead Nebula.

All at once, Cos' fear of the Hagions had meaning for me.

The Hagions were not a race to trifle with. They would do what they wanted, without regard, without conscience, without remorse.

Staggering out of the washroom, not even curious as to how I had found my quarters without help, I went to the far wall to bring the comfort of Antarctica into view. It felt good to be home. My soul would be replenished by the time Cos came to take me to the election finals.

The ship had returned and settled in orbit at an odd angle. Antarctica sprawled dead ahead instead of below. It was beautiful—so white, mostly cloud-covered, with the bare Palmer Peninsula poking out into the Drake Passage, flicking towards Tierra del Fuego to the north. I'd heard people actually lived on bases down there, researching all manner of things: global climate, the ozone hole, auroras, earthquakes, the blood of polar animals, the limits of human sanity. It seemed a place I'd want to visit sometime. If only I had the—

Rita. I need to talk to Rita. She knows, a thought-voice pleaded.

Rita froze. *Cos? Are you OK? You sound—*

Where are you? How am I hearing this? the thought-voice answered.

A shock of realization shoved me into a complete panic. I held my breath. This was *not* Cosmigellan, his voice, his thoughts. It wasn't anyone of The One. I could draw only one conclusion. The Hagions had finally done it: They owned my mind. There would be nowhere for me to run, nothing left of me that belonged to me alone. Oh god, how could they do this? How will I survive with them in my head?

I beat my head against the clear wall, watching the transparent surface oscillate silently, waves distorting the continent of Antarctica with each impact.

You can't have me! You can't have my mind!

Crying, I turned and dashed to my bed, throwing myself on it, wrapping my head in the spongy slab that passed for a pillow, beating my fists on the wall, trying to drive the intruder away with the pain. I beat the wall again and again until my knuckles bled from the scratches etched in the wall....

I froze. I lifted and uncovered my head. My fingers obscured the scratches on the wall. All I saw was the mangled knuckles. The voice was gone.

I pulled my fingers away and there in even letters was etched the anagram *QWF.*

At the foot of my bed hurried footsteps slapped the floor. "Rita, what's wrong?" Cos panted. "I came as quickly as I could."

I rolled over onto my side, stared into his frightened, sweaty face. "Someone else was in here." I pointed to my temple with a bloody right hand. "They've done it. They know how to get inside of me. It's all over."

"Why did you do this?" he gasped, sitting on the edge of the bed, reaching for my injured hand.

"To get them to leave. It worked."

"Listen," he said, still breathing heavy. "They can't get inside your head. I swear to you, there's no way." He cradled my hand between his. "You scared me, Rita. I heard you call me, and when I listened I was greeted with all that pain. What the hell's wrong with you?"

"I'm not kidding," I sobbed. "Someone else was in here. Someone I don't know."

"Was it male or female?"

"Definitely male. He said he needed to talk with me. At first I thought it was you, but it wasn't. Then he said, 'She knows.'"

"He said, *she?*"

"Yes."

"Then it couldn't have been a Hagion, don't you see? Hagions use the genderless *zhe.*"

I gushed a sigh of partial relief. "It wasn't a familiar voice, Cos."

He shook his head, eyes fixated on my swelling hand. "I think you broke it, Rita. Let's get you to Procedure."

"It was worth it. I'll do it again if I have to."

He pulled me gently to my feet, holding the hand protectively.

"Wait. Look over there, at the head of my bed."

He leaned close, squinting his eyes. "*Qwiff.* Again. You sure you told no one about us?"

"Yes. What do you think? I'm crazy?"

He brought my hand up within inches of my face. "What do *you* think?"

I blushed and looked away.

"We'll need your transmitter. You have to be careful about being seen in public without it. If they catch on to what we've done...."

"Uh oh. I told Macro to put it at the head of my bed. I doubt if it's still there."

Cos released my hand and lifted the sponge slab, plucking a tiny trinket from the folds in the blanket. "Don't lose this, dammit." He dropped the transmitter in the gaping hip pocket of my caftan and patted my bottom.

In Procedure I allowed Cos to talk me into a rather ominous-sounding treatment—to be performed by an army of molychines within a liquid metal ball.

The silver sphere locked and floated around my injured hand, numbing it to the point where I barely felt the frenzy of a thousand molychines crawling through my mangled flesh, sewing the meat together with my own fibers, tugging the small bones into alignment, knitting the breaks.

"You'll be a little tender for a few days until you heal completely," Cos said, dragging the cold liquid sphere off my hand like a blob of mercury. Tight, pink flesh emerged, my hand fully repaired.

A quick spurt of tears danced in my eyes. "So much wonderful technology in such a brutal race."

"The paradox should not be unfamiliar to a human. Let's go. The final election is underway."

I did not know the Hagion who spoke at the podium in Society. I had never heard such gentle assurance from a Hagion. The roach's voice penetrated, mesmerized with its soft monotone. It paused at peculiar places within its speech, as if listening to internal cues, instructions.

"I wonder if that's caused by a Billboard molychine," I mused.

Cos snapped his head around and stared at me.

"What?" I said. "Is something wrong?"

"How do you know about that?"

"Billboard molychines? Tmait told me."

His speech became choppy, accusatory. "Did zhe tell you what they do? What they say?"

"Not really. What does it matter?"

"Forget about Billboard molychines."

"What's the big deal? What dif—"

"Just *don't* speak of them, Rita."

I hoped I'd seen the last of that cement-headed secretiveness he often manifested. In self-defense I tuned his presence out and concentrated instead on the creamy words of the speaker.

"Resolutions five...through nine will pass should our votes... favor Vtekdao. Our civilization will continue as now, progressing under Vtekdao's wise guidance.

"Resolutions one through four will...pass should Tmait defeat Vtekdao. These resolutions will...call for rapid change. Though Tmait proposes reductions in...duty cycles for all Obligants, as well as...*voluntary* product donation for all Ignorants, such an upheaval...will be a challenge of adaptation. Be wise in your... choice, cherished Ignorants.

"Should the elected official be...unable to fulfill zhaz duty in the capacity of Honorable Altruist, zhaz...opponent shall claim the title and position of said office.

"Hope is gratified for your support and participation...and extends blessings of prosperity that your...product shall thrive in the next...generation. Hallowed be The Purpose!"

Society roared with repetitions of the last statement, and fell to a hush just as suddenly. At that moment it became apparent who would prevail. Vtekdao must have known too or he wouldn't have tried to raise an heir so quickly.

"And now, all present," the podium roach said, "please cast your votes."

I waited. Nothing happened. I expected some kind of activity, but only the podium roach stirred, shifting from one zygodactyl foot to the other, then rocking rhythmically from side to side as soft utterances escaped its yawning mouth. I crept closer, slowly at first to avoid disturbing anyone in the audience, then, seeing that my presence was unacknowledged, forged forward until I stood right beneath the podium. The roach above was oblivious to me, burping fractions of familiar words from its throat. "Mate, mate, mate, tek, mate, tek, tek, mate, mate," it said faster than I could count.

Counting! Its pupils were motionless, frozen. I whirled around to face an audience of spinning pupils. Wading back through the motionless crowd to a smiling Cos. I whispered, "They count votes...mentally?"

"You got it."

"So, they're linked, like the Phaedrans?"

"Precisely. What one knows, they all know. All the more reason to avoid confiding in any of them, telling any of them the meaning of *QWF*."

"I told you—I didn't tell anyone. Why won't you believe me?"

"You still think you can find an ally among them. You are wrong. Promise me you won't try to."

"You're right," I lied. "It's too risky."

"The final tally is in," the roach at the podium announced. "Welcome your Honorable...Altruist, Tmait." The auditorium erupted into a synchronized cawing, a sound that I could only interpret as the cheer of victory. Through the cawing I heard another voice from the podium: Tmait's.

"My citizens! My citizens! You have chosen wisely. No longer will your product be taken from you, dictated by a schedule that kills! No longer will Ignorants lead a life of purposeless despair and exploitation! No longer will Obligant workers surrender half their credits to non-working Ignorants. No longer will Obligants toil in Assembly until their vision fails and they must be transferred to Restructure where they ultimately become the product they process!"

The cawing swelled loudly, then fell silent.

"Vtekdao's oppressive reign is over and a New Hagion race will emerge from his waste and obsession!"

A glimmer of hope sparked inside me. I pictured Cos and Macro and myself back on the ranch, Shana purring in my arms, the colony feasting and bathing naked in the pool by the orchard, free of strife. Vtekdao had lost his strangle-hold on not only me and the colony, but his own race, his demands and dreams of omnipotence burned to the ground. There might be a chance for us—all of us—now. Even though Cos did not accept it, I knew I could negotiate with Tmait. Tmait could be reasoned with. "Cos, do you know what this means?"

Cos chuckled softly. "It means nothing. Nothing will change."

Before I could attack his negativity, a roach passed us. "Ingrates," it grumbled in a familiar deep voice. Vtekdao then faded through the wall as I followed him with my stare.

"Pissed, is he? Why, that warms my heart," I mumbled.

"Let us feast!" Tmait said from the podium.

I turned around to see Society transform before my eyes. Round tables emerged from the floor, growing up and blossoming out like daffodils, their surfaces uneven, lumpy, the lumpiness becoming metal bowls and eating utensils. Hagions milled and chattered, arranging themselves in cozy circles around the tables where they commenced feeding each other.

Tmait clicked down from the stage and weaved back and forth from table to table, apparently looking for an opening where he could join in the feeding.

I stood by an unclaimed table. "Hey!" I waved. "Hey, Tmait! Over here! The Savior needs to speak with the new Honorable Altruist."

"What the hell are you doing, Rita?" Cos growled through a clenched jaw.

"Sucking up to the new guy. What does it look like?"

"You're wasting your time and endangering us more than I can make you understand."

"I'll be the judge of that," I muttered.

Tmait threaded his way towards us and folded down to the stool. "Ree-tah, I am honored you've joined us in this glorious event."

"Congratulations, Tmait." I extended my hand to his fingers. He wadded. I withdrew my hand. "I guess the Hagions can look forward to a more compassionate administration now that you're in charge."

"Compassion is not of concern. It is a matter of economics. The Purpose must be implemented, but with care and planning."

I sighed, suddenly deflated. "And you will still require me to bring the Benefactors?"

"You are the Savior."

Dammit. "What about my cat? Will you give her back to me?"

"I have no use for the creature. Zhe will be returned to you."

That tiny victory was just enough to keep me from beating my head on the table. My hopes for further negotiation descended into the abyss of despair. Cos' stare all but screamed *I told you so.*

I lowered myself to a stool, slumping over at the table, staring into the array of bowls of brownish-green sliced Hagion foodstuff, and the big center bowl of golf-ball-sized rocks. Beyond Cos, I caught a glimpse of a Hagion shoot through the wall and head straight for our table.

"Well done, Tmait," Vtekdao said in a definite upswing in mood as he settled on the stool next to his successor. He leaned across the table, utensil in hand, and plucked a sparkling gray stone from the center bowl, offering it to Tmait, who leaned in and folded his rubbery mouth around it, reciprocating. They chewed the rocks, sparks shooting from between their boulder-like teeth. The piezoelectricity emitted from the stones turned the air over the table musty-sweet with the release of ozone.

"It is curious," Vtekdao said between dainty nibbles of the mystery food, "that you actually believe you can change millennia of tradition within the Ignorant social structure. The Ignorants will never deposit their product at will. They are incapable of free choice."

"You are wrong. How can you know Truth if you never test it, if you never give it a chance to surface?"

"Truth never needs testing. Truth is the will of Hope," Vtekdao said, standing abruptly, dropping his utensil with a loud clang. "You will know Truth in time, my opponent." He turned, walking behind Tmait, subtly flicking the six fingers of his left hand as he brushed by. I heard a tiny click near Tmait's bowl.

I stared at the departing Vtekdao, unbelieving. "I could have sworn he—"

"Well, it looks like you'll be feeding Tmait now, Rita," Cos said abruptly, standing. "I have to get back to Application and check on Macro's work. Good to serve under you, Honorable Altruist. My potential is fulfilled." He bowed and slipped through the wall before it even dawned on me what he'd done.

Damn him. What the hell was with him?

Tmait sat balancing the curling iron utensil as if unsure whether I would help him. Before I decided to try this odd arrangement, another roach filled Vtekdao's seat and began the feeding ritual with Tmait, much to my relief. I didn't recognize this one; the brow folds were unfamiliar.

"Hello. Your name is...."

"Ngishkaok—Ignorant to the Honorable Altruist, Tmait."

Shalf had been the only other Ignorant I'd spoken to. Perhaps this one would be as open and gentle. "I understand life will be a little more tolerable for Ignorants now that Tmait reigns."

"It is the will of Hope."

Oh, Jesus. Maybe a more direct approach would be in order. "I don't know if it's OK to ask, so tell me if I'm out of line, but, can you tell me what the Billboard molychines do?"

"Information," Ngishkaok said.

"No, I mean, specifically, what do they *do?* Do they play advertisements? Public service announcements? Prayers? What?"

"Different for each of us."

I was getting nowhere but at least I had established that the subject was taboo only with Cos, and it was eating me alive to know why.

"Is it in words? Pictures?"

"Both," Ngishkaok answered.

Tmait's pupils stopped spinning and he stiffened in mid-chew, captivated by his own Billboard, I assumed.

"What words? What pictures? Tell me."

"Dramatization of The Purpose when the Holy Ones at last will be free to live as before, when the Benefactors come and—"

Tmait hissed and choked, dropping his curling iron from trembling rubber fingers. He shuddered on his tuffet for several seconds as both Ngishkaok and I sat there helplessly watching the creases and arteries of his exposed brain balloon and fill with thick black fluid that shot through the vessels in his eyes, blackening the yellow orbs like hot tar poured over raw eggs. He emitted a final shrill hiss and keeled over face down in the center bowl of rocks, black fluid oozing from his gaping mouth onto the gray stones.

A tiny silvery object glinted in the flowing black slime; before it disappeared between the rocks I plucked it up with the utensil, holding it inches from me. From one end of it, tiny mechanical pincers flexed menacingly. "Ugh." I dropped the utensil, watching the machine scurry across the table.

Feeling for Tmait's pulse, I found none and looked up at Ngishkaok's brow creases, studying the folds while avoiding the spinning pupils, and whispered, "I think he's dead. That machine... Vtekdao...."

"We're doomed! The New Society will not come to pass! Vtekdao reigns again!" Ngishkaok wailed, trembling and wadding.

"Shhh. Vtekdao committed a murder. He won't be reinstated."

"What's *murder?*"

Oh boy. I held my head, hunched over, elbows propped on the table, clamping down on an impending headache. Ngishkaok was right. It was all over. Nothing would change. Vtekdao had won.

Unable to remove myself from the table where Tmait lay dead beside me, I stared into the metallic table surface, emotionally defeated by this horrible turn of events. I felt the walls close in around me, a shadow drop over me; a shroud of resignation. I looked up. Hagions surrounded the table, silent, pupils spinning. They glowered at me, ignoring their dead newly elected leader. Sweat trickled down my sides.

"We did not expect such behavior from the Savior," the roach standing behind Ngishkaok said.

"Huh? What behavior? You're not accusing me of—"

"Why else would you summon zhan to your table?"

"No. No, you've got it all wrong! I didn't...I couldn't. Vtekdao's the one who profits from this, not me."

"Vtekdao remains our Honorable Altruist and you must answer to zhan. We will escort you to zhaz chambers. Please do not be difficult."

Rubber fingers tugged at my left arm. "I have no reason to kill Tmait. Don't you understand that?" I stood, allowed myself to be towed through the thickening crowd, through the wall. A Hagion on each side of me, I trudged up the spiral, driven not by fear, but by my seething hatred for Vtekdao. The son-of-a-bitch had framed me; if it took me the rest of my life, I'd pay him back for that. He had it all now, using me as a tool to get it. And what was I to make of Cos' timely exit? Did he know what would happen?

I couldn't seem to do anything right here. King Midas had nothing on me. I had the Senokot touch: Everything I touched turned to shit.

When I felt the two roaches steering me to the wall, I burst through ahead of them, ready to face my nemesis. The roaches that held me tottered through on their small hooves, caught by surprise by my sudden move forward.

Vtekdao lounged in his cocoon-like throne, a roach stationed on each side of him. A wave of nausea and grief swelled inside me at the sight of Shana floating in the glass jar on the bench behind him.

"Tmait is dead, Honorable One. We bring the perpetrator," the roach on my right said.

"Bsouk, Bzheyant, you honor me well with your expediency. Leave us now." The roaches left.

I broke up into laughter. "You stupid fuck. You don't really think you'll get away with this, do you? I *saw* you. I know what you did."

"It matters not. I am in control of my civilization's destiny now. The Purpose will be fulfilled. You will now honor your agreement."

"What will you do when I tell everyone you killed Tmait?"

"No one will believe you. They will believe your loyalty to me caused you to commit a desperate act."

"You consider killing Tmait desperate." So, murder did matter—in an odd sense. Probably only if one didn't get caught.

"An act of instability, at least. Your credibility has been destroyed." He began to shake and wheeze, blushing light blue.

"You don't get it, do you? If I'm such a degenerate, won't you look like a fool for trusting me, for asserting that I am the instrument of The Purpose, the will of Hope?"

He stopped laughing. "That is an...unfortunate, however minor, inconven—" He slipped into a fugue.

What kind of advertisement would play for this dictator? That everyone else was under some kind of mental control was no surprise, but who, or what, controlled Vtekdao from the inside? Why would he *let* them? I wanted so badly to reach out and stroke his brain, do to him what I'd once done to Tmait, but I knew the other two roaches would be on me in an instant.

" . . .ience. You will not embarrass me. You will cooperate. Must I offer further demonstrations of why your complicity is in your best interest?"

The worst had already happened. He needed us all alive. What else could he do?

I had a sinister idea. "You're right," I said calmly, pulling my caftan open, wrestling out of it and standing before him dressed only in my convictions.

"What is the meaning of this? It is uncommon for humans to—"

"Your Savior is out of her fucking mind! Your Savior is a murderer! How can The Purpose be fulfilled by a crazy human? How will you convince your followers you know what you're doing? You're entrusting the future of the race to a psychotic!" I screamed as I ran as fast as I could through the wall and down the spiral. "Your Savior killed Tmait! Vtekdao trusts your Savior! Your Savior is a killer!" I kept screaming, all the time hearing the clacking of Hagion hooves closing in behind me. Instantly two sets of cold rubber fingers closed around my wrists. "I killed Tmait. I'll kill your children!"

Jerking free was not difficult; escaping was. In seconds dozens of roaches circled me. Each time I broke away from them, crashing through a tangle of rubber and chitin and horn, they formed a new circle. They closed in, cold fingers probing, groping, gripping, slipping off every part of me in an attempt to hold me. Fighting their speed and numbers exhausted me, reducing me to a quivering mass of sweaty flesh.

It took eight roaches to drag me back to Vtekdao, who stood at his throne, quaking and wheezing in light blue flushes.

"Impulsive, you are. You don't seem to be impressed with the gravity of your situation." He wadded both hands. "You *must* bring the colony. There is no more time for these games you seem to enjoy."

"Why should I comply?" I panted, sweat running from my neck and down between my bare breasts.

"The Benefactors are necessary to The Purpose."

Here we go again. "Dammit! The Purpose! The Purpose! What the fuck is The Purpose? I need to have a reason for my actions. *Please,* tell me what The Purpose is."

The crowd of roaches behind me clacked and mumbled nervously.

"Dismissed!" Vtekdao yelled. He huffed once. "You are the Savior. You know what The Purpose is. You have been sent by the will of Hope."

"Wrong, roach. You know damn well I'm no savior. Now why don't you just cut the bullshit and level with me? Before I embarrass you again."

Vtekdao didn't move or speak. He hadn't fugued; his pupils still spun. By god, I do believe he was *thinking.*

"Vnoim, program a Billboard for our Savior."

Oh shit, I'd done it now. "You're not going to plant one of those advertising molychines in me, are you? I protest."

"You wish to know The Purpose? Then accept my offer."

Offer? Like free cable TV? I was supposed to thank him for converting my thoughts into a station break? "No, I don't want any more implants."

"It will be removed after two cycles. We doubt the human brain would be able to function with it in place—your species is so primitive. We require you to operate at full capacity in bringing the Benefactors."

It is beyond words how I felt about being called a primitive by a roach. My curiosity, my need to understand, to know, superseded my distrust of Vtekdao. "OK. If you promise to remove it after I've seen what you want me to see." Not that his promise meant anything to me. I knew Cos would remove the molychine if I asked him.

"Certainly. Vnoim, place it."

The roach came at me with a pair of long tweezers. I couldn't see what they gripped, it was too small. I kneeled, bowing my head. A sharp sting shot through my neck. I grabbed my caftan as I rose.

"It will be some time before the first cycle. You are free to go," Vnoim said.

Just like that? After all that scrambling and fighting to bring me here, recapture me, he'd let me go? I didn't like the way that felt. "You lied, didn't you?"

Vtekdao folded into his cocoon-throne. "I speak necessary words. Return to me when you understand."

What had I done? How stupid could I be? Of course he lied. I let him set me up again.

I walked through the wall, not bothering to dress, dazed, resigned to whatever I'd permitted Vtekdao to implant. I no longer believed it had been a Billboard. It was something else, perhaps another executioner, or a brain cannibal like he gave Tmait.

Why did I keep trusting him? How could I hate him so much and still let him suck me in? It was some kind of sickness, something dark and ugly inside me that would destroy me.

These feelings, this recurring self-doubt was not unfamiliar to me. It had been that way with my father. The worse he treated me, the harder I tried to please him. As if I could. He fed on my suffering—until the day when I decided he'd never hurt anyone ever again. It would have to be the same with Vtekdao.

My lack of creativity in finding a different solution depressed me. I should choose another option besides murder this time—I'd done that, and I'd felt a thousand feelings at war inside me because of it. But also because of it, my potential had changed; my choices should change. That was the Qwiffian way.

Again unaided, I dissolved through the wall into my quarters, only to meet twelve yellow eyes. I stopped dead, still clutching my caftan at my side. "I'm not in the mood for this, whatever the hell it is."

"Please, we need—"

"I don't give a shit what you need. Tell Vtekdao I'm not ready yet."

"Vtekdao did not send us. We came for Qwiff."

My heart squeezed in an extra beat. "Who...What's Qwiff?"

"Teach us, Honorable Ree-tah."

I shook my head furiously. "Who *are* you?"

"We are the Ignorants Ngishkaok, Bsouk, Bzheyant, Sphoiashth, Javanaugh, and the Obligant C'toikth," the roach in the front said, wadding to each as he introduced them. "We want

Qwiff."

"Bsouk? Bzheyant? You're the assholes who turned me in to Vtekdao. I don't owe you a goddamn thing. By the way, I didn't kill Tmait. Vtekdao did."

"We know. We had to turn you over to Vtekdao, to deflect suspicion. We have splintered from The Purpose. You will lead us. With Qwiff."

I laughed. "I'm not doing anything with you. My loyalty is to Vtekdao and The Purpose." Go tell Vtekdao how he failed in his treachery, asshole. "I don't want you around me. It's dangerous for you to be here."

"It is safe, Ree-tah. Sympathizers carry our transmitters within them. Our whereabouts and our thoughts are unknowable."

My hair spanked my face as I vigorously shook my head. "Please leave. I do not wish to offend Vtekdao. You must go."

Saying nothing more, they filed through the wall.

I sighed in relief. From now on I'd have to consider every contact a set-up, or at best, a test of my loyalty. Did Vtekdao really think I'd buy the story of dissidents? God, he was a work of pomposity! Dissenters would never be tolerated aboard this ship; they'd be absorbed.

Pulling on my caftan, I shot through the wall and up the spiral to Application where the coward Cosmigellan had said he'd be. I had to tell him about the fake dissidents, about Tmait's murder, about...No, I wouldn't tell him about my naked tantrum—I'd just get another ass-chewing.

I felt oddly triumphant in the way I'd handled the incident in my quarters. If I was to survive, I'd have to do a lot more of that kind of thing.

Pressing the red dot on the wall, I didn't even have time to look for Cos in the bloody red glow of Application. Pictures flickered behind my eyes, growing, widening until they played before me like a giant hologram. An image of row upon row of jars on shelves, superimposed itself over the actual view of Application. In the image the jars were filled with developed Hagion young. Humans in white caftans, their backs to me, pulled wet folded roaches from the jars and placed them gently in glass boxes, where they then attached tubes and small fluid-filled cylinders to the sides of the boxes. An offstage narrator spoke softly, lovingly:

"And when the Benefactors are recovered the product of thousands of loyal Ignorants will be placed in vivigenesis. Our Benefactors will tend the incubation of the next generation of our great race." *It was my voice!*

I tried to move, to walk; not one muscle worked. I felt adrenalin course through my veins, my muscles unable to respond to it.

The picture flickered and changed to a view of a different room. Hagion young lied stretched out on dozens of silver tables, their limbs strapped down while humans poked, prodded, sliced, injected, and inserted tools and devices like Nazi vivisectionists in a psychotic sci-fi movie. My duplicated voice continued in the same loving tone:

"Through skilled surgery, the Benefactors will insure that our progeny are fit for natural reproduction." The view swelled, showing a close-up of human hands inserting a small tube in the groin of a Hagion youngster. "The Holy Ones will procreate freely, sexually, prolifically. Our civilization will be restored at last! The natural order of The All That Is will be reclaimed!

The view flickered again, to the vast reaches of space, zooming in to a star system—Sol's star system. Huge cylindrical ships etched their way through the firmament, blinking out, re-emerging elsewhere in quantum jumps across space. There were thousands, tens of thousands of them, the collective mass of the ships cluttering, consuming the space between the planets, reducing the nine worlds to mere trinkets bejeweling a sea of Hagion technology.

"Again the Holy Ones will flourish and multiply throughout the universe. Baryonic supremacy will fall! Holy Life is sacred! It is the fulfillment of the Purpose, the will of Hope!"

The view flickered back to the human surgeons who turned as one, chanting in unison, "We are here to fulfill The Purpose. It is our destiny. Holy Life is sacred. It is the will of Hope."

My heart galloped in the tight reins of the implant. I wanted to scream. The Billboard held me fast in its will-thieving grip. I gazed at all the familiar faces. I knew every one of them.

The picture winked out and my muscles spasmed with the sudden effusion of adrenalin. Jerking spasmodically, I folded over and fell, catching myself before my face hit. "Cos!" I screamed into the floor. "Cos!"

In the red light of Application two bare feet padded up into view. I turned my head as Cos crouched down and poked a finger between my lips, waiting for me to unclench my teeth before shoving a hard bitter bead beneath my tongue. "So, you've gone and done it. I told you not to interfere. What the hell's the matter with you, Rita? You had a Billboard *implanted?* Are you crazy?"

"Cos," I moaned, muscles quieting, heartbeat slowing. "I saw you—all of you: Jaynah, Pascalia, every neohuman. I heard my own voice. How'd they do that? They've only seen you and Macro."

"Simulation. They know who we are. They won't stop until they have us. You must not interfere."

"You're their goddamn caretakers! Their nannies! You're going to help them breed like maggots! They're going to take over the whole universe!"

"They are domestically incompetent. They've tried for millennia to recruit other species, but were unsuccessful. We are their only hope."

I pushed myself to my feet. "You can't do this! This can't happen!"

"We have no choice." He turned and walked away.

I followed him into the extraction room. "The hell you don't! Refuse! You can't let these roaches fill up the universe, swallow up every beautiful thing in the sky—"

"They already have. They are nine-tenths of everything. It's just not organized quite yet."

"Cos! Cos, how can you call me insane when you're going to let them—*help* them—choke off everything we know with their darkness, their evil? How can you do that?"

He whirled around and gripped my wrists. "Stop it!" He shook me. His eyes were aflame with more fury than I'd ever seen from him.

"Cos, you're hurting me."

"Stop it, then! You don't understand!"

"Then *make* me understand! Tell me *why!* What penalty is there if you refuse them?" I jerked my wrists away and promptly hammered his chest.

"I can't," he said, holding his hands out as my fists struck his arms over and over again. "I can't." He backed up, tears running down his face.

I stopped, unable to look at his pain. "I'm sorry," I whispered through my own tears.

He came to me and embraced me. "I know. I know you are."

For several minutes we held each other, sobbing softly, he torn by his knowledge; I by my need of it.

Then he vanished, replaced by a replay of the Billboard presentation. I couldn't even feel his body against mine, his warmth, his breath on my neck, as my voice droned on of the plan for massive hatching of Hagion eggs, the rampant breeding, the frenzied universal domination—all through the gracious succor of their Benefactors.

The sickening image blinked off and my consciousness folded around Cos, still warm, face wet in my embrace. "Cos, can you remove the Billboard? I don't want to see that hideous film ever again."

He pulled away and returned with a long tweezers. The sting was welcome.

I sighed, calming, remembering why I'd come here to see him. "I almost forgot to tell you. Tmait's sort of abdicated the throne. Vtekdao killed him and tried to make it look like I did it."

"I know."

"Is that why you bailed, chickenshit? I could have used some support."

"Not true. You did fine," he said, smiling.

If I hadn't used up my anger, I'd have slapped him. "You know what else?"

"I'm confident you'll tell me."

"I found out who's been etching *QWF* all over my walls."

His eyes widened, bloodshot from our fight.

"Well, not exactly who, but maybe why. A group of dissident Ignorants plus C'toikth. They want me to teach them about Qwiffianism."

He pursed his lips. "Dissidents? And what did you say?"

"I refused. They were obviously sent by Vtekdao. I figure one or the other of us leaked the word `Qwiff' when we first came here, maybe I talked in my sleep or something, and Vtekdao's trying like hell to find out what it is."

"I see. And what will you do if they persist?"

"Oh, I don't think they'll be back."

He stared down at the floor, saying nothing.

"Cos?"

With a slight smile, he said, "Rita, whatever you choose, be careful. And *do not* challenge Vtekdao. That's of paramount importance."

"I hate that fucker and he knows it."

"Do as he says. He can do more harm than you can even imagine."

In mid-laugh someone walked into my brain.

Rita. Rita speak to me. Tell me what—

"Cos! Listen! The voice is back, that same strange voice."

Who is this?

I searched Cos' face for a reaction. He shrugged. "Didn't you hear it?"

"No."

"You didn't listen, did you?"

He lowered his gaze. "I'm sorry. I can't."

"Locking me out of The One, again?

"I have to."

"Then how can I hear this voice?"

He didn't answer.

I eased down on the end of the low central table, staring into the watery walls of the extraction booth where Shalf had died. The voice never returned. I jumped up to leave.

"Promise me you'll obey Vtekdao," Cos said. "When zhe comes for you—and zhe will—cooperate. You'll endanger much if you do not."

I nodded, unsure whether I had lied or not.

"And remember to pretend you still have the Billboard installed."

"He might try remove it, as he said."

He smiled. "No, Rita. He won't. It was meant to stay with you, that you would be swayed to fulfill The Purpose."

"Oh. I see. I arranged for my own brainwashing. Great."

"And keep your transmitter with you at all times."

Fondling the tiny spiked piece of metal in my pocket, I left with a nod and no words. I couldn't shake the feeling that he talked as if he would never see me again.

Out of Duty and in the red light of Application, I slinked up to the first row and scanned the jars of preserved eggs: the new generation of roaches waiting for their caretakers to bring them to life.

Lifting the lid off the third jar, I dropped the transmitter in the fluid and watched it disappear behind the egg.

CHAPTER 14

DISILLUSION and DISSOLUTION

Objects are events.
—Qwiffian Handbook of Sapience

Descending into thick cool mist. Jade green, everything is jade green. Huge valleys of opal glint in the dim dripping sunlight. Fine tendrils reach from slow quiet streams up to the canopy of mist; their terminal pods burst, spraying glittery spores into the viscous, sweet air.

The clear, hard shell encasing me cracks and falls away, releasing me. My body sways, shines a turbid, gelatinous gray-green. All around, similar bodies mill, dance in rejoice. Close by, a thin minaret spears through the cloudy dome—at once a sarcophagus and a monument for those who have succumbed to The Ancient Way, that I and my kind may continue.

Beings identical to me close in around me, blush lavender, extend pseudopods, touch, flow into and through me. An immense flood of experience and knowing passes from their minds to mine, from mine to theirs. We are holographic existence multiplied to infinity, complete in each self, duplicates of The Whole. We are of The One.

Fading. Returning as something else. A dark comet shears through the heavy sky, absorbing light. The planet shudders. Geysers gush plumes of hot vapor and sparkling dust. Streams become rivers, rushing in a hideous rolling green froth. Opal cliffs crack and collapse, crumbling into yawning electricity-laced crevasses. The air is choked with sweet chemical screams. We are dying.

Black void absorbs my consciousness, it becoming part of me, I becoming part of it, until we are the same.

Uncoiling, unraveling, unclumping, diffusing. The darkness tears the light asunder, disposing of its hold, its brilliant fifteen-billion-year dance.

Dissolution, fragmentation, crumbling worlds. Decayed dreams, dissolved lives. Disorder.

Turbulence gone awry. Chaos out of rhythm. Disarrangement.

Displaced plans, scattered hopes. Disintegrated futures, squandered potentials.

Expulsion from the cradle of creation.

Universal evanescence.

When the thumping in his head finally forced him awake, Jason Childress couldn't decide whether to ask *where* he was or *how* he was. His eyes still closed, he reached up and ran his fingers over his right temple. His forehead felt rough and numb. Gauze, he speculated.

He pushed his elbows into the softness beneath his supine body and strained to raise himself, opening his eyes slowly, letting just a sliver of photons leak in before trusting to flood his throbbing brain with his whereabouts. "My car. My car," he moaned, his head beating with every word.

A shadow filled his view, obliterating the bright light from the kitchen window. Childress recoiled down into the blankets.

"Don't get up yet, Jason." Nancy's voice wrapped him in its warmth. "Here, drink this." She caressed his hand, curling his fingers around a warm cup. "It's comfrey tea. For the nausea."

He hadn't noticed nausea until she mentioned it; it lurked just under the surface, upstaged by the pain in his head. He sipped the honey-laced liquid, feeling it splash to the bottom of an empty stomach. "How long have I been like this?"

"Two days. You hit your head pretty hard. Twenty stitches."

"Who...?" He reached up again to feel the bandage.

"Sabina. She's our trauma surgeon."

"One of the *children?*"

"She's quite competent."

His stomach growled in approval of the tea and his eyes focused better on Nancy's smiling face. "My animals. I have to get home." He set the cup on the arm of the sofa. Swinging his legs to the floor and planting his knuckles in the layer of blankets, he attempted to stand. He looked down into his lap. "What the hell is *this?*"

"A diaper. Two days, Jason. You couldn't be moved."

"Great." His headache eased as he sat up. "Bring me my

clothes, will you?"

"Take it easy, Jason. There's no rush. Jaynah and Darwinia are taking care of your animals. Everything's OK." She checked her watch, a pleat of concern between her brows.

Childress relaxed, leaning back on the sofa. "God, what have I done? I must be losing it. Got to lay off the cognac," he mumbled, finishing his tea. "How bad is my car?"

"No serious damage. Volta and Fermiana managed to hammer out the grill. It runs."

He smiled when he heard the names, then sighed. "You won't believe the dreams I had. Planets blowing up, talking amoebas, the whole universe coming apart. Voices! Dozens of voices, pulling me towards—" He stopped, puzzled, looking into Nancy's wide blue eyes. "Not a dream. An hallucination. Like the one in the car...."

"It's OK, sweetheart," she said, placing her hand on his arm, the only hand he'd never squirmed out from under. "You've somehow tapped into The One. Be happy about that."

"The one? The one wha—" Then he remembered. The children. The story they told. His disbelief, and his hasty departure because of it. He shook his head, instantly wishing he hadn't. When his brains sloshed to a standstill he asked for more tea, captivated by the foggy place that had opened up between dream and reality.

"When you refine your new talent, you'll never be alone again, Jason," Nancy said, offering the tea.

He chuckled, cautiously. "I spend all my money on creating aloneness. It's who I am."

"Perhaps... no longer." Nancy smiled again. It was beginning to irritate him.

"Mind if I shower before I leave?"

"Your clothes are in the master bath."

He eased to his feet, the wet crotch of his diaper sagging between his legs. Smiling sheepishly, he waddled down the hall to the last bedroom on the left, and entered the shower room. Through a glass ceiling, sunlight shone down on a row of ten shower heads. On a corner clothes rack hung his jeans, jacket, and sneakers, all freshly washed. His white shirt was not there; a green T-shirt hung in its place. Nancy always did like him in green; it brought out the green in his eyes, she'd often said. There was a time when that had mattered to him.

Looking in the mirror, a clean shaven but drawn face stared back. He fingered the bandage, found the end and unraveled the wrapping from around his skull. A small gauze patch fell from what he expected to be a rather large and gruesome gash in his head. There was only a ragged scar and some mild bruising. No stitches and no little white stitch marks at all. That Sabina girl must be some seamstress.

Childress let lukewarm water pour over his head as he pondered his circumstances. What the hell had driven him to come down off Palomar Mountain two days ago, to this ranch? Ever since that meeting things just didn't seem real. Strike that. Ever since the earthquake—in actuality an earth*slip* from being suddenly released from whatever had retarded its rotation—ever since Antarctica, ever since being put on the Beta Team at WCPW, nothing seemed real.

Especially the voices.

Gentle voices. Accepting voices. Telling him he was of The One as Nancy just had. What did it mean? That they spoke to him telepathically? How could a no-nonsense scientist like himself abide such fantasy?

Yet....

Undoubtedly his fellow astronomers regarded his wild ideas with the same skepticism as he did the beliefs of the people on this settlement. He would have to forgive his peers, and himself, for that. Years of schooling had done it to them.

Though he rejected orthodox religion as outdated metaphor, he knew there was something more, something important missing from standard scientific explanations. Life had patterns, had meaning beyond empiricism. Maybe if he listened, opened up to the possibilities....

As if on a timer, the stream of water dribbled to a stop, signaling the end of his reverie.

"What does it mean," he asked, pulling on the green T-shirt as he entered the living room where Nancy spoke softly with two adolescents, "to be of The One? Do I get a secret decoder ring or something?" He twirled his long dark hair into a rope, looping it through itself to hold at the back of his neck.

"It means you have opened yourself up to the All That Is. You are not bonded... yet it happened. No need to analyze it," Nancy said.

"Wait. Wait. Bonded?"

"Emotionally, psychically joined with one of the neohumans. To be so, automatically links one with all others of the colony."

"So that's what the voices are? *Everybody here?*"

"Yes. Only, you're not bonded. Unless your residual affection for me somehow allowed you to....“

Yes, he still cared for Nancy; he always would. But his caring by no means could be interpreted as being "in love" with her. "So, if I'm connected to you, I'm connected to all through you. Is that what you're saying?"

"Yes...except it's backwards. Usually the only way to become linked with The One is through bonding with a Phaedran, not a human."

"Oh, I see." He fought with himself to maintain an active, inquisitive mind, open to such strange possibilities—if not to embrace these odd concepts, then to understand where Nancy was coming from, what made the colony tick. "To which one are you bonded, Nancy?"

"Why, Doron. I thought you knew that."

"Doron is your son. Of course there is that special bond between mother and—"

"Doron is more than my son. He was my neohuman lover, Alabaster. When he could no longer maintain human form, he injected his DNA into one of my ova."

"Maintain human form?" he caught himself repeating her words.

"Yes. When the Phaedrans took human form, all physiological processes were under conscious control. But aging disables that ability shortly, and they revert to native form."

"And that native form is..."

"Something resembling a very large amoeba."

A flash from his dreams invaded his thoughts. He swallowed, mumbling, "Green. It's all green and wet where they come from," staring out the picture window to the east pasture.

"Phaedra! You've seen it!" Nancy said. "Jason, you *are* of The One."

"Of The One," Doron and the young girl said together.

"Well," Childress said, "that explains those weird dreams." He gulped and pulled out a chair to sit at the dining room table with the children as Nancy brought him a glass of something green. He drank it eagerly, the minty vapors diffusing up into his sinuses.

"Welcome to the universe," Nancy said.

Childress finished the cold aromatic tea. "So why don't I hear the voices now? Why haven't I heard them since the accident?"

"They frighten you," Doron said. "Until you accept them, they cannot be a normal part of your consciousness. And it will take effort. You must train your mind, first accepting yourself as one voice of many, a complete whole of The One Mind. Then the hard work begins: filtering each voice, responding when contacted."

"Yeah, well, it sounds like I have a hell of an apprenticeship ahead of me. Right now, I'd like to get back to the house and check on my animals."

"Jason, I told you. They're well looked after. There's no need—"

"Nancy, I'm indebted to you—all of you—for everything. I'd love to stay, but that puppy of mine won't like it that I haven't come home for two days. You've had animals, you understand their comfort does not stop at food and shelter. Now, where's my keys?"

"Jason, you can't go. It's not safe out there."

"That so-called earthquake didn't cause that much damage. I drove out here the day it happened, didn't I?"

"It's not that, it's..."

"Tell him, Nancy," the girl said.

"Volta, it's hard enough accepting *us,* I don't think—"

"Tell him."

Nancy dropped her gaze, her long orange lashes a fortress against her apparent unwillingness to divulge facts of great weight. Childress waited.

"It's contaminated," Volta finally said, her green eyes flashing beneath cornsilk-blond bangs. "It started in the city yesterday. We estimate the spread to the outskirts, then to rural areas, will take about twenty-four hours. Nothing manmade will be left untouched."

Childress leapt to his feet. "Contaminated? With what? What the hell are you talking about? Did somebody drop the Big One during my vacation at Club Coma?"

"Nothing like that," Nancy said. "It's not life-threatening, per se. But we expect in time—"

"*What* isn't life-threatening?" He looked around the kitchen, spotting his keys on top of the refrigerator. "Shit, I have to go. Phoebe. My birds."

"Jason," Nancy said, launching from her chair and grabbing for his arm as he reached for his keys. "Jaynah and Darwinia are bringing your animals. It has to be this way. Trust me. Trust *us*."

"You know me better than that, Nancy. I only trust those who have no burning need to demand that I do. I shouldn't have humored you as long as I have. No, Nancy. I'm leaving." He stopped, doorknob in his grip. "Why can't you accept that it's all over between us? We're *friends,* nothing more. You can't keep me here. Frankly Nancy, your manipulations shock me. Do you really think I'm that gullible?" He pulled open the door.

"Jason, wait!"

He didn't hear the rest of her pleas as he slammed the door behind him, loping down the steps to his car. He gave the damage to the grill only slight acknowledgement as he jammed the key in the ignition, starting the engine, angrily stomping the gas pedal and shooting forward in a scratch of gravel. Damn her. The whole settlement must have been in on her plan.

At the end of the driveway he had to get out to open the chain-link gate. Just as he lifted the catch he saw it: a moat. A goddamn moat, half filled with water, stretched beneath the twelve-foot-high cinder-block wall that ringed the ranch. Had this been here before? He couldn't remember. Off in the distance to the west ten or twelve figures worked, pulling what looked like huge hoses over the wall. The only patch of solid ground remaining was fifteen or so feet in front of the gate. Childress shook his head, remembering too late the probable results. The throb abating, he went through the ritual of opening the gate, getting back in the car, driving through, getting out of the car again, closing the gate, getting back in, before edging onto the country road that lead to the freeway. Turning onto the freeway he passed two identical light blue vans. In his rearview mirror he saw them stop at the gate to the ranch.

The traffic on the freeway was peculiarly non-existent. It was more than unusual for a freeway that emptied to and from the U.S.-Mexico Border—it was eerie. Until ten at night this freeway, he recalled, was congested with both U.S. and Mexican traffic, Border Patrol vehicles, Highway Patrol, San Diego Police—all occasionally interrupted by the excitement of illegal aliens running across the freeway in search of a new life... or a novel death. It was rare to drive this stretch without hearing a siren coming at you in pursuit of some zonal violator.

Now, as his car moved smoothly along the freeway, silence, and a sense of abandonment permeated the air, impelling him to imagine himself the last man on earth. He smiled to himself.

Approaching the first traffic signal, he didn't have to prepare to stop or speed up: The light was dead. It was the same with the next signal, and the next. Passing the tower of the recently expanded municipal airport, he pulled over to the side of the road. Across the freeway, a row of new warehouses was devoid of activity, seemingly abandoned. The earthslip had caused more damage down here than elsewhere, Childress surmised.

Jason, come back. A single voice in his head.

Leave me alone, Nancy.

Don't go any farther.

Why? Why, Nancy? He closed his eyes tightly. A faint throb began in his right temple. "Ok. Ok, I'm not going crazy. You're really in here," he muttered.

Come back. There's nothing for you out there.

I'm going home, Nancy. He pulled back onto the freeway. By the time he got to 805-North, the landscape had taken on a decidedly derelict appearance. Everywhere he looked, warehouses, homes, crumbled to the ground. The freeway itself was getting rougher, more cracked and pot-holed as he drove north. Up ahead at the Palm Avenue Bridge exit, the tall, metallic-green glass bank building had been reduced to a heap of glass shards and twisted metal. He ascended the offramp to Palm Avenue and parked at the dead traffic signal at the top of the bridge, killing the engine.

Leaving the car, he walked east on what should have been a concrete sidewalk, but amounted to nothing more than a ribbon of soft gray powder. At what had been the entrance to the California-Mexican National Bank, Childress contemplated a stream of sparkling green sand sifting through bolt holes in a crumpled steel girder. This destruction had not been caused by earthslip. This was something entirely different. Something perhaps, alien. No natural force could result in such fine disintegration. The building had not just fallen, it had dissolved. As Childress listened in the near-silence, he knew the process was still going on.

He climbed over and through the tangle of brittle metal; it crumbled away with the brush of his legs. Piles of glass crunched under his feet, reduced to sand with each step. He stood now in what he guessed would be the center of the lobby, scanning for desks, vaults, safety deposit boxes, finding only variously-colored heaps of dust and sand framed by crumbling steel. The hiss of flowing granular matter surrounded him.

Suddenly a grumbling sensation droned through the soles of his feet. He whirled around, alarmed, staring off at the bridge where he'd parked his car. Almost imperceptibly, the ground beneath the wheels sagged. A sharp pop split the air. There, in the dead center of the bridge pavement, a bulge of cracked asphalt swelled up like a muffin cooking in fast forward. The sounds of metal snapping and groaning sent Childress hurdling over the debris and running to his car, scratching at the hood as it slowly slipped back down the offramp. He scrambled over shifting ground around to the driver's side of his car, clawing at the door handle as it receded from his grasp. His foot crunched through the pavement as he vaulted over the door, landing in a seat that crumbled beneath his haunches. Breathing fast, hands shaking, he turned the key. It snapped. He quickly glanced up, helpless as his car crept backwards down the ramp, retreating from the rumbling bridge.

Stomping on the brake to somehow stop the backslide, Childress' sneaker exploded in tatters from his foot as the brake pedal fractured into fragments. The steering wheel disintegrated in his grip. Staring unbelieving at the small particles of steering wheel imbedded in his palms, he screamed and smashed through the door, feeling it crinkle then dissolve against his shoulder. He fell sideways onto the road and right through the asphalt in a puff of black powder to the dirt below.

"God! What's happening? God, it's all falling apart!" he screamed, scrambling to his feet as first the left front tire, then the other three tires on his decaying Mustang detonated in powdery black clouds, the remainder of the car collapsing in a heap of disordered fragments.

Childress ran. He ran as fast as his nearly bare feet would take him, screaming for redemption in his mind, pounding through the soft pavement, the cloth shreds of what was left of his shoes whipping his ankles. Behind him, a final crash made him turn to

witness the last of the Palm Avenue Bridge drop and thunder to the dissolving freeway in a thick mushroom of powder.

He reamed the black silt from his nostrils, eyes, and mouth, continuing south in a slow jog. He would turn east back to the ranch. He didn't know why or how, but he would be safe there.

The overpass to the south had not collapsed yet, and the further south he jogged, the more sure his footing became. Whatever had eaten away at the structural material just a half mile up the freeway had not got down here yet. He slowed to a walk, conserving energy for the seven-mile trek back to the ranch. Clearing the last of the black powder from his nose and mouth, he was able to appreciate the easy spring sun on his back, the sweet breeze on his sweaty scalp.

No traffic. It was incredible to imagine that all of humanity was somewhere else, trembling in fear, no doubt, at the dissolution of their plastic world. Childress' only regret was the loss of his beloved '65 Mustang. For Childress, there was no more fear. He believed Nancy now. He had no choice.

In the distance, as he walked east, he heard the high RPM whine of an engine. He looked up. A light blue van screamed towards him, headlights flashing. It screeched to a halt beside him.

"Get in!" Jaynah yelled across the cab from the driver's seat.

Childress yanked the door open, half surprised the handle hadn't crumbled in his hand, and launched himself up beside her. "Well, it's a beautiful day in the neighborhood, as Mr. Rogers would say."

"Who?"

"Mr. Rogers. Children's show host from the last century. Never mind. What's happening out there is nothing to joke about."

"Nancy told you not to go."

"I was just trying to get to my animals."

"They're at the ranch. We brought them."

He looked at her, unbelieving. "You caught two-hundred birds?"

"Took us two days."

Where would they put them all? There was no aviary on the ranch, that he remembered. "Two days? So, you knew in advance what was going to happen?"

"Yes, Jason. We did. Everything's going to be all right."

Did being of The One entail knowing the future? Is that what he had to look forward to? A shiver coursed through him. Precognition would certainly set him far apart from his already incredulous peers, much further than he'd feel comfortable with. He chuckled to himself. His whole life had been a delicately choreographed dance between isolation from and submersion in humanity. He'd probably never find a balance.

"Get out and strip down," Jaynah ordered as she parked the van across the street from the entrance to the ranch.

"Pardon me?"

"We're contaminated. We've got to strip down. And we'll have to leave the van here. There won't be much of it left after a few hours, anyway."

"Contaminated? With what?"

"Molecular machines. They're all over us. Hundreds of millions of them."

Childress gasped and ejected from the van, beating and brushing his hands over his clothes.

Jaynah stepped beside him, removing her blouse, revealing smooth white breasts, laughing. "They won't hurt you. They're designed to dissolve concrete, asphalt, rubber, metal, things like that. Manmade things."

He jerked his T-shirt over his head, tearing a lock of hair from his scalp in his panic. Jaynah unzipped her shorts and stepped out of them, oblivious to Childress' stare. He felt himself stiffen and looked away. It had been too long; she was half his age.

"Jump in," she said, stepping into the full moat. "They can't operate in water. They'll short circuit."

Childress stepped into the cold water where an hour before he had driven his car across solid ground. The chill sent his gonads to the core of his body, erasing any sexual pangs.

"Go under for a few seconds. They're probably in your hair, too."

He squatted, holding his breath, letting the water gush into his ears, up his nose. Steadying himself by holding the bottom of the chain-link gate, he felt a thumb-clip closed around a heavy chain. He realized then that no one was meant to come or go. He felt a pat on his head and came up for air.

"That's fine. They should be inactivated by now."

Childress coiled his hair into a rope, again self-tying it at his neck. "How...how do you know all of this?"

"Cosmigellan warned us."

CHAPTER 15

REVELATIONS

Everything is force and interaction with velocity.
—Qwiffian Handbook of Sapience

Enveloped in bright blue light, exultant. Swirling, diffusing, one into the other: of The One. Share the light, the Beingness, the knowing, the All That Is.

Boundaries dissolve.

Darkness encroaches, pouring into the glow of The One, diminishing the light, violating secret cavities, raping, snuffing out radiation, engulfing.

Eclipsing forever.

I snorted myself awake. What an ugly dream. I lay on my side, my back to Antarctica, willing each part of my body to wakefulness. My ears were the last to respond.

"... be here soon. We must be patient," a soft voice said from behind me.

I rolled over...and gasped, clamoring back against the wall, my knees drawn up beneath my chin. The room was filled with roaches. "What the hell are you doing here?"

"Ree-tah does not accept our intentions, C'toikth. Our Savior distrusts us, believes we have been sent by Vtekdao."

"Zhe will come. We will convince zhan of our dissatisfaction with Vtekdao's rule. We must."

I slid off the edge of my bed. "I told you I didn't want to be involved. I have nothing for you. Get out."

From the rear of the pack, another roach spoke. "It will be difficult, C'toikth."

"Our Savior is not unintelligent."

"Ngishkaok, is it true? The legend? Ree-tah made Vtekdao laugh?"

"Zhe did."

I stood now, smoothing the twists from my caftan. "Look, your presence here is unwanted. Do I have to get physical?" I eyed the group. Dominoes. One push....

"What can zhe be doing in Application so long? Zhe surely has not been assigned there."

I didn't hear the answer. All at once I understood and caught myself cackling like a fool. Not that it really mattered. As they speculated on my return, I danced around the room, making faces and other obscene gestures at the cluster of unaware Hagions.

A most interesting development, indeed. How would a rebel like myself take advantage of such a turn of events? Where should I go; what should I do? If this ship contained all the Hagions, and not just a scout party, I could conceivably bring this civilization to its knees.

I decided Vtekdao's death would be the grand finale. If I killed him right away, he might live long enough to transmit my whereabouts to the others. I would save him till last. I'd screw with the gears of this society first, starting in Restructure. If they couldn't expand the ship, they couldn't engage in Harvest.

I waded through the chattering group of roaches and punched the pyramid key on the wall console. A metal bowl of quasagna and a curling iron utensil appeared. Punching the key again, I snapped up both utensils and made my way down to Restructure.

I didn't expect to see anyone on my way down the spiral, but I did. Coming towards me up the walkway clicked a roach. Walking backwards in front of it, I studied its brow creases, deciding I did not know this one. As I stepped aside, something evil made me hesitate in withdrawing my left leg out of the roach's path. It tumbled and crashed to the floor with a sickening crunch. I continued on.

Entrance to Restructure was met with the bang of the virtual particle generator. As before, the hazy gloom of this warehouse-like area was abuzz with dozens of Obligants lost in their scatological duty.

From the vats, effluence gurgled through clear pipes and hoses into the wall. The metal sheet banged to a halt, quivered just inches from a ring of Obligants, and shot down the alley, shrinking to a small square in the distance. I stared down at the utensils in my hands, grinning at the hardness of the metal.

Shuffling my way along the wall, the metal sheet whizzing

by many times, I moved deliberately towards the stationary metal sheet. The movable sheet slid rapidly towards me from the far end as I pressed myself against the wall. Rushing in, it banged to an ear-rending stop, a mess of sparks discharging in the small gap between the plates as it trembled there for a few seconds before speeding away again. My exposed skin tingled.

Before the sheet returned, I leaned in and tossed a curling iron utensil at the bottom of the stationary plate. "This one's for the Horsehead Nebula," I said, as if performing a ritual.

I vacated my post before the sheet returned. When it did, it slammed to a standstill, quivered, and hung there, impotent and useless.

Passing the vats on my way out, I saw the clear tubes squirm and buck, clogged from vats all the way to the Restructure wall. No Obligant even looked up. They just stood there, waiting to complete the job I had aborted. I had no idea how long they'd wait there before they realized their processor had stopped. Next stop: Assembly. Then to my final destination of Vtekdao's chambers.

I estimated the walk up the spiral would take over an hour, and it would be grueling. I had plenty of time to plan my strategy, to fantasize what I'd do when I faced the Head Roach. I hoped I had the opportunity to grab his velvety exposed brain and squeeze it like a dirty sponge. I hated him enough to do that. He'd die in my grip, black ooze seeping between my fingers, shrill cry hissing in my ears. Satisfaction, extraordinary satisfaction.

Rita.

I stopped, heart galloping. Voices again? *Who is this?*

It works! Uh, it's Jason. Is it true? You're on a ship?

Jason? Jason who? Who the fuck's Jason?

Jason Childress. We met, remember?

Oh god, that asshole, I thought, knowing well that he would "hear" it. I suddenly became aware of his accent. *Are you bonded with a neohuman? How did you get into The One?*

That's not important. Are you on a ship? Made of dark matter?

Yes. How did you find out?

Please. Tell me, are you in geosynchronous orbit over Antarctica? Did the ship leave at any time?

Yes, and yes. They told you, didn't they? The colony broke their promise.

Not exactly. Rita, listen carefully. It's all falling apart here. Roads, buildings, everything manmade is—

I don't have time for your emotionalism! Don't you ever break into my mind again, you understand?

Rita, wait!

Shut up and leave me alone. I slammed my mind down against him, locking my thoughts, my vengeance inside. No one would know what I'd planned. Especially not Cos.

I stomped up the spiral, even more determined than before. Assembly was on the way to Vtekdao's chambers, a quick detour before I indulged in the utter joy of mangling his brain, watching his bulbous yellow eyes explode from his head like tennis balls launched from a serving machine. A sickening loneliness crawled through me as I pounded upwards, legs burning, lungs heaving, heart pulsing with hatred. This was it. By god, it was going to happen. I'd defeat the Hagions with nothing more than viciousness. A lone human against—

The spiral flickered. I hung in silent blackness, the blood rushing in my ears. I dropped the utensil, leaving it in space. My bare feet settled on sub-zero temperature metal as my surroundings solidified around me.

"Very clever," a deep voice boomed from the rim of the dish. "But not clever enough."

I wondered to which act of malice he referred as I lost all feeling in my feet up to my ankles. The sensation was like wearing a pair of Novocaine socks. I wasn't happy about being in the interrogation bowl again, but was too ripped on adrenalin to get all depressed about it.

"Did you really think you'd succeed?" he bellowed.

"Well, it was worth a shot." I fished for clues. "How long did it take you to find out? Who told you?"

"It was a simple matter. After isolating the two Benefactors, yours was the only other single heartbeat on Lolbah. As you know, the Holy Ones have two hearts. Locating you was no trouble at all."

Ah, the transmitter—he'd found it. I should have figured that out, since he had in fact zapped me here and obviously saw me.

Grinning, I said, "And you thought I was clever...."

He wheezed and trembled from the rim. His laughter echoed across the bowl. "So, my resourcefulness impresses you."

"Oh, immeasurably, Honorable One."

"Ree-tah," he said softly, "you honor me with your games. I so enjoy them."

"Happy to accommodate." Stay tuned for coming attractions, you fuck.

"And now, the matter of the Benefactors. I do not regard this as a game, you understand."

"Zap me out of this dish and we'll discuss it."

"Not so hasty, Ree-tah. I do believe your present circumstances may help you better appreciate the urgency of bringing the Benefactors to Lolbah." The dark figure above me wadded against the hazy blue back-glow.

The air in the dish began to shimmer, to take on substance, form. An Earth city. Los Angeles, maybe. I hadn't traveled enough in my past modeling career to know what city this represented. I craned my neck. The city wrapped around the inside of the bowl like a huge hologram. If I dared reach out, I imagined I could touch concrete.

"Observe, Ree-tah. The results of any further delays from you."

I looked around me—at the rows of shops, the tall skyscrapers, the congested city streets—my eyes jumping from one structure to another. Slowly, a rumble grew—from what point in the distorted wraparound city, I couldn't tell.

The flagpole on the courthouse to my left began to list, sagging from the crumbling concrete where it was attached. Then the steps collapsed in clouds of powder. The side columns folded away in crumbling fragments onto the sidewalk where people screamed and ran. Six cars collided, one into the rear of the other in a chain of disaster that suddenly took hold of the entire city, dissolving it to shuddering piles of debris and dust. People clawed their way out of cars, buildings, their feet crunching through the asphalt in black puffs. A woman fell with her toddler in her arms. Before she could regain her footing, an overhang cascaded down on her and buried both her and her child in a ton of concrete rubble. Neither of then even had time to scream.

I staggered, light-headed and queasy. This was it—the reason Cos had locked me out of The One. He couldn't tell me what the Hagions were planning. He knew I'd do exactly what I now knew

I had to do: kill Vtekdao—at all cost.

But this had to be a simulation. He was bluffing; so then, would I. When he sent me back down to the surface, I'd have Jaynah make more weapons and stuff so many up me I'd generate my own magnetic field.

I pressed my hands over my face and cried. "Stop it!" I sobbed over the roar and panic. "Stop it! I'll go. I'll bring the colony!" I never thought I'd hear those words of defeat come from my mouth.

"You have five-sixths of a sextet."

Blackness blinked on, then off.

I didn't have the chance to ask him if I'd be rigged with an Executioner again. I guess that would be redundant, now that he held the whole planet for ransom. My knees felt the pressure of my weight as I fell forward, catching myself on the kitchen counter.

Childress rushed towards me, reaching for my arm, then withdrawing as he touched the sleeve. "Rita. Please forgive me for my contact," he whispered.

"So, it was you all along. I beat my hand to a pulp because of your intrusions." I glanced at the microwave clock; it was ten-thirty in the morning.

"I...I don't know what you're talking about. This is the first time I've tried to—"

"You've been in my head twice before, asshole. You *amateur.*"

"I'm sorry. It must have been involuntary. I'm afraid my telepathic talents are somewhat erratic, at best."

"Would you mind getting me a hot towel? My feet are freezing." I minced painfully to the dining room table. "What are you doing here, anyway? Where is everybody? I need to talk to Jaynah."

"They're all outside." He knelt and wrapped the towel around my feet, patting it down.

The gesture surprised me. "Thanks." I smiled down at him, more in regret than appreciation. I remembered all too well his self-righteous attitude that first day we met; it had somehow dulled his exceptional good looks—then. A twinge of desire sparked through me, but was quickly doused by the awareness of my purpose here.

He removed the towel from my feet, touching my ankle gingerly as if afraid he'd catch some fungus from me. My feet tingled with warmth.

"So, what *are* you doing here?"

"I tried to leave...after my accident. I didn't get far. No one can leave here."

"Accident?"

"Yes, well, we won't get into that. Suffice it to say my inclusion in The One was a rather traumatic incident and I wasn't quite accepting at first. It's a whole new world for me."

"Yeah. I used to think I liked being alone. I only liked it because the alternative was worse—being with cruel and stupid humans." I paused, vacillating as to whether I should ask yet another favor of him. "I've been locked out of The One. You're the only one I've had contact with. How can you and I... Could you ask if I can be let back in?"

"I'll see what I can do." He sat at the table beside me and closed his eyes.

I studied his face. He was younger than I, by perhaps ten years.

"Cosmigellan says...'Not now,'" he said, grimacing as if in pain, flashing his eyes open.

"Damn him." That could only mean one thing: Cos had another secret. They all did. And Jason Childress could tell me what it was.

"No, I can't. I don't *know* what it is."

"But I thought—"

"I don't know how to express it. It's not in words—it's more like a feeling. Sorrow...and...obligation. Something inevitable, and close to them." He shrugged.

"They're so willing to give themselves to the Hagions, violating codes we all wrote. Codes of living to one's potential, not allowing another to rob you of that right. They're willing to discard that. And I'm stuck in the middle, not knowing what I should do."

"So you're opposing their choice to go with the Hagions."

"I have to. Don't you see? I have to honor my *own* potential by doing what I know is right."

He sighed, nodding. "When you and the colony are collected, include me."

"*What?*"

"Take me with you. You need help."

"You don't know what you're saying."

"Oh yes, I do. I want to go. I want to help you."

"Don't say that! The neohumans won't like it."

"They can't read me if I don't want them to."

"You've learned well. And... quickly." It took me months to learn such selectivity, such control. "I still don't think it's a good idea. Cos occasionally peeks in to see what I'm up to. I can feel him do it. If he found out—"

"Rita, I've seen what the Hagions have done. They've congealed, changed the natural order of things. They don't belong here." He leaned in close. "I can show you. Let me show you."

I stared into his verdant eyes. Images began to swim through my mind. Nebulas dispersing; galaxies unraveling, clusters flying apart. Earthquakes, volcanoes, tidal waves, long hot March days, teams of scientists struggling to understand the expanding ozone hole over Antarctica, collapsing bridge—

His mind suddenly slammed shut.

"Oh god," I said, laying my head down on the table. "I had no idea. All the destruction seems to be just side-effects of their presence." I laughed at the irony of it all. "Kind of puts the concern over disposable diapers in perspective, doesn't it?"

"Yeah," he chuckled. He got up, rattled through the upper cupboard and brought out two glasses, then brought a carton of milk from the refrigerator. "Don't you see how remarkable this is? I'll be the first astrophysicist ever to board an alien ship. This calls for a celebration," he said, pouring the milk and raising his glass. "A toast. Here's to making fantasies come true."

Such confidence. I hadn't agreed to take him. "Here's to flushing *yours* down the toilet."

He laughed, his eyes glistening with sudden moisture. "I do hope to change your mind." He sipped his milk. "My own colleagues refused to accept that the seismic and atmospheric phenomena were correlated with deep space aberrations, that it all has something to do with dark matter. That's why I came here. To talk to you."

"What do I have for you? I'm no astronomer."

"You do have a plan, don't you?"

I laughed lightly. "Not exactly. I've been playing it as it comes. I monkey-wrenched their virtual particle generator. I don't know if it's permanent or not."

His eyes widened. "Virtual part...A *Casimir* generator? A

working *Casimir* generator?"

"That's right. We're dealing not only with a soul-murdering social structure, but some pretty sophisticated technology."

His face lit up, like I'd just told him he'd won a sweepstakes. "You need me, Rita," he said, fingers lightly touching my arm, reluctant to caress it.

"Maybe." I leaned in close and kissed him. From his mind I read shock, uncertainty. "I'm sorry. I didn't mean to—"

"It's OK. Just... unexpected."

"I guess I'm just happy to have someone on my side for once." Then my words hit me: I was wrong. Jason was not the only one on my side; there were others. I don't know why I hadn't seen it before. "The dissidents. My god, they're for real. They didn't see me and talked amongst themselves. They're for real."

"Dissidents? This could be just what we need."

"Yeah. A splinter group of Ignorants. Breeders. They've had it with dying for The Purpose. They want me to teach them what Qwiffianism is."

"I'm afraid you've lost me." He pushed away from the table and stood. "Let's walk. Tell me what you know about them."

We strolled through the apricot orchard as I described the Hagion social hierarchy in as much detail as I could recall. Jason asked important, intelligent questions, triggering memories and new ideas. It was good for me to talk to him, to unload it all on someone who didn't need me to shut up. The conversation, the fresh warmth of the country air stirred suppressed urges in me. Jason was unexpectedly pleasant, not at all the self-absorbed pedant I'd decided he was when I'd first met him. There was a peacefulness about him; the creases in his face told of a history of many smiles. By the time we reached the hedge that concealed the swimming pool, I found I'd told him the whole story of how I had found Cos on a hot mound in the garden one spring day, how I'd rescued that stinking lump of gelatin, witnessed the transmutation from amoebic form to a human male resembling an actor I had a crush on, become Cosmigellan's friend and lover, participated in the recovery of many of his kind, helped establish the colony and the philosophy that bound us to each other. Jason never interrupted. I instead felt his hand slide lightly into mine, his longing for affection exuding from every pore. This peculiar man walked a tightrope between

his need for solitude and his drive to connect with someone. His doubt, his indecision attracted me to him.

"Tell me, Jason. Tell me why you're afraid." Hadn't Cos asked a similar question of me so many years ago?

"I just don't...." He sighed, pulling his hand from mine, folding his arms across his chest. "Why does it matter?"

"For the reason that makes you ask." Another Cosmigellan remark.

Jason laughed heartily. "People bother me. I don't trust them."

"Old hurt or recent hurt?"

"Both, I guess. Starting when I was five, maybe six, and recurring quite regularly."

"Tell me. I want to know."

He looked down at his feet, apparently unsure as to whether he should divulge any of his pain.

"I understand psychological abuse. It took me all of my adult life to defuse my growing hostility and helplessness." I proceeded to tell him of my experiences, how my father had belittled, threatened, stole from, lied to, cheated me while his demands escalated to the point of downright slavery; how I'd hated him so much it spilled over and mutated into self-hatred, self-destruction. I told Jason everything...except the one thing I couldn't tell him. When I finally finished, I pulled Jason through the concealed passage in the hedge and we sat at the pool's edge dangling our feet in the emerald water.

"I was abandoned at a baseball stadium shortly after coming to this country from England," he began, staring into the green water as if finding the words there. "My father made such a big deal out of taking me. Then he went to get beer. He never came back. I stayed in my seat like he'd told me, until the game ended. When the stadium began to empty, I went looking for him. I was pushed, trampled and crushed by the crowd until I fell. Twenty feet to field level." His face grew slack, melancholy. "I woke up in the hospital with two broken legs. Alone. No one ever found my parents."

"Jesus." That was all I could think of saying.

"I spent till age fifteen in foster homes, enduring a variety of for-your-own-good tyrannies. Then I ran away. I looked for my family for seven years. No luck. I stopped looking for them because I was afraid if I ever saw my father again, I'd kill him."

I almost choked on that last statement.

Jason looked up at me. "It doesn't ever go away, does it?"

"No. It just changes meaning. It'll be with you forever." I rubbed his shoulder in sympathy, feeling him begin to twist out from under my hand, then relax. "If it's any consolation, I've learned that humans rarely excel at anything unless they're either perpetually disappointed, or tormented by wrongs done to them."

He smiled and pulled me close, hugging me briefly, then releasing.

I suddenly felt close to him, closer than I'd felt to any man besides Cos. Maybe it was his extraordinary good looks. Maybe it was his distrust of people. Maybe it was his childhood, a childhood as painful as my own. More than likely, it was all of that.

He looked away when I grinned at him, Would this hurting man ever relax enough to let nature take its course? By my estimates I had very little time left. Once the colony and I were on the ship, I had no idea what Vtekdao would do with me. Once the roach had his Benefactors, what would he need me for? For all I knew, a romp with Jason would be next to my last act on Earth, just before I gathered up my best friends and handed them over to Satan, in hopes of using them as decoys for my ultimate plan of destruction of the Hagion race.

Funny, how when one is sick, or otherwise staring their own mortality in the face, the sexual urges surface with a vengeance. Like sex will somehow allow you to transcend the crisis, make you immortal. Like it's a last effort to procreate before dissolving into the substrate of The All That Is.

Procreation was not possible for me, and the furthest thing from my mind. Jason Childress was not safe near me: I wanted him. I wanted to make him feel good, help him forget his origins, forget who he was, forget his name. I stood and unzipped my caftan, slipping sensuously out of it a limb at a time until he was captured by his own passions.

He pushed to his feet and just stood there, eyes wide.

I bent down and snapped a bloom from the Lily pad floating at the edge of the pool, and stepped up to him, pushing the stem behind his ear. *You're mine.*

He closed his eyes and shivered, his breath coming in shallow shudders.

For god's sake, Jason. What do you need? Written instructions?

I pulled the leather tie from his ponytail, releasing a mane of long dark brown hair.

He teetered backwards a few steps, catching himself.

His shyness, his nervousness, aroused me. Time to crank up the gain on this seduction. I ran my hands over my breasts, pinching the nipples erect, smoothing my hands down my belly until they met wetness. I drew a moist finger across his upper lip, leaving a shiny streak beneath his nose.

I was unprepared for what happened next.

Breathing heavy, he suddenly grasped my upper arms, threw his head back in a grimace and yelled.

I froze, dumbfounded.

He took a deep breath and stared into my eyes, grinning. "Thank you, Rita," he said, pulling me in, kissing me all over my face and neck.

"You mean... you mean, it's all over?"

"Yes. No." He tore off his shirt, buttons spraying from his chest, unbelted and pushed his pants down, stepping out of them.

Damn. Nothing like this had happened to me since I was sixteen. This man was a lot younger than I'd guessed....

Rolling his clothes into a bundle, he came towards me, deliberately, eyes aflame, and hugged me tightly, moving us closer to the edge of the pool. Through his kisses and nibbles I felt us fall sideways, a shock of cold water crashing over us. Breaching the surface, gasping, still locked in his embrace, I felt his insistent lips, tongue, and teeth traveling down my throat, over my breasts. The chill of the waist-high water disappeared, warmed by the heat of our bodies, I imagined. He slid his open mouth between my breasts and descended down my body until I could see nothing but his hair fanning out on top of the water.

Electricity and silly thoughts shot through me. What was the record for holding one's breath under water? What kind of a man could hold so much passion in him after climaxing? Cos had always fallen asleep after sex. Oh god. Jason. Not Cos. Don't think of Cos. Think of Jason's full white-toothed smile. Cos' Hershey-syrup eyes—no! Jason's eyes of green fire, Jason's long silky hair, Jason's sensitive probing fingers, Jason's talented tongue....

I convulsed to climax, moaning, "Oh Cos," just as Jason surfaced, gulping for air.

He held me close, breathing hard. "It's Ok. I know."

The embarrassment, the guilt, made me want to sit on the bottom of the pool and take a deep breath. "I'm sorry. I don't know what—"

"Shhh," he said, walking me backwards, pinning me against the cement rim of the pool. He reached down behind my left knee and lifted my leg, entering me. "Don't close your eyes."

We caressed each other in the wordless language of the rapt mind, speaking to each other in images, impressions, experiences, expectations, seething emotions.

Minutes, maybe hours later, he did it again: threw his head back and cried out like his soul had been ripped from him.

I couldn't help it: I laughed; he joined me. I was glad he was in my life, that he was here on this ranch with me and my best friends.

A flurry of yellow and green streaked the skies. Birds. Hundreds of them, flying with a joy that could only follow confinement. Jason looked up, smiling as the birds fluttered overhead, arching a pathway as if avoiding an unseen barrier. "Those are mine. They're aware of the tension net, see?"

My head snapped around. "A what?"

"A tension net, a dome of a sort stretching along the walls. The moat won't prevent dust from carrying the molychines in on the wind."

"Moat? Molychines?" My pulse quickened.

"Molecular machines—dissolving everything. That's what I was trying to tell you. The roads, the buildings, bridges... dissolving. That's why I'm here. I couldn't leave."

"My god, the simulation. It *wasn't* a simulation. It was a report. Vtekdao told me he'd do this. The fucker already *has*."

Before he could answer, a collection of black spots dashed through the hedge, its body wiggling to and fro as the puppy charged up to the edge of the pool, whining, licking Jason's sweaty face as he leaned back. "It's Ok, Phoebe," he said, chuckling, cuddling the puppy to his chest. "It's Ok."

"How'd *that* get here?"

"Jaynah brought her. Along with all my birds."

Horror shredded through me. "My god, Jason, you don't plan to take her?" The horror grew. "Shit, what time is it? We've been screwing when we should have been seeing to it—"

"It's all right, Rita. The colony's waiting for us inside."

I couldn't decide whether to tell him what might happen to her. Vtekdao would surely confiscate the puppy, certain it was another gift. But, I knew he wouldn't leave the puppy here. The complication was unresolvable. I looked into Jason's eyes, trying to think of how to tell him.

"It's Ok, Rita. It'll work out. Let's go in."

All sixteen of the neohuman children stood in the kitchen and living room, dressed in white caftans in preparation for their restored roles as roach-sitters. Their human mothers stood with them, patting them, saying goodbye forever—without tears, without mourning. How could they do it?

I stared beyond them out the picture window to the east pasture. The ranch had been transformed, born of the ashes of my childhood pain, risen and renewed like the legendary Phoenix. This colony. This settlement. The Qwiffian philosophy that created them. Was I the only one who grieved their end?

Weapons. We needed more weapons—one for each of us. I looked to Jaynah, who shook her head silently. "There's no time," Jason said for her, wrapping his arm around my waist, pointing at the microwave clock with the fingers of the other hand as he hugged his puppy close. It was one minute before the five-hour limit. No time at all.

The neohumans gathered in a tight circle in the kitchen, standing shoulder to shoulder, faces expressionless. I looked to Jason, who winked, a tiny smile quivering on his lips. Through my tears, the kitchen started to evaporate, never to be occupied by our kind again.

Just as we began the atomic flux, my sister, Stella stumbled through the door, beer in hand, tripping through the wall of bodies and becoming part of what she would never understand.

CHAPTER 16

RESONANCES

The universe is non-local.
Non-locality means that reality in a quantum universe is all one point.
—Qwiffian Handbook of Sapience

In Procedure, Cosmigellan and Macro rushed from one low table to another, shoving pills beneath unfeeling tongues, calibrating newly implanted phase-shift modulators, securing lingual decoders within molars. I'd been through it all before and was more than relieved I didn't have to go through it again.

Hagions descended upon the waking Benefactors, hurriedly sequestering them. Stella awoke, screaming herself hoarse.

"What the fuck?" she said, rolling off the examining table, turning unsteadily in place as she gawked up at the high dome ceiling. "What happened? Where are we? What were those things?"

"Shut up, Stella! They're not going to hurt you," I said, my hands itching I wanted so badly to strangle her, or at least slap her sober. I glanced quickly at Jason, who eased slowly off his examining table, in awe of his surroundings.

Damn her. What would I do with her? What use would she have to my purpose, much less the Hagions'? It wasn't bad enough I still didn't know what Vtekdao would do with me, that I had brought a non-Benefactor and his pet. I now had to deal with my hysterical alcoholic sister.

"Why did you just walk in like that, Stella? You have no idea what you've done. How much trouble we're probably in."

"Hey, you weren't home. I waited over at your house for two hours. I figured your friends in *Deady's* house would know where the hell you went." She broke into laughter. "God, I need a beer."

It was going to be hard to keep from punching her out. "Dammit, Stella. Damn you." I debated telling her where she was; my temper won. "You're on a ship. In space. Miles above Earth.

There's no beer here. You've always been a pain in the ass, but never more so than now."

She laughed hysterically. "A spaceship! Well, doesn't that just beat all! Little Miss Know-it-all finally cracked! And everyone thought it'd be me."

"Come here," I said, my breaths coming in measured gusts. "I have something to show you." I went to the wall and touched it. Antarctica glared white and cloudy dead ahead.

Stella crept closer, on her face I could see she wasn't impressed. "That's some video screen. Biggest one I've ever seen. How much you s'pose something like that costs?"

"It's not a video screen, Stella. It's a viewport. Come closer." Both she and Jason stepped forward. "Look down."

Stella inhaled audibly.

"When's the last time you could look *down* a video screen?"

Jason looked from me to Antarctica, back to me again. "So... what kind of entertainment do we have on the Promenade deck?"

I had to laugh. I needed that little break in tension. "Bobbing for photons."

I looked quickly to Stella who fell silent, eyes veiled in tears. "It's true—we've left Earth. Shit, we've left Earth," she whimpered.

"That's right. No liquor stores." I knew I needed to lighten up on her, but couldn't resist poking at her. She had calmed. If I handled her right, the next few hours with her could be more reasonable than I'd anticipated. Stella was never one to endure dry periods gracefully. It was imperative that I keep her calm. That is, if I could stay calm.

"Rita, I don't like it here," she said. "I wanna go home."

"We can't leave. Not yet anyway." How could I tell her that we may never leave? That what I had planned could get us all killed and I needed her to help?

"They took Phoebe, didn't they?" Jason asked softly.

"Jason, I've got all I can handle here," I said through clenched teeth. "It was your choice to come here. To bring that goddamn puppy. Vtekdao probably has her doing the Charleston, for all I know."

He nodded, the mirth sagging from his face.

I shook my head in self-reprimand. "Sorry. I didn't mean to sound so insensitive. I expect Phoebe's OK." Suddenly, I felt overwhelmed. There was so much to do, so much I had to work out in my head before I proceeded. And there stood Stella and Jason with their *needs*. Now I know how mothers feel. How would I keep it all together? It was a waste of time trying to guess why we three humans had been left alone in Procedure. I didn't want to hang around to find out. "Let's get out of here. I'll treat you to lunch."

The walk down the spiral to my quarters was punctuated by gasps and complaints from the ever discontented Stella. At once I loathed and pitied her. Jason, in a wisdom I appreciated, kept his mouth shut.

I stopped abruptly at the place in the wall where I knew the entrance to my wedge to be. "Don't give me any lip here, Stella. Just follow me, OK?" I glanced at Jason, meaning to include him in those orders as well. They both nodded. I slipped slowly through the wall, stopping halfway, my left arm and head beckoning them.

Inside, my nostrils stung with the odor of burnt pine. We could hardly move. My quarters were packed wall to wall with stinking roaches—more than I'd ever seen before in my quarters. The splinter group was growing. Stella emitted a short shriek, cutting it off as I clamped down on her wrist.

Jason whispered, "Only you can prevent forest fires. What's that ghastly smell?"

"Pheromones," I answered.

"Uh-oh," he mumbled. He must have learned through The One of Hagion sexual taboos.

Stella jumped back as the roach in the front stepped forward. Two long brow creases. A comma on the right. I recognized him as C'toikth.

"We are here for Qwiff. Tell us of Qwiff," he said.

"Yeah. I know. That's a tall order."

Stella covered her ears, a pained expression on her face. Jason stared at me questioningly.

"Oh," I said. "Bite down. It activates the lingual decoders."

They did. Their eyes got wider.

I used to take great pleasure in showing friends things they'd never seen before; it was like re-living the wonder of discovery through them. I didn't have time for such indulgence now. Everything I did from now on would be a product of my own internal panic.

"Qwiff is short for a philosophy of the self's potential through quantum cosmology," I said.

The small room erupted in chatter. "We know cosmology. We know quantum physics. Tell us of Qwiff," C'toikth said over the noise, sounding disappointed, impatient.

"Please. Quiet!" I felt my hands tremble; I couldn't tell if it was testiness or the growing discomfort from their perfume.

Silence descended. "Cosmology isn't just," I waved towards the opaque window-wall, "out there. It's *in here.*" I pressed my fist between my breasts.

There were a few murmurs, then quiet again. "Your potential sparks from the All That Is and changes with every choice you make."

"Choices. Potentials. *We* choose. Yes, we understand," C'toikth said.

A roach from the back pushed its way through the knot of Hagions to stand before me. It was particularly odiferous, its lower abdomen shiny and round with a ripened egg. "We choose. I choose...not to go to Duty."

I dare say the effluvium was about to hit the propeller, now. "I thought any who defied the Purpose—Vtekdao's mandates—would be absorbed. Killed."

"Our Savior will report us to the Honorable Altruist?" another roach asked me.

"No. Absolutely not—I would never. But, how will you keep him from finding out?"

"We will not be discovered, if we *choose* not to be."

I had to smile.

Stella cautiously eased up beside me. "Rita, Rita what are they talking about?"

"Little sister, we've just stepped into the middle of a revolution."

She inhaled sharply, coughing.

I grasped her by the shoulders. "And I need your help. It's important."

She stared into my eyes, mouth agape, shaking her head subtly. "I...I can't. I don't know what—"

"I'll tell you what I need as we go along. Don't worry. Everything'll be fine."

She closed her mouth and nodded. "OK. I guess so."

If there was one thing I knew about Stella, it was her need to be useful. She would be amenable to whatever I asked of her... up until the time she began to feel used. Then I'd have to drop my requests, until she started complaining how she was being left out, treated like a nothing. It was a delicate balance I'd walked with her all her life. Though no one in the family had become an expert in dealing with her, I figured I had an advantage because I'd recognized and named the problem. I was glad to have her cooperation for now, however long it lasted.

"So, what's on the agenda, C'toikth?"

"To recruit our own."

C'toikth was an Obligant, leading a group of Ignorant dissidents. Which social group did he mean? "Ignorants? Obligants?"

"Yes." With that the crowd filed through the wall, and—I hoped—took their stench with them.

"Whew!" Stella said. "What *was* that?"

"That was the smell of all hell breaking loose." The burnt pine scent still lingered. Nevertheless, I was starving. "Anybody for quasagna?"

Jason and Stella stared.

I laughed. "Looks like lasagna. Smells like lasagna. T'aint lasagna." Then apologetically, "It's all there is." I pushed the pyramid button three times, taking a utensil and a bowl. "Hagion chopsticks. You'll get the hang of it."

I wolfed my pea-soup-flavored meal, watching with amusement as Jason and Stella sniffed their bowls, poked at the contents, snapped the clips on their curling-iron utensils, and finally begin to eat.

"Not bad," Stella said. "What's it made of?"

"Don't know. Packs a hell of a lot of energy, though. We'll need that." *Could be made of the same stuff as this ship, for all I know.*

Do you really think so?

I hope not, Jason. Don't say anything to Stella. In fact, we can't say anything very specific at all. Got to handle her very carefully.

Got it. "Well, I for one am thrilled about being here. How many people have ever had such an opportunity, to mingle not with one but two alien cul—"

No, Jason! She doesn't know about the Phaedrans—the neohumans.

"—tures. Hagions and humans!"

Stella looked up from her bowl. "You got that right."

Just then I realized that I was treating Stella just like Cos treated me. It made me wonder if he had similar ulterior motives.

Jason finished his meal, putting the bowl and utensil back on the table beneath the rows of keys on the wall, a pleat between his brows. "Hmm. That's interesting," he mumbled.

"Oh yeah. I only know what two of those keys do. Don't go punching any, OK?"

"No. I didn't mean that. I just thought of something. They didn't bother me."

"What?"

"All the Hagions huddled in here—there must have been thirty of them. If they'd have been humans, I would have gone berserk."

I looked squarely into his eyes. Before words could form in my mind, a Hagion darted through the wall into my quarters.

"Vtekdao requests your presence in his—" It stopped, pupils spinning, head bobbing lightly. "You must report the violator at once. Who was zhe?"

"What? Who was who?" I asked, knowing damn well what he meant. My pulse quickened.

"Someone in breeding mode. Pheromone has been released in great quantities here."

Indeed, there was enough scent left to make eating somewhat unpleasant. "I don't know what you mean. There's just us."

The roach paused. At last it said, "Perhaps humans do not sense the pheromone. My apologies. Vtekdao waits."

"Tell him to wait. I'll be there as soon as we've finished eating."

"Now, Ree-tah. And bring these...these Non-functionals."

Stella stepped up close behind the roach. "Hey, who you calling non-functional, frog-eyes?"

I shot a mean glare at her over the roach's head. "Sure," I said to the roach. "No problem, uh...you are?"

"Vnoim—First Flagellant to the Honorable Altruist."

I studied his brow creases, fearing I'd mentally catalogued too many roaches to keep them all separate in my head. I'd have to be more selective in memorizing specific individuals, if I wanted to avoid any mistakes. "Vnoim. Yes. Lead on." *Promoted to Tmait's previous rank.*

Jason glanced my way. *I wonder if he has the same ambition as his predecessor.*

He'd better not. Ambition's a terminal disease around here.

"Where are we going?" Stella asked.

"To see the head honcho. You'll like him. He has a wonderful sense of humor. Oh, and please, Stella, be on your best behavior."

She rolled her big blue eyes. Jason smiled at her, probably taken by her beauty. It was hard for me to think of her as beautiful, to see it through all that self-loathing and hostility. The way she dressed didn't help, either. She deliberately down-played her looks by wearing military fatigues—khaki shorts, boots, camouflage T-shirt, padded utility vest, even dog tags with *Bitch from Hell* stamped on them. Jason must have caught a rare glimpse of the real Stella beneath all of that, and responded as so many men had tried to respond to her before—only to be met with a tirade of nastiness marinated in a pitcher of beer.

Halfway past Assembly, Stella complained of pain in her legs.

"We're almost there," I said. "You ought to be glad the ship won't be expanding, the walk getting longer every time you—"

"How do you know of this?" Vnoim barked, spinning around on his tiny hard hooves.

"What?" I froze, my insides grinding into a corrosive lump. What had I said?

"That the ship will no longer be expanding," the roach yipped.

"I...I uh...Cosmigellan told me. What happened?"

"The generator in Restructure has ceased to operate. It is an unprecedented disaster."

No kidding?

"It is non-functional. We must hurry to construct a new one in Assembly. Without it, we will be unable to go to Harvest. We will starve. Our civilization will perish."

"Oh, my." *My, my, my. They don't know how to fix it.* One thing was for sure, after my chat with Vtekdao, I'd have to get my ass back down to Assembly—fast. Another thing—I'd have to learn to keep my mouth shut about what I knew.

In ignorance there is conquest, Jason thought-voiced.

In feigned *ignorance there is conquest. Spying on my machinations? Shame on you.*

As I thought that, Vnoim turned and passed through the wall. We followed.

Vtekdao sat wrapped in his cocoon-throne, and as usual, he was flanked by two guards. "Ree-tah!" he bellowed. "You have done splendidly!"

He waited for my response; I withheld it. What would I say? Thank you for making me betray my friends?

"And now, Ree-tah, your reward. An eventide celebration to honor our Savior. Your presence in Society is required following the ceremonies."

Following the ceremonies? Not *for* the ceremonies? "That sounds real nice and all, but what happens after that? What will you have me do now that I've brought your Benefactors?" I braced for his reply.

"The Savior's continuing responsibilities are many. You will oversee the Benefactors, guide the Ignorants in their duties. You will report to me, apprising me of any difficulties."

He'd just appointed me supervisor of what I vowed to subjugate? There *is* a god. "Thank you, Honorable One."

Vnoim quickly clicked forward. "Honorable One, this decision may be premature, at best. I have information regarding a possible disobedience. The Savior's quarters smell of pheromone. Zhe claims no knowledge—"

"Is this true, Ree-tah?" Vtekdao asked softly.

"I don't know. Vnoim says he smelled something; we sensed nothing." I looked to Stella and Jason; they both shook their heads vigorously.

"You *will* report any such disobedience, won't you, Ree-tah?"

"Not to do so would endanger The Purpose."

"Then we understand each other. I am satisfied with my appointment, Vnoim. Perhaps you should check your own emissions." Vtekdao and the two guards wheezed and quaked in laughter, blushing light blue.

I laughed, my voice out of place, but a necessary added touch to the illusion of my confederacy. I heard Jason and Stella begin to laugh as well. We'd done it. We were in.

Then Jason damn near blew it. "Where's my puppy?"

Everyone stopped laughing and wheezing as Vtekdao rose from his seat, eyes bulging, pupils whirling. With rubbery fingers, he pulled back the red drape hanging behind his throne. My first impulse was to look for what I could barely endure seeing—the jar where my beloved Shana floated, suspended in her prison of quasi-death. There she was, staring out at me with unconscious eyes. Below her, on a red velvety slab, curled a tiny speckled ball, her sides heaving up and down in peaceful breaths.

"Thank you for this additional gift. Unfortunately, it is much more active than the other. I had to render it dormant."

"Phoebe!" Jason called, stepping forward. I thrust my arm out, stopping him, knowing the horror and grief he felt. The puppy had not responded to his voice.

"It will be awakened when the chip is ready," Vtekdao said. "The creature does not vibrate as the other did. I wish it to vibrate."

He's going to make the puppy purr? Kee-reist. Jason's face blanched as he strained against my arm. *Don't, Jason. You'll ruin everything we've gained. Phoebe's OK. Move into The One; they'll tell you.* He closed his eyes and I felt him relax.

"And now, Ree-tah, I must consult with my advisory council in preparation for the celebration. Someone will come for you when we are ready for your speech."

Speech? What speech? Nobody said anything to me about a speech. "What will you have me say, Honorable One?"

"A simple acceptance of your canonization. Reiteration of the tenets of The Purpose. As dictated through your Billboard."

I remembered what my simulated self had spewed. I'd repeat those words, and then some. "Yes, Vtekdao. Until then, I'll show my disciples the ship. With your permission, of course."

Vtekdao stepped forward, eyes bulging. "Disciples? These Non-functionals?"

Had I overstepped my piety? "They are my assistants. To better implement The Purpose."

He was silent for a moment. At last he said, "Very well. They shall assist you."

"Come, my proselytes. Let us partake of the wonders of the Holy Ones' technology," I said. Stella glared at me.

Jason raised an eyebrow. *You're laying it on a little thick, don't you think?*

For a Hagion? Never. I bowed to Vtekdao, who acknowledged with a nod as we turned and left his chambers, slipping out into the spiral. "First stop: Assembly."

"What the fuck was all that in there?" Stella said, her walk becoming a stomp. "Savior? Disciples? Oh god, you're really eating this up, aren't you?"

"Stella, I'm doing what I have to do."

She stopped and faced me. Her crystal eyes sizzled with contempt as she rocked back on one leg, hands on hips.

"Stella, I need you more than ever now. We can bring these bastards down, but only if we act together, and play their game. If they need to believe I'm their friggin' Savior, then that's how I'll play it. I don't like it any more than you do."

Stella sighed, relaxing her arms, lowering her gaze. "Yeah, I guess you're right. But I still think you're enjoying it a little too much."

I smiled at her. She was right. I was enjoying it, but not for the reason she thought. We continued down the spiral, the fire of carefully engineered betrayal scorching the edges of my mind.

"This is Assembly," I said, standing at the red dot at the entrance. "It's where they make their molecular machines." I pressed the red dot and slipped through the wall, Jason and Stella following.

The virtual particle generator banged in the background as a large circle of perhaps two hundred Obligants worked hand to hand, their fingers dancing in a flurry of meticulous coordination.

Jason leaned his head back, staring up into the expanse of the high ceiling, the blue light washing over his face, making him look like a corpse.

I gulped. Thoughts like that were not conducive to conquest.

Jason's jaw slipped a cog as his eyes devoured the advancing metal plate. "A working Casimir generator. I never would have believed it if I hadn't seen it with my own eyes," he said, walking closer to the metal sheet, flinching as it banged to a halt just inches from him and the circle of roaches who worked oblivious to his presence.

"What are they doing?" Stella asked.

"Making molecular machines. And that moving metal sheet, that's the heart of their technology. Without it, their world falls—damn!"

"What?"

"I don't have anything to throw in the gap. I need something that'll keep the moving plate from meeting with the stationary one behind it." Shit. A trip down the spiral to my room for a utensil, then back up again, would be prohibitively exhausting.

"Will this help?" Stella opened her vest and withdrew an unopened bottle of beer.

"Field rations, Stella?" Then I caught myself, softened. "You're going to sacrifice your last bottle of beer?"

She nodded, dangling the bottle in her fingers.

I almost kissed her. "You want to do the honors?"

"What? Outrun that thing?"

"No. Just weasel along the wall. It won't hurt you—I've done it myself."

"Yeah, but *I'm* not a canonized saint."

I laughed. "Knock it off, will you? All you have to do is toss the bottle at the base of the stationary plate. Got to do it right the first time. There is no second chance."

She grinned and bounced away, flattening against the wall of the long corridor in which the plate traveled. It whizzed by her time and again. She surprised me. I didn't expect so much enthusiasm, so much synergism from her.

In less than a minute, the sheet banged to a final stop at the far end of the corridor. I glanced at Jason, who still studied the generator and the Hagions in their impossible work. He turned and looked back at me, glaring disappointment on his face.

The generator had stopped; not one Hagion finger moved. All was still and silent. Like an ancient tomb.

Stella bounced back up beside me; Jason sauntered. "You did good, Stella," I said. "Let's get out of here."

We walked briskly, then jogged down the spiral. I could only guess at the time, how soon "eventide" would come, and decided I didn't have time to pull another stunt. Besides, too many disasters in succession would look suspicious.

"It's incredible," Jason said through his panting as he jogged.

I slowed to a walk, the others matching my pace.

"The intricate finger movements," he said. "The extraordinary cooperation. I wonder which came first evolution-wise: the hands that don't meet their own, or the manner in which the Hagions work together."

"They do everything together: eating, grooming—if you want to call preventing sexual union grooming."

"There's no sex?" Stella said. "I'd die."

Jason stopped. "You mean they can't even eat unless someone feeds them?"

"Exactly. They depend on each other—each other's hands— for *everything.*"

"The bonding force."

"Huh?"

"The bonding force. All systems are cohesive as long as the bonding force is intact. For a system of gears, it's enmeshment and movement. For planetary systems, galaxies, galaxy clusters—it's gravity."

"So what's your point?"

"In living systems, the bonding force is more subtle— behavioral. In herd animals, it's safety in numbers; for humans, it's sex; for Phaedrans, it's knowledge. And for the Hagions...it's dependency on another's hands."

Scientists irritated me. Come to think of it, so did interstellar philosophers. "Get to the point, Jason."

"Eliminate the bonding force and the system fails."

"What are you saying? Cut off their hands?"

"Well, no. Not literally. Not unless we have to. I...I don't know what I mean. Never mind." He shook his head and began to walk.

But Jason's observations had sparked something in me, a new hope that swelled with every step I took. Why hadn't I seen it? The hands. The hands were the key. Hagion interdependence on hands was literally all that kept their society together. But that alone would not be their downfall. What I'd already done with the generators was apparently enough to guarantee a slow demise. If I needed to cause death on a more personal level, I'd go for the hands. Starting with Vnoim, First Flagellant to the Honorable Altruist slash stool-pigeon.

Feeling the alternating densities in the wall, I prepared to push through into my own quarters.

Darkness converged on us with all the daintiness of a stroke.

Stella whimpered as our feet settled on cold hard metal. Jason's demeanor belied his churning mind. There was barely room for us three to stand on the flat spot in the bottom of the dish. Before we could adjust for the cramped spacing, Stella's scream sheared through my head, ricocheting around the sides of the bowl and tearing through me many times again before she finally stopped. She scrabbled up the slick sides of the dish, her effort nearly successful in the army boots. She went limp near the top, unable to grip the rim, and slid down in a lump between my legs. My ears still rang from her screams. Jason simply pressed his lips together, shaking his head as he stared at Stella. The dark figure above us spoke.

"Ree-tah. You disappoint me."

It was Vtekdao. Damn, how did he find out so fast? "I am grieved to hear that, Honorable One. I am equally unhappy I don't have the foggiest idea what you're talking about."

"I appoint you, our Savior, to a very important government position, and immediately you fail me."

How would I maintain my composure when I could feel the guilt seeping to the surface, ready to admit my treason?

Stella began to cry. I could only hope her fear would disable her speech centers.

Volunteer nothing, Jason thought-voiced.

"I'm sorry. What is it about my performance that bothers you?"

"The generator in Assembly—you did not report it!" he boomed.

"I...We...What about it?"

"It too has stopped! I know you were there. Did you not see that it was stopped?"

"No. No, Honorable One. When we went there, it was working fine. I swear on the will of Hope."

He was silent for several seconds. "And when you left?"

Omission has its uses, but is ineffective when your opponent asks too goddamn many questions—especially appropriate ones. "One gets used to the noise after a while and learns to ignore it. Whether it was working or not when I left, I couldn't tell you." I couldn't. Not ever. My face blushed hot while my bare feet froze numb. If he ever suspected I was responsible, I'd become siding for the ship. Come to think of it, no I wouldn't. I'd eliminated that possibility when I'd trashed the generator in Restructure. There were other unknown, perhaps nastier fates waiting for me if I couldn't pull off my innocence.

He stared down into the dish for too long. I imagined yellow eyes I couldn't see, crushing me, spinning pupils sweeping through me, whipping me into a whirlpool of gristle and gore. Even the shadow of his hideous bug-body, spilling over the side of the silver dish, was menacing. He was up to something, the gears of his evil brain manufacturing a perfect torture for me.

"Maybe this will jog your memory," he said, sneering, I was sure.

Around us in the metal dish wrapped a familiar 360 degree scene from my private life. My father's living room. The hospice living room before it had been remodeled for the neohuman colony. My father lay face down in his overstuffed rump-sprung chair, his pants pulled down, exposing bare buttocks.

Where did Vtekdao get this? How could he know this? Cos had told me the Hagions couldn't get inside my head...yet, here before us was a scene no one had witnessed but myself.

I saw myself enter the room with a full hypodermic syringe and plunge the needle into his right ass-cheek.

That isn't how it happened!

I had the syringe before I rolled him over, and I had injected him on the inside of the anus so there would be no visible needle mark. I'd planned a perfect murder: killing him with potassium after overdosing him on his own heart medication at dinner—extra oregano in the spaghetti sauce to mask the bitterness.

After coming back unexpectedly from the nursing home and reclaiming a home no longer his, he had shot and killed two Phaedrans. Their human bodies reverting to native amoeboid form after death, there was no evidence of murder.

That's when I'd decided. My father had earned my final interaction with him.

But this play before me—it was like it had been compiled of a collection of memory fragments not mine. I carried the entire act within me, a secret from everyone but Cos—and by extension the whole colony—for six years. No one else knew.

Except the colony. They wouldn't have....

Then to my horror, my simulated father stirred and rose, pants around his ankles, pointing an accusing finger at me. "Why did you do it, Rita? Why did you murder me?"

Stella screamed.

CHAPTER 17

CONVICTIONS

The quantum world is a microworld of randomness and indeterminacy in which seemingly absurd and miraculous events occur....
—Qwiffian Handbook of Sapience

Reviving Stella took some doing on Cos' part. In my wedge, he worked over her with a variety of instruments.

"If you can, tranq her," I suggested. "She's out of control."

Without looking up, he said, "I know why she's here: It was an accident. But why is *he* here?"

I knew better than to think Cos was jealous. Yet, there was an edge of irritation in his voice. "He wanted to be with me. Nancy was right—he's a fine man."

"And of The One, I understand. A disconcerting development." His voice was flat.

I didn't like his tone at all. "How's Stella?"

"She'll be fine," he said, straightening. "I've implanted a neuroleptic pump—mild continuous dose. It'll help her through alcoholic withdrawal. Over the next two days you'd better keep an eye on her. She'll be volatile, irrational at times. If I increase the dose, she'll never be able to function as your disciple."

"You know about that?"

"I know everything." He pocketed the tools and went to the end of the bed. "You're expected in Society soon. Someone will be sent for you. Congratulations, Savior." He left.

I stood at the head of the bed, staring over Stella, not really seeing her. All I could see was Cos' slack face, hear his dull voice. It was as if all the life had been drained out of him and what was left walking around, performing his assigned duties, was a soulless automaton. Was it resignation to his fate now that the whole colony was on board, or was it something else, like embarrassment that I'd found out why he'd locked me out of The One?

But, except for my communion with Jason, I was still locked out. What reason could he have to deny me full access now? As I pondered that, Jason reached around my shoulders and squeezed.

"He loves you. Even if he can't share everything with you, *know* that he loves you."

As I turned to him, a roach dissolved through the wall. I immediately focused on its brow wrinkles. C'toikth.

"Please come with me to Society. Our Savior must speak to zhaz subjects."

"What do I say? I have nothing planned."

"You will speak of the will of Hope and the glory of The Purpose."

"Yeah, right. But what do I *say?*"

C'toikth's eyes bugged. "The Savior does not *know?*"

"Of course. I just thought you'd want me to mention the *realities* of The Purpose, how it oppresses freedom of personal choice and individual potential. You know—Qwiff. What you and the dissidents asked me to—"

"Qwiff? You will speak of the glory of The Purpose and the will of Hope. That is all that is required." He spun on his tiny hooves and wadded. "Follow me, please."

Fearing I'd somehow misidentified the roach, wanting to kick myself for my presumption, I rousted Stella. We walked her—Jason on one side, I on the other—up the spiral to Society, the roach leading.

Once inside the huge crowded auditorium, Stella shook the drug-fog from her head. We threaded our way through the mass of chitin to a table that had been reserved for us near the front of the auditorium. Jason clutched Stella as they sank to their low seats.

Stella seemed subdued, any impending anxiety submerged in a continuous pulse of narcotics. I hope she stayed that way. I didn't have time to discuss why I'd killed our father, or why I hadn't told her the truth all these years. Not that I thought she missed her dear "Deady," as she liked to refer to him—even when he was alive.

Vtekdao's voice dredged me from my wallow of family troubles.

"Citizens! The will of Hope is with us. Our Savior has provided us with our long-awaited Benefactors. The Purpose shall be implemented!"

The huge auditorium vibrated with a chorus of caws. All around us roaches wadded, leapt from their seats, cawing shrilly, the sounds so loud and piercing I could only feel blowing vibrations in my ears. Stella pressed her palms to her ears, mild distress creasing her forehead.

"Bring our Savior!" Vtekdao boomed from the podium.

Before the cheering died, cold rubbery fingers grasped my right upper arm. I turned to find C'toikth tugging at me, more in gesture than force. I obliged, somewhat oblivious to the crowd and the noise, as words, sentences, phrases, scurried and collided in my head. What would I say when I got up there? How would I pull this off?

I stepped up on the stage and slipped behind the podium, thousands of pairs of spinning pupils pulling me out to them. Vtekdao remained on stage, ostensibly out of my view, but I still felt his yellow-eyed stare searing through my left shoulder.

Thinking of nothing better than repeating the obvious and oft-chanted, I said, "The Purpose will be fulfilled. It is the will of Hope."

Cawing overtook the auditorium. Over their cheering, I said, "The purpose of life, is a life of purpose," quoting not from Hagion axioms, but from the Qwiffian Handbook of Sapience.

There was immediate silence. Not one roach stirred, not one spoke. My words had not been new; the way they fit together was. Had I baffled them? Angered them? Intrigued them? I glanced sideways, catching a glimpse of Vtekdao, rigid and silent.

"It is the will of Hope that you honor your potential," I went on. "Your potential must have no arbitrary restrictions."

Off in a far corner of the auditorium, a small group of Hagions grew restless. Again I glanced at Vtekdao, who remained motionless.

"This is a glorious day for all. Not only because I have brought you the Benefactors, but because I have brought you something much more valuable than a handful of caretakers."

Still, the only movement, the only sounds, came from the small gathering in the distance. Had my audience gone into a collective trance?

My pulse was charged with the adrenalin of daring. I continued, quickly, boldly. "It is the will of Hope that I bring you wisdom. I bring you the courage to look into your own souls and see what's there. You cannot see it? Is it shrouded in axioms, rigid maxims, unyielding dogma? Custom and tradition have become your drugs—disabling independent creative thought.

"Look closer. Do you see it now? Do you see the will of Hope, the *real* Purpose?" I paused, nearly breathless with fear.

A squeal tore through the auditorium. It must have been my imagination, the fear, that made me think I smelled something familiar.

But I pressed on. "I have a message from Hope: The Purpose is not to create more *of* you; The Purpose is to create more *in* you."

The odor was stronger now, the ashy pine scent of pheromone curling into my nostrils, coating the membranes like lard on a truffle.

"Anything you want from another must be earned!" I yelled, reveling in the echoes of my own voice as it skipped off the sides of the huge auditorium. The sea of chitin below me became restless, shifting, clicking, still riveted on the podium. I knew then that I had very little time.

"Do not seek what you value through the favor or slavery of others!" I stared up into the clear ceiling, arms outspread to black space above. "Hope deliver us from our delusions that we may honor You and our holy potentials!"

The group in the far corner rushed and diffused into the crowd. Chaos took over.

"Live through your own ideals! It is the will of Hope! The ultimate authority is oneself!"

The auditorium was saturated with pheromone. Hagions groped, mounted, fused with each other in sexual frenzy.

Vtekdao was at my side in an instant. "What is the meaning of this?" he howled, clicking to the edge of the stage, overlooking the pandemonium below.

It wouldn't be long before it was all over for me. I shouted a last few words over the din. "Anything can happen if it happens quickly enough! It is the will of Hope! Things are only impossible until they are not!"

The auditorium floor became slick with bodily fluids. Roaches fed each other pebbles from bowls in the center of each table. Cloacae pressed together; piezoelectricity passed from one roach to another. Eggs dropped and skidded across the slimy floor. The stench of pheromone and ozone hung in the air thick and sweet, penetrating my skin, my brain.

The whole auditorium was consumed in an orgy of free sex. I caught a glimpse of Jason hugging Stella, isolating her from the disorder, just before blackness enveloped me, pouring me back into the cold metal interrogation dish.

I didn't give Vtekdao a chance to tear into me. I had a gallon of adrenalin to burn, so broke down in tears. "What happened? Why did they—oh god, it was horrible!"

A dark shadow loomed above. "What you have done is unforgivable."

I couldn't really say I hadn't expected that. It was just a matter of time, and I was hoping I could buy more of that before he came after me.

Time's up.

"You can't blame me for what happened," I sobbed dramatically.

"I most certainly can! Your words have incited a riot, a disgraceful display of immorality and dereliction of duty to The Purpose."

"But...but, I spoke of The Purpose. I spoke the words as I received them. From Hope. Maybe you are afraid of losing control. Maybe what you want and what your constituents want is discordant."

"Blasphemy! The words are *yours!* You continued with your filth when I myself could smell the pheromone, feel the impending catastrophe. You did not stop."

"I smelled nothing," I said, adhering to my previous lie. "How could I have known these words of salvation—the will of Hope—would result in such a...such a—" I exploded into tears again, only half faking this time.

I heard a rattling sigh above me.

"Perhaps...it is true that humans are insensitive to the pheromone...." Vtekdao said, a distinct tone of regret lacing his deep voice.

About then I could have sworn the will of Hope was shining down on me. The fickle bitch.

"However," he said, "you did continue when you saw what

your words had done. Let me show you what your transgression means, that you may know the error of your ways."

As before, the silver walls of the interrogation dish gave way to a circular simulation. Wrapped around me was a line-up of maybe a dozen Hagions, heavy and bulging with developed eggs.

They stood in Restructure, vats in the background, their hands bound with white ligature, effectively disabling the wadding movements—or any ability to conjoin with another. Another Hagion stepped into the foreground from thin air beneath the holographic display. It turned. Two long brow ridges, a comma on the left. It was C'toikth.

He held a small black marble in his right hand and turned to face the line-up of bound breeders. A cold black smudge escaped from the marble, speeding towards the Ignorants, discharging a black cloud that spread like a tentacled cancer on its target. One by one, the hands of the roaches dissolved from their stubby attachments. The roaches screamed hideously, the pitch so high it amounted to nothing more than a hiss that grated the air and made the hairs on the back of my neck stand up.

"The result of your evil words!" Vtekdao asserted.

"The words of Hope are evil?" I retorted.

"They are not the words of Hope. They are *your* words!"

"I am the Savior. Hope speaks through me. It is mandated."

The discomfort of waiting for his reply escalated to pain. Making him believe I spoke with Hope, had a direct line he could not access, was *my* only hope. He could not disprove, and therefore refute it. I was the Savior. He'd told everyone, and I think he believed it himself.

"There is a movement developing on Lolbah. A movement that threatens to subvert The Purpose and the will of Hope. Tell me now—who are the Dissidents?"

That's right, when you've been had, change the subject. "Dissidents?"

"They have been in your quarters!"

"So says Vnoim. I have seen no one." I ransacked my mind for something useful, something dangerous and disguised—like piranhas in your soup. "What motive, do you think, would Vnoim have for telling you such a lie about the Savior?"

He paused again. A mental stutter, I imagined. "Need I remind you that when I require the truth, it shall be mine?"

"As well it should be, Great One."

"Your disciples—perhaps they will tell me what you will not."

Something sharp poked me in the guts. Jason could handle himself well, but Stella....."They cannot tell you what they do not know." Then I asked what I dared not keep to myself. "Vtekdao, is it wise to be destroying the very tools you need to implement The Purpose? Destroying the breeders is not the will of Hope." Wise up, Torquemada.

He spoke rapidly, uncertainty tainting his authority. "This small detour is necessary. In the long run The Purpose will be unaffected."

Again, outer space swallowed me as I hung in the void, my quarters sluggishly materializing around me. The slowness of my transport back to my room was only a minor curiosity. I knew I had to get to Society. Stella had begun to fall apart as I was zapped to Interrogation. I hoped she and Jason were still there.

Bolting down two bowls of that increasingly insipid quasagna, I charged up the spiral, invigorated not only by the Hagion rations, but by a renewed determination and confidence. I had made Vtekdao stumble in his certitude, question his faith. It felt good.

Rounding the corner at level six—Obligant level—I passed two Hagions in a sticky embrace, exchanging fluids and piezoelectricity. Had sexual abandon spread throughout the ship? Could I hope for that? I quickened my pace, running up the spiral. Finally, I made it to the red dot at level five, pressing it and entering Society, where my nostrils stung with pheromone, my eyes feasted on anarchy.

It was all out of control. A handful of Hagions were involved in attempting to arrest the madly mating couples, prying at them to release their hold on each other. How these few had escaped succumbing to the pheromone, I had no idea. But I knew what would happen to the roaches who had yielded to their natural drives: They'd have their hands amputated. Worse than death.

It sickened me. That fact bothered me a great deal. Had I not been the one to instigate this riot? Had I not been the one who demanded Jaynah make weapons, who insisted the Hagions could be conquered and the colony restored? Wasn't I prepared for massive death, suffering, misery, on both sides? Why then, did I suddenly feel sorry for the Ignorants and what happened to them?

Quickly I shook the guilt and scanned the chaos for Stella and Jason. They were nowhere to be found. *Jason. Jason, where are you? Where is Stella?*

Rita. Come to Application, Cos thought-voiced. *Stella needs you.*

Without answering, I left the uproar and rushed the one level up to Application. Cos was waiting for me when I dissolved through the wall, his face worried in the bloody glow.

"She tried to kill herself," he said.

I thought I would pass out right there. "How? Why?"

"You'll have to find out why." He turned.

I followed him through an inner wall into Duty. Stella was rigid and immobile on the low examination table in the middle of the room, her wrists enclosed in silver orbs. "What did she do? Slash her wrists? How? There's nothing sharp—"

"Broken beer bottle," Jason said. "She had another beer hidden in that damn vest. When the crowd went crazy and I saw she was about to go off too, I hugged her to me. That's when I felt it." He gulped, his voice shaking. "All I did was ask her to give it to me. But she just freaked, broke it on the edge of the table, and gouged herself open right then and there. There was nothing I could do. It happened too fast."

I eased up to the table and looked down at her, a distant stare in her blue eyes. "Why, Stella? Why?"

She closed her eyes tightly. I touched her arm; her skin seemed to flinch, as if repulsed by my caring. "You took him from me," she whispered.

My mind reeled in an attempt to understand what she meant. "Took who? Jason? You want Jason?" Could it be that she had misinterpreted Jason's kindness so horribly?

"You took him," she said again, louder. She opened her eyes to stare into mine. "You're always the one. You get it all while I get nothing."

I looked to Cos. "Why did you bring her here, instead of Procedure? She needs more attention, more drugs, something," I said accusingly.

"Procedure is full to capacity with Hagions undergoing desensitization. Your speech required it."

There was no reprimand in his voice. There was no emotion at all. I probed his mind, finding a blockade of secrecy where I'd wanted to find acceptance, entrance into The One. I felt Jason's mind pull me from Cos, pity and guilt in him as he coaxed me back to Stella.

"Stella. What could be so horrible that you'd want to kill yourself? Suicide isn't reversible like a drunken stupor. It's forever." I regretted those last words just as I spoke them.

She stared up at me, hatred seething behind those eyes. "You took him. You killed him and now...."

Realization slapped me in the face. Dad. I should have known I'd have to answer for that sooner or later. I didn't expect my deed would make her want to die, however. It didn't make sense. She had hated our father as much as I did, she wanted him dead as much as I did. There was something terribly twisted about her reaction. "I had to do it, Stella. I had to do it for us. Are you upset because I didn't tell you? That I didn't ask you to help?"

"You just don't get it, do you? You whore."

I'd heard that nastiness before. It was best to just ignore it. "No, I guess I don't. Tell me, Stella."

"You took him away from me! You take everything away from me! All my life, *you* were the pretty one, *you* were the smart one, *you* were the one who got the college degree, *you* were the one with all the boyfriends. And even when you got crippled up, and I thought I had a chance at last to stand out of your shadow, you started a new career and succeeded at it."

"You think my successes somehow prevented you from getting yours? From excelling at something on your own? Christ, Stella. It doesn't work that way. There isn't a limited amount of achievement in the universe. I didn't take anything from you. You're using that as an excuse not to prosper, to stay where you are."

"Goddamn you!" she screamed, fighting against her rigid body, tears streaming down her cheeks. "All my life I fantasized about killing him. I must have killed him in every way conceivable—I shot him, slit his throat, ran over him with a car, disemboweled him with a machete, set him on fire. He died a thousand times a day. It kept me alive. It was all I had. I knew someday it would be me who killed him—he would die by *my* hand. You took him from me!"

And now all that was left to kill...was herself. I cried. I

couldn't help her. No one could. "Let her go," I said through my sobs. "Let her go."

Cos hesitated, searching my face for a reason, or maybe just hoping I'd change my mind. When I didn't, he released her from her molychine restraint. Then, I released her. To whatever she chose for herself.

Jason reached for my hand. His touch was somehow less exciting, less comforting than I remembered it. "You can do nothing else," he said softly.

I know. Whatever happens is supposed to happen.

Cosmigellan had taught me well.

CHAPTER 18

INTERFERENCE PATTERNS

There are no natural laws. Laws are products of concepts.
We experience what we experience because that's all we can
experience.
—Qwiffian Handbook of Sapience

Stella had disappeared into the bowels of the ship with her self-packed emotional baggage before I could even talk myself into accepting the fate she had chosen for herself.

My plan to follow her was short-circuited by the sudden appearance of a Hagion. It hadn't bothered to enter in the standard way, but had just "happened" right there beside me, though slowly, liquidly as it dripped into form. Vnoim.

"Vtekdao requires your presence in his chambers immediately."

Well, that didn't take long. I hoped Vtekdao hadn't done too much thinking about what I'd said. I meant for him to react emotionally, thereby disabling rational thought. That was the way to confound an opponent, wasn't it? At least it was true for humans....

I didn't argue or stall this time; I simply left with the roach, knowing Jason would follow. A tiny surge of triumph swelled inside me as we passed Assembly on our way up the spiral. Jesus, I was tired of hauling my weary carcass up and down this ship. How many times had it been? My two bowls of quasagna were proving inadequate; I'd have to refortify myself soon if I wanted to keep up this pace.

Not that I knew what my next step would be. That would depend on what Vtekdao had on his mind. I could only guess what nasty little demo he'd cooked up for me now—if indeed that last scene had been a simulation; apparently some of the holograms were not. Distinguishing them was impossible.

When I went through the wall into Vtekdao's chambers, I knew I'd been set up big time. A sharp stench stabbed at my nostrils.

Jason coughed. A roach, hands bound, stood before Vtekdao, who glowered at us from his throne with bulging eyes.

"Ree-tah!" Vtekdao greeted me. "Step beside this traitor and identify zhan to me. The truth."

Traitor? I looked over at the roach's brow creases. "It is C'toikth," I said, swallowing hard.

"The leader of the dissidents! Zhe has told me so!"

My mind cringed in confusion. Why would C'toikth do that? Why would he operate with such secrecy and then expose himself, his followers, so readily? "Well then, you seem to have solved your problem. Congratulations. Why do you need *me* here?"

Vtekdao leaned forward in his crusty throne. "You *knew* of the dissidents, of C'toikth's disloyalty. You did not tell me."

This had to be another of Vtekdao's sick games, and I was growing tired of being pulled into them. "I know nothing. I told you—"

Vtekdao wadded his right hand, where he fondled a dull, threatening black marble. He aligned his hand with C'toikth's left hand.

I didn't have to guess what his intentions were.

"Tell me who the dissidents are," he said low.

My brain spun. I couldn't decide if C'toikth was a dissident, or part of an elaborate plan to trick me into revealing myself, or a double agent. But, I knew there was indeed a real movement against the Hagion social structure, a revolt underway that would succeed with or without C'toikth. If C'toikth were playing both sides, then surely he had taken into account he might be found out, and was prepared for the consequences. If he was part of Vtekdao's game, Vtekdao probably wouldn't kill him. All I knew for sure was that I couldn't betray the others—Ngishkaok, Bsouk, Bzheyant, Sphoiashth, dozens of others. The loss of this one would not threaten their cause. Besides, C'toikth was only a roach.

So why then, did I feel so bad about what I decided to do?

Before I could utter a word, a black puff raced towards C'toikth's hand, dissolving it. His shrill hiss-scream tore through my head.

My mouth felt all furry and liquid with impending nausea. "Stop! Stop! There is a plan. I overheard a plan."

Vtekdao lowered his hand and leaned forward again. "Plan?

To subvert the natural order? To secede?"

"No. I don't know anything about that. It's something...I don't know exactly what to make of it. I heard someone say, 'Vtekdao must be absorbed.'" Put *that* in your cloaca and smoke it.

What are you doing now? Jason thought-voiced.

Playing Vtekdao's favorite game. Don't interfere.

Vtekdao did not respond for a long time, then wheezing filled the room as he and his two guards blushed light blue. The bastard was laughing! So much for spreading nasty rumors. Vtekdao then stood, raising his weapon, and fired black smudges at C'toikth.

C'toikth shrieked and hissed as his right hand vanished in a stinking plume. With another shot a tar-rimmed hole melted through his chest, exposing two mangled and fibrillating hearts, as he toppled to the floor in a gruesome clatter, jerking and quivering and hissing.

I closed my eyes and buried my head in Jason's chest. Some little bit of me had cared about C'toikth. There was nothing I could do now. My plan, my silly rumor had backfired.

"Tell me who the dissidents are!" Vtekdao roared, his chest vibrating visibly. He wasn't going to drop this, was he?

"I don't *know!*" I screamed back. "I just know that I heard that someone plans to kill you. Doesn't that *mean* anything to you?"

He wheezed again. The guard to his left leaned in close to Vtekdao's mouth and mumbled. Vtekdao's pupils screeched to a halt, then backed up and spun the other direction. "Leave me. I tire of your obstinacy," he finally said.

I bowed to him. "Thank you, Honorable One." Jason and I turned; I stepped sideways, avoiding the spreading pool of black fluid beside C'toikth's shattered body, acknowledging just a twinge of grief. Was it true, had I learned to see some of these creatures as benevolent, not as part of the collective "roaches"? Though acknowledging the individual was an admirable trait for a Qwiffian, how could one do battle with enemies one saw as separate identities? After all, what infantryman could gun down a gook if he'd been introduced to him and his family? What bombardier could drop explosives on Najib at the dinner table with his adoring wife and five sultry-eyed children if he didn't see them as ragheads and sand niggers?

Such ideas gnawed at me often, but never more so than now as we descended the spiral in silence back to my quarters. I fleetingly thought of Stella, wondered where she would be now that I was the scourge of her life.

We were exhausted by the time we reached my room and we collapsed in each others' arms on the narrow bed. I had hoped for just a moment that Stella would be waiting for us here, and was disappointed only slightly that she wasn't. If she chose life, if she chose our relationship, she would come to me. She hadn't.

Unable to sleep after what I guessed had been a couple of hours, I disentangled myself from Jason's flaccid embrace, somewhat disgusted with the ease with which he'd slipped into REM sleep. I watched his eyeballs dart under their lids, his mind frolic with Universe knew what delights.

Men. So cat-like in many ways, though I'd never say so. Watching Jason sleep, I thought of Shana, how often I'd stared at her as she slept. It was a wonderful thing, to see a cat wake up—from what looked like deep sleep—to scratch a biting flea, merely to dissolve again into that liquid relaxation only a cat can embody.

I wondered if Jason was like that. So peaceful, so restful... when this whole fucking ship was about to fall apart, when he'd lost his puppy, his new friends, maybe even me. Damn him.

I leaned down close to his face. "Wake up!" I yelled, clapping my hands together with a loud pop.

Jason spasmed to consciousness, a scowl on his pasty face. "What?"

I turned and went to the keyboard console, punching the pyramid key once, twice. A single bowl of quasagna materialized on the desk. It was only half full. I beat on the key again; nothing happened. "Well, I guess we'll have to share," I said, taking the bowl and utensil to Jason, who sat on the edge of the bed, grinning. "Something's wrong with the computer. Here." I shoved the bowl at him.

He smiled, hands on his thighs. "Feed me."

"Oh for crying out loud, grow up!"

He made an exaggerated sour-face.

"I don't feed men. It encourages infantilism." I put the bowl on his lap, wondering if he'd catch it before it slid to the floor.

"You're such a romantic, darling," he said. "Are we dealing with PMS here? Have I done something wrong?"

"Not PMS. Not you. Me. And this place. This *place!*" I wheeled around and stomped to the keyboard, and though a Hagion was the last thing I wanted to see, I punched the tornado button. Vnoim seeped slowly through the air, solidifying inches from me.

"Why have you summoned me?"

"Something's wrong with the food server thing. I need two bowls. It gave me one—half full."

"Due to the non-operation of the generators, all food rations will be reduced to half."

"There are two of us here. If we have to share a single half-ration—"

"Very well," Vnoim said. Another bowl slowly appeared on the desk below the keyboard. "Please do not summon me again. Energy must be conserved. We must all—" He had an absence.

As I watched his pupils stop turning, the membranes slide and flutter across those yellow eyes, I remembered how Vnoim had tried to make points with Vtekdao by compromising me. I had only twenty seconds in which to act.

Squeezing as hard as I could, I bent back the fingers of his right hand, cringing with the multiple pops of knuckles slipping out of joint, breaking, crunching in my grip. The roach never flinched. I mutilated the other hand.

"What the hell are you doing? My god, wasn't your father enough? Are you going to take this up as a hobby?" Jason howled, launching from the bed.

Only mildly shaken by his accusations, I ran my fingernails viciously down both velvety lobes of Vnoim's brain, shocking him to a screaming, trembling convulsion of consciousness. He opened and closed his mouth, gnashing his teeth threateningly, shrieking wordless sounds. Revolving at an unbelievable velocity, his features a blur, he clacked and rattled in a circle like an unbalanced top, spinning, rebounding off the furniture, smashing into the corner of the desk, slashing through crushed chitin to soft flesh and spraying streams of black fluid around the room. Everywhere I stepped to avoid him, he came after me, spattering me with black.

Suddenly he whirled sideways into the hygiene area, Jason and I dashing after him as he dove into the fountain, triggering the water spray, tumbling into the grate gagging and vomiting black sludge. One final jerk and the roach was still. Forever.

"Shit, Rita. Why?"

"He finked on me. Not for the sake of The Purpose—which I might have been able to excuse—but for his own aggrandizement. That pisses me off."

I looked around the room, to Jason, my own caftan. We were spattered with Hagion blood, black as ink. "We can't be seen in these," I said, kicking the mangled carcass aside, its head rolling, blackened eyes staring up at me like dead eggplants. Stepping into the fountain, the spray doused us, but the black stains remained fast as laundry marker. "No choice. Strip down. No one will care."

Removing our clothes and rinsing the ink from our hair, we picked our way through the splatters and gobs of black gore that decorated my quarters. Every wall, my bed, the keyboard, was bespeckled in Hagion blood. Scene of a murder.

By some peculiar luck, none of the ink had fallen in my uneaten gruel, so I bolted it, knowing I'd need the energy, my mind whirring with the implications of my dirty deeds. The effects of the generator sabotage were just now being felt. "Could explain the slowness of the transport, too," I said, mostly to myself through a mouthful of tasteless mush.

"Huh?" Jason asked, eyeing his bowl, disgust on his face.

"They're running low on fuel. There won't be a Harvest, so... there's going to have to be some serious belt-tightening around here."

"Do you realize that if we just sit tight, the whole civilization will fall apart all by itself?"

"Yeah, but who'd die of starvation first—us or them? Besides, do you really think I'm the type to sit around and *wait?*"

He laughed uneasily. "No way."

"Let's go."

"Where? What do you have up your sleeve—so to speak— now?"

"I need to see Cos."

About halfway up the spiral we saw a most astounding thing: twenty or so Hagions tied in a chain, their hands bound, being marched forcefully up the spiral by two other unbound Hagions wielding those nasty death marbles. Jason and I stayed behind them for a while, then boldly walked beside the bound prisoners, eyeing their swollen and dripping cloacae, our nostrils stinging with the ashy pine pheromone. Dissidents, every one.

"Where are you taking these infidels?" I asked the Hagion at the rear of the chain.

"Public execution in Society, by orders of Vtekdao. You are invited, Savior, to witness the result of their disgraceful behavior."

I recognized its voice, but couldn't identify it. "And you operate in what capacity to our Honorable Altruist?"

"I am Shwength, Second Flagellant to His Worthiness."

And unbeknownst to him, probably just promoted to First Flagellant. "Thank you. We would be honored to accompany you."

Why, Rita? Jason said in my mind.

I have to, don't you understand? I don't want to watch them die. They've done nothing to me. It's killing me knowing I am the cause—

You are not! They came to you, remember? They would have revolted eventually, don't you think?

I don't know. But if I don't agree to watch their deaths, and pretend I approve, my credibility with Vtekdao will suffer.

I see.

We trekked beside them all the way to Society, their hooves clicking and slipping in cloacal fluid. Once inside the huge auditorium, I forgot all about being naked and exposed.

The stench was overwhelming. In the center fountain were heaped dozens, maybe hundreds of dismembered Hagions. My impulsive little murder paled in comparison to this mass slaughter of citizens.

"My god," Jason croaked.

"Wait!" I yelled to Shwength, who prodded the chain of prisoners to the fountain. "How many have you sac...executed thus far?"

"Twelve hundred thirty-one. Including these."

That number would be in base six. In base ten it was a lesser number. But it didn't matter. I had never actually taken a census, but from the gathering I'd seen during Harvest, that had to be half the population on the ship. "Vtekdao's will be done," I added, clamping down on the scream clawing its way out of my throat.

Untied from each other, their hands still individually bound, the prisoners arranged themselves around the fountain, seemingly resigned to becoming part of the carnage.

I shivered, my arms crossed over my breasts as Jason wrapped his arm around my shoulders, providing my only connection to reality in this Hitleristic nightmare.

The two Hagion guards were dismissed by a single executioner who approached the ring of prisoners. I blinked. At first I thought I was hallucinating, revulsion distorting my vision. I stepped closer, feeling Jason's restraining embrace. Breaking free, I scrutinized the brow creases: two long flat ones, a comma at the left. There was no mistake. It was C'toikth.

"What the hell?" I whispered. Vtekdao must have staged C'toikth's death via hologram. Yet it had looked so real. More than real.

C'toikth raised his right hand and fired black smudges at the circle of Dissidents. Hands vaporized, hissing screams sheared through the auditorium, bodies flailed backwards into the fountain, spinning, churning fluids and chitin chips in all directions as if the lid had been left off a blender.

Something lightweight, hard, and wet flew into my hair and dangled in a gooey strand before my eyes. That was all it took.

I turned and ran, a burning wave searing my throat. Under a table near the exit, I vomited my paltry tasteless dinner, now soured and curdled. Wiping my mouth and eyes, I returned to Jason, who stared numbly at the fountain.

"They committed suicide," he said.

"What? They were murdered," I whispered.

"No. Their hands were taken; they killed themselves."

"How do you know that? Maybe the pain—"

I glared at him. His face was slack, his voice monotone. "There is no pain greater than the horror of uselessness."

I stared at him for several seconds. "Come on, Jason. We have to go."

"I know. It's time."

I bid my dinner adieu, knowing I would have been better off with a full stomach, and walked arm in arm with Jason up to Application. *It's time,* I said to myself. *It's time.* I know it's time. Jason knows it's time. What I didn't know was...time for *what?*

Just past Society, we passed a stinking Hagion lying against the inside wall to our right, apparently dead from an impacted oviduct, its cloaca ruptured, the veins in its eyes black with strain. The Dissidents had gone nuts, withholding eggs until they died. Even as revolutionaries they couldn't act rationally, instead sacrificing themselves to a *new* cause. The insanity of so much death, so much waste, ached and throbbed in my gut. Was all this *my* doing?

As we climbed to Application, we gave little notice to the soft clicking of hooves far behind us. That was a mistake.

Before curiosity made me turn to see who followed, a loud pop split the air at my left. Jason grabbed me as we both whirled around.

C'toikth advanced slowly, again fired a black smudge at me, just missing my wrist as the bolus popped against the wall beside me. I jumped sideways, crashing into Jason as he staggered to keep from falling with me.

"Hide your hands!" Jason yelled as we ran up the spiral, the clicking behind us accelerating to a mad clatter, growing louder, closer. Another pop to my left, then to Jason's right. I scanned the wall to my left for a red dot. Where the hell were the red dots?

The roach zoomed ahead of us, spinning around to face us. We split up. Jason dashed to the right; I to the left, sagging into the wall and springing back as the roach fired between us. Jason rushed towards the roach, shoving it against the wall with a sickening crunch as I scrambled up the spiral, desperate for a red dot.

There! "Jason!" I screamed, pressing the dot and shooting through, Jason pounding behind, breathing hard.

We dashed into Procedure, a level above where I wanted to be. I'd missed the red dot to Application. There was only the one central exam table; the other tables were gone. Nowhere to hide. The roach tore through the wall, firing the black marble randomly. I fell to the floor, scrambling to the table as black smudges popped overhead. Jason tripped over my legs and fell on top of me with a grunt. We struggled to keep covered as the roach came around the end of the table, glaring directly at me.

The room flickered, darkness exchanging with light, light overtaking darkness as the lounge, C'toikth's murderous yellow stare, began to fade away. I clutched Jason tightly as C'toikth clicked closer and fired. A black smudge passed through the ghost of my hand to my ribs underneath, as the room dissolved away and we crouched naked before the leering stars of the Milky Way.

Deep red flowed around us, Vtekdao's chambers seeping

into a tangible reality. I had never been so glad to be transported against my will as I was now. My hand burned; I was afraid to look down, fearing I'd find a stump where it had been. Then I felt Jason's warm hand fold around it. I sighed in relief: Phantom limbs felt pain, not affection.

"Who is it that wishes me dead?" Vtekdao said.

The question surprised me. He'd laughed when I told him he was a marked roach. He'd dismissed it. I was gratified learning that it was eating him alive.

I looked down at my hand, a red stripe singed across the back of it to the wrist. "Honorable One. C'toikth is trying to kill me. Please, I beg of you, order him to stop."

Vtekdao's eyes bulged. "Nonsense. Zhe would do no such thing without my decreeing it."

And have you, you bastard? I raised my hand, the wound facing him. "Look. I narrowly escaped amputation. You brought me here just as he fired."

"Then the Savior is unharmed."

"For now. But will he continue to pursue me? How will you protect your Savior?"

"The Savior requests *assistance?*"

"Please. Make him stop. Or . . ." Did I have the nerve to ask? ". . . or provide me with a weapon that I may defend myself."

"The Savior requires assistance!" he wheezed. He leaned forward, nearly standing. His voice grew stern and cold. "The Savior shall survive through the will of Hope." He rocked back. "Now, tell me of my would-be assassin."

I knew I dared not press the issue. It was I, after all, who had insisted that I had an inside line to Hope. When you aspired to greatness, you didn't expect handouts. Jason and I were on our own.

Vtekdao sat, waiting for my answer, consuming our cool bare bodies with his bilious glower.

What would I say? If in doubt, stall for time. "Honorable One, may I suggest summoning me and my disciple by other means? I understand the energy supply is critical."

"I will decide when energy is conserved and when it is used!" he bellowed. "Who is this would-be assassin?"

So much for delay tactics. I'd have to take advantage of a situation I wasn't sure he knew about. He'd never be able to verify my confabulation. "It was Vnoim, Honorable One. But he was not alone. I am grieved to say that I do not know the identity of his co-conspirator."

Jason's mind erupted into mine. *What the hell are you doing now?*

Killing two birds with one stone. Just back off, Jason.

Vtekdao rocked back and forth in his throne. I had no idea what it meant.

"It was zhe, was it? I should have known. Zhe died in your quarters. Do you have an explanation for this?"

"Vnoim confessed to me he was a dissident. I confronted him with what I'd overheard him say regarding your death. He begged me not to tell. I did the only honorable thing I could do: I caused him to end his own life." *You'd better be right about that, Jason.*

I am.

"Yes, yes," Vtekdao said, calming. "You had no other choice. You do not know the other? The co-conspirator is still at large?"

"I do not know his identity, so therefore don't know whether he still lives or has met with the same fate as the other infidels. I pray for your sake, he has been eliminated and you don't have to worry yourself with such subversive nonsense." Keep squirming, you son-of-a-bitch.

"Indeed. You are to be commended for your faithfulness and service to The Purpose. You may go."

I bowed and turned in one motion, hesitating in leaving. What if C'toikth was out there, waiting for us? When we'd vanished, he had to have guessed that we'd been taken to Vtekdao.

We had to get to Cos in Application. I locked eyes with Jason and it was understood what we'd do. Simultaneously, we dashed through the wall. I ran up the spiral; Jason ran down. The roach spun in place like a lawn sprinkler, showering the walkway with a flurry of black smudges, just missing my ankle as I leapt sideways and darted down the spiral to join Jason.

We ran, arms held tightly against our chests, zigzagging down the spiral. Without my arms for balance, I was sure I'd break a leg. Deadly black puffs popped all around us. It was only a matter of time and being in the wrong position at the wrong instant before one of us was fatally hit.

We raced by the red dots of Assembly and Procedure, popping

shots in pursuit. My legs burned, my lungs heaved for more air. Just as I saw the red dot to Application, Cos stepped through the wall. I fell into him, clutching at his robe. He caught his balance and, raising his arms, a silver cylinder in his hands, he aimed over my head at the roach. Before he could fire, something popped close behind me, searing through my right shoulder, sending jagged blades of pain through my chest. There was no air left in my lungs to scream.

I heard another pop, Jason's scream like an echo in the distance as I clutched the front of Cos' caftan, fighting to hold myself up. Through the hideous roar in my head, a loud pop banged overhead, followed by a shrill hiss behind me. A tsunami of sound, darkness, burning flesh, my arms liquid, body descending....

CHAPTER 19

VARIABLES

It is impossible to simultaneously know both the velocity
and the position of a particle (Heisenberg Uncertainty Principle).
—Qwiffian Handbook of Sapience

When I opened my eyes I saw Jason laid out in a white caftan on a low table beside me, his eyes closed, long dark hair flowing to the floor. I could detect no movement in his chest. *Jason. Jason, say something.* No response. I squeezed my eyes shut and silently cried, knowing he had to be dead.

My left cheekbone and hips bit into the hard surface beneath me as I lay on my stomach, unable to move, unable to turn my head away from the funeral scene across from me. How had it happened that I had survived and Jason had not?

"Cos," I moaned through an immovable jaw.

"I'm right here." I felt his warm hand on my bare shoulder. "Be still. I'm nearly finished. You were very lucky, Rita. There was minimal damage to the scapula. Please don't move."

Like I had a choice. I heard a zipping sound at my right ear and felt a warm pressure over my right shoulder blade. An exquisite sting at the back of my neck and every muscle in my rigid body suddenly released with a tingle.

"You can get up now. Slowly."

Cos helped me turn over and sit up. I was still naked. We were apparently in Duty. Two armed Hagions stood at the far wall. "Is Jason...did he...*die?*"

"No. He'll be fine. He lost his right calf muscle; it's being restructured." Cos reached under the exam table on which I sat and pulled out a silky white caftan. "Put this on. It is time," he said, placing a gentle hand on my shoulder.

I sighed in relief and pulled the caftan over my head; it reached to my ankles.

"You'll like the large pockets," he said, looking intently into my eyes. "Try them."

I shoved my hands in the pockets. In the right one I felt a cold hard cylinder about the size of a double-A battery. Grinning, I remembered how much I loved this alien. "Nice. Does Jason's caftan have...pockets as well?"

"Oh yes. When he recovers you must both go to Vtekdao. It is time. Those two will escort you." He jerked his head sideways. "Do the right thing, Savior." He nodded almost imperceptibly, twitching an eyebrow in punctuation.

The whole universe had been turned sideways during my unconsciousness. I found it hard to believe Cos was telling me what I thought he was telling me. I had to be cautious; I couldn't afford to misinterpret anything ever again.

Bring Vtekdao to me, he thought-voiced, slamming his mind down before I could probe him for details, as he undoubtedly feared I would.

A noisy inhalation broke me from Cos' stare. Jason moaned and rolled his head from side to side. "Wha? Where am I?" He rolled his shoulders towards me in an effort to get up, a horrified expression on his face. "I can't move my legs. I can't move!"

I rushed to him. Linea intercepted me, stabbing a long tweezers at the back of his neck. He squinted and pressed his lips together.

"What happened?" he said, transfixed on the silver orb encircling his lower leg.

"We got hit," I said. "Bad. Lucky to be alive." I pointed at the molychine repair ball. "Your leg was blown apart, so they tell me. I think you'll be pleased with the results of Hagion technology." *Jason, we're being monitored, watched. Listen carefully. In one of your pockets you have a weapon—a small cylinder. It's incredibly powerful.*

He put his hands in his pockets.

No! Don't raise suspicion. Don't do anything, yet. That weapon releases a laser blast by scraping the thumbnail up the barrel. It doesn't matter which end is pointing at your target, just remember to always scrape away from you. Got it?

Got it. What's up?

We have to kidnap Vtekdao. Bring him here. For now, play it cool.

He smiled up at me. "Marvelous technology. When can I walk?"

"Relax, Dr. Childress," Linea said, her short blond hair hanging in disarray before weary blue eyes. "Microsurgery is one thing that can't be rushed."

His response was lost to my ears as a complaining female voice grated the airspace behind me.

"The goddamn pump stopped working. If you want me to do your nigger-work you better keep the equipment working."

I turned, unsure as to how I felt about seeing Stella at this time, in this potentially volatile situation.

Cos rushed to her. "Which pump?" His voice had a worried edge that didn't indicate minor inconvenience. "Which one, Stella?"

"I don't know! The pump thingy that goes to the incubators."

"Show me." Cos jerked Stella around by the arm and pushed her through the wall to Application.

I shot through after them. "What's going on? What's the crisis?" I insisted, walking the aisles close behind them, rows of shelves whipping by in the red glow. I heard a single roach clicking behind us.

"Up there." Stella pointed towards the high tube-entangled ceiling.

Cos traced the spaghetti-works with his eyes, finally focusing on a single clear pipe coming from the wall and feeding into several smaller tubes, each connected to a separate aquarium-like tank. In the tanks, dead water held motionless half-formed miniature Hagions. Infants. Not one stirred.

Cos jiggled the tubes in two tanks, tapped the glass. He ran his hands through his hair. "It's the nutrient fluid. It's run dry. They're all in shock. Not your fault, Stella. Not your fault."

Stella stared at him. "Then do something. They can't stay like this forev—"

"They're dying. There's nothing I can do." Cos shook his head.

He glanced at me, then, and suddenly I felt his dagger of accusation. "The generators?" I asked in a creaky whisper. "It's because of the generators?" Somewhere, a steady metallic dripping droned.

He nodded. Stella looked away—away from her murdering

sister. I had taken *this* from her, too.

"Five hundred of them. Gone. Just like that," she said, raising her arms and letting them slap to her sides in resignation as she turned and walked away. "All that work. For nothing. . . ." Her voice trailed off as she wandered down the last row, disappearing into deep red shadows...and the horror of uselessness.

Cos brushed by me, past the Hagion guard who stood at the wall, and passed back into Duty. The guard hurried after him, chattering.

I didn't understand. Did everyone hate me right now, including myself? If it was wrong to foul the generators, why hadn't the neohumans stopped me, or at least reprimanded me? I dipped my hands into my pocket, fondling the cylinder. It gave me comfort to know it was there, ready for me. I turned to go back to Duty, my pace slower. I peered down each row I passed. Neohumans tended the jars of eggs and developing Hagion fetuses. To what end?

The bright light of Duty bleached everything but the guilt from my soul. At the far wall, Cosmigellan was engaged in debate with the two sentries, his hands flying in gesture; theirs wadding furiously. I couldn't hear what they were saying, but surmised there was trouble.

Jason was on his feet testing his rebuilt leg. He grinned broadly, looking absolutely messianic in his white robe, dark hair hanging free around his shoulders. My eyes wanted to linger on him; my distressed mind would not let me.

"How are you doing?" I asked him, trying to hide my anxiety.

"It is time, Savior. Vtekdao waits," he said. *The lid's about to blow right off this place. Say nothing of your involvement with the generators. Let's move.*

I didn't like the tone of his thoughts. *You know something I don't know?*

I'll say. Let's go.

The two sentries clicked up to us, black marbles poised. "Vtekdao waits," one of them said, wadding towards Application.

We followed them into the red glow and through the wall to the outside. Anger and an indefinable terror began to grow inside me. I hated being locked out of The One, ignorant, dependant upon what someone else *chose* to reveal to me. Now Jason was starting with the same crap that had driven a wedge between Cos and I. He was hiding something, something dark and ominous. Something he'd decided would be too much for me to handle. *Jason, dammit. Don't do this to me.*

He sighed as we trekked up the spiral. *OK. But first I have to make a confession. My timing is horrible, I know. But I've grown quite fond of you. I can't bear the idea of never seeing you again, of never—*

Jason! You're scaring me!

He paused, his emotions pouring into my mind. *They're coming after you, Rita. They're coming to kill their Savior.*

What spilled from my mind then, contained no words. My heart was an impotent click in my throat. Someone else would come after me, as C'toikth had. The Hagions were determined to succeed. *How do you know this?*

I am of The One.

How do any of you know this?

We just do.

So why are we going after Vtekdao when I'm about to be hunted down like a coyote and killed?

Insurance, Rita. Insurance.

All at once I understood. It was the only sure way of saving my neck.

Jason tapped into my thoughts again. *We'll have to waste the two guards just before we enter Vtekdao's chambers. Ready?*

I was numb with fear. *I guess so.*

The guards turned left. Instantly I yanked the weapon from my pocket and scraped my thumbnail up the cylinder. Jason had already aimed and we fired two shots each. The roaches fell, handless, spinning and hissing on the floor.

Jason yelled, "Vtekdao's guards. Go!"

We bolted through the wall. A black smudge tore through my left sleeve, burning a shallow furrow in my arm. I raised my weapon and scraped twice. Then Jason fired. The roaches at Vtekdao's sides scream-hissed and spun around the room, one getting tangled in the drape behind the throne, exposing a sleeping puppy and a drowned cat. Prostrate, the wounded roaches convulsed and died.

"What's the meaning of this?" Vtekdao bellowed, clamoring to his feet.

"You're coming with us," I said, aiming my weapon at one

hand, Jason aiming at the other. "The game's over."

"I will do no such thing! You are not long for this universe, Savior! Your demise is imminent. I can provide sanctuary. Hide yourself now."

"Why, so you can kill me more easily? Is that why you faked C'toikth's death? So you could send him after me and I'd never suspect your plan?"

"The traitor's death was real. You have my word. What zhaz twin did was a regrettable mistake. I should have foreseen it. I apologize."

Twins. Damn. I hadn't thought of that. A sudden realization coursed through my guts: The attempt on my life had been my fault. I'd asked the wrong roach what I should say to the dissidents at my canonization. Shit. Cos had been right: reveal nothing to anyone.

"Others are coming after me? Why do they want me dead?"

"Your words. Your evil words—they have confused, disturbed. Do not misunderstand me. I have the greatest respect for you, Ree-tah. My subjects, however, do not share my adoration. They have lost many of their own. The Dissidents were important to The Purpose, and they chose your words over their duties. It is natural that they—"

"You stupid fuck! Don't you see? *You* are the one who ordered their executions! Had you just left them alone, let them adjust to their new-found personal freedom, they would have resumed their duties."

"They violated the codes of the elders, the will of Hope. They had to be punished, their deaths serve as an example to others who would betray The Purpose. It is the Ancient Way."

That damn phrase again. I hated it. What were the chances of both Phaedrans and Hagions adopting the same dogmatism? There was something very disturbing about it. "How many have you killed? Half? All? And your wasting energy when no more can be generated. Do you know that the fetuses in Application are dying? Your civilization is dead. How will you explain this to your subjects? How can you face them, knowing it is you who have destroyed them, their future? This is the end of the line, roach."

He sank into a fugue. When he came out of it, Jason and I were at each side of him, holding him at the joints where hands met thorax. "You're coming with us."

"You can't! They wait for you! Outside—hundreds of them! We'll all be killed!" Vtekdao howled.

I looked over the roach's head to Jason and gulped. There was no turning back now. I had to do as Cos asked, to finally trust that he had some kind of plan.

"Would they kill their Honorable Altruist?" I pressed the weapon into his six-fingered palm. "You're dead if anyone so much as breathes on me."

Jason and I pulled him from the raised platform and walked him to the wall. *This better work, Jason. I'm not real happy about dying in the Roach Motel.*

It will.

I took a deep breath and we stepped through the wall, Vtekdao firmly wedged between us. There were Hagions as far down the spiral as I could see.

"Leave us! Do not endanger your Honorable Altruist!" Vtekdao screamed into the crowd. The chickenshit took the words right out of my mouth.

We inched ahead, parting the sea of roaches as it receded back down the spiral. Every muscle in my body quivered in readiness to flee, escape, abandon this absurd scheme. I glanced quickly at Jason; his breathing quickened to shuddering gasps, sweat dripped from his scalp. It was no comfort realizing I wasn't alone in my terror.

Finally our way was clear. No one threatened us as we hauled our captive down to Application. Finding the fourth dot, I leaned down to press it with my elbow.

"Rita wait!" Jason said. "Something's wrong in there. Something's gone terribly wrong."

"What? What is it?" In that moment of indecision, Vtekdao twisted and jerked out of my grip. Jason dropped his weapon and it rolled down the spiral as he flailed, fighting to hold Vtekdao. I ran past him, diving for the weapon, snapping it up just as Vtekdao dashed to the inner wall, pressing himself forcefully into the fabric. Before Jason and I could grab him, the wall opened up and he plunged into a glowing green tube, a silvery pod ballooning around him as he descended. He dwindled to a shiny speck as the wall sucked back in like an irritated sphincter. We'd lost him.

"Shit." Something about that silvery pod bothered me: its

familiarity. For just an instant, it made the loss of our hostage seem of secondary importance.

"Rita," Jason panted, clutching my left arm, rubbing his thumb across the burn, "The colony's in danger. Hagions, dozens of them."

"Oh god." My stomach crawled into a ball. Cos must have known something like this was going to happen. That's why he needed me to bring Vtekdao. And I'd failed him. "We can't just go in there shooting...." Suddenly an idea hit me. It was a longshot, but it was all I had.

"You can't tell them. You can't. Not yet," Jason responded to my thoughts.

"I'll have to."

"You'll be their prime target if you do."

"Hell, Jason. I already *am* now that Vtekdao's gone. We've lost our bargaining power. There's nothing left to lose."

"But your life."

Without answering him, I dashed to the red dot, pressed it and entered Application. In the bloody light a circle of Hagions surrounded an apathetic knot of neohumans.

A single Hagion clicked forward. I remembered the brow furrows. Ngishkaok. One of the original Dissidents. "You, Savior, will surrender your life in exchange for the lives of the Benefactors."

My mind spasmed. His demand made no sense. "And if I do not relinquish my life? You would exterminate your Benefactors? What of The Purpose?"

"It...it does not matter. The generators are dead. The Purpose is doomed. We wish only retribution."

I sensed uncertainty, a definite paucity of conviction in its voice. "Your vengeance is misdirected. It is Vtekdao that you want, not I. Don't forget, you dissidents came to *me*."

"It is no longer important. Our movement is now meaningless. The Purpose is meaningless. You will accept your failure, Savior."

The roach beside Ngishkaok stepped forward, a black marble balanced in its fingers. It had a clear shot.

"Wait," I said. "I am still your Savior, no matter how disappointed you may be in my efforts to free you. I can still help you. I know how to fix your generators."

There was a brief moment of wheezing laughter before the roach beside Ngishkaok fired. I didn't see the smudge as it popped a fraction of an inch from my arm. Through the bedlam of my own panic and anger I did what no one, not even myself, expected: I rushed the crowd.

Like brittle bowling pins, dozens of chitinous bodies crunched to the floor. I fired at the perimeter of the fallen roaches, the blasts eliciting scream-hisses from the wounded and insulted. To my astonishment, a black smudge escaped from the end of my weapon.

The neohumans scattered, screaming, climbing shelves, pulling jars to the floor in watery explosions, splashing waves of fluid and embryos across the room. They had gone into spindle.

I fell to my belly, sliding through the fluid and glass shards, mowing through a tangle of spindly legs as shrieking roaches smashed into each other in an effort to gain their footing in the slime. Crouching, I turned and fired into the chaos. Peals of pain and rage filled Application. Over the din I heard Jason's weapon discharge beside me from the other side of the shelving. He was still alive. That braced me.

A loud pop rang over my head. I flattened on the floor, glass fragments biting into my palms and chin. A glass jar smashed in the middle of my back and I felt a cold squirming fetus gasp its first and last breath between my shoulder blades.

Stella ran up beside me, screaming, and fell to her hands and knees.

"Get down! Get down!" I yelled, scraping my thumbnail up the cylinder again and again, firing into the snarl of furious and screaming roaches.

"I want a weapon! Give me a weapon!" she shouted over the din.

"There are only two! Jason has the other!"

Pop! Less than a foot from me, a hole opened up in a Hagion's brain, sending it hissing, spinning, spraying black liquid. Nearly headless and mangled beyond recognition, it turned back and came toward me, firing rapidly, pops exploding fractions of an inch from my face. I aimed at its hands, vaporizing them. The roach shrieked and collapsed in a sucking, quivering mass.

Clicking approached quickly from behind. I glanced over my shoulder. A roach aimed its marble. Before I could roll over and fire, Stella grabbed a jar and threw it, crushing the roach's segmented middle like a rotten Easter egg. I fired at its hands and watched it die.

When I rolled back over on my belly, Hagion hooves clicked inches from my face. I looked up into the face of instant extinction: Ngishkaok.

Reflexively I tried to scrape the cylinder—my hand was trapped under my belly. In my last seconds of life my brain chose to focus on anything but the matter at hand.

All at once I noticed the screaming and hissing had ceased. No shots popped in the air. I could hear Jason's breathing on the other side of the shelf. I wanted to hug him, say goodbye.

My eyes were riveted on the spinning pupils above me, drawing me inwards, into the whirlpool of eternity that beckoned. Suddenly, the roach's head dropped from view. I looked down to see Stella's hands wrapped around Ngishkaok's ankles as he squealed and hissed on his back on the floor.

"You're getting good at this," I said, scrambling in the slime for my footing. Glass sliced into my feet as I positioned myself over the writhing roach.

"Kill him! Kill him—I can't hold him much longer!" Stella screamed.

Scraping forward on the cylinder, I watched as one hand, then the other evaporated. With a hiss and a convulsion the roach's eyes blacked over. It was dead.

The only sounds in Application were the soft hisses, clatters, and gurgles of dying Hagions. I scanned the black-slime-encrusted disorder of dismembered bodies, amputated and broken limbs, crushed chitin, blackened and dislodged eyeballs, ruptured and bleeding brains, glistening bowels. My handshake with death dispelled the need to vomit. I knew the nausea would be with me for a long time, unrelieved. What I had to do next would only amplify my misery: look for wounded neohumans.

"Jason. Jason, are you OK?"

"Yeah," he moaned.

I stepped around the end of the shelf and found him kneeling over a dead Hagion, clutching a fistful of fingers he had manually torn from the roach. "Jesus, did you have to get up close and personal? Where's your weapon?"

"I dunno," he drawled. "I dropped it." He inhaled deeply, a whimper escaping.

"Let go of...those things, OK? Open your hand."

His hand flew open; the gooey rubber fingers dropped. He began to shiver. The first casualty.

Why in the hell did they call them casualties, anyway? There was nothing casual about victims of war. I pulled him up. He stood, still staring down at his victim. Black splotches stained the front of his gown. "Stella, will you look around and see if you can find one of these?" I held up my weapon.

Without hesitating she plunged both hands into the gore, turning the dead roach, picking through chitin chips and black tar until she came up with a dripping black object.

"That's it. Good work." I had to put Jason somewhere before I went searching for the neohumans. Putting my arm around his waist, I coaxed him into the brightness of Duty. His hand went up, shielding his eyes. At least he was still aware of his surroundings.

Three exam tables had emerged from the floor, each occupied by someone I knew and cared about. Cos was hunched over a tray of instruments at the counter near the entrance. He limped slightly as he shifted from leg to leg. There was a lot of damage to take care of. Jason's shock state would have to wait.

"Cos, are you...are you all right? Are the others going to be all right?"

He snapped up his head. His dark eyes burned with everything that hurt. "Of course I'm not all right. And I don't know about them yet."

I put my hand on his arm. "Cos, I—"

"Don't." He raised his left hand as if to push me back.

"What else could I have done? What options did I have?"

He looked squarely into my eyes. "Brought Vtekdao, as I asked. With zhan in custody, this disaster could have been avoided."

Everything that happens is supposed to happen? That was a tenet he lived by. I wanted to throw it back in his face. "Well, shit happens, doesn't it? He got away. Just broke free and slipped through the inner wall down a green tube where he—"

"The inner wall? Are you sure?"

"Yeah. In a big silver bubble."

"That could be very good for us," he said, turning back to the tray, busying himself with his left hand as he hugged his right arm to his stomach. "It's the launch bay. If Vtekdao decides to leave...."

"What's wrong with your arm?"

"Not important. Where's Stella? I need her."

I slipped back into Application. Stella came towards me carrying Caylene in her arms. "She's dead," she said without emotion. "So's Ureyana. The others are coming." She walked past me into Duty. I caught a glimpse of Caylene's face and neck. A whole side of her throat had been blasted out. The colony's only aeronautics buff, struck down before she had even been in a plane.

I wouldn't allow myself to cry, to break down when there was so much to do. We had to recover as quickly as possible. That's what the Hagions would be doing; they'd be back.

Robed figures emerged from the rows of shelves and came forward, filing past me. No one spoke. No one exchanged glances, acknowledged my presence. There was Macro, tired but well. He passed me as if I were invisible.

Locked out of The One, now shunned. What was next, ostracism from the colony altogether? I wasn't about to stand by and let *that* happen.

"Listen up, *friends*," I said upon returning to Duty. Cos, Linea, and Decartesana worked over their fellow neohumans, patching wounds I knew they'd mostly incurred during spindle. "I admit I fucked up. But why, for Universe sakes, have you placed all of your hopes on *me?* If you wanted Vtekdao, you could have gone after him yourselves."

"No," Jaynah said, cradling her left wrist in her right hand. "Vtekdao's abduction required weapons. The promise of death. We could not abide by such desecration of the codes." She lowered her eyes. "You are human. You do not suffer such constraints on your behavior."

"I am Qwiffian, just like you!"

"But you are not Phaedran. Not on this quantum branch."

"But I *am* on others. What is this separatist horseshit?" Was I never to be of The One again? Had they decided? I summoned the nerve to ask. "Will I be ostracized?"

Darwinia stepped forward from the group, apparently uninjured. "We are not angry with you, Rita. We are simply... impotent."

"No. No! I don't accept that. Not for a second. We can still get out of this," I said, charged with a stubborn optimism that bordered on mania. My mind was a maelstrom of ideas. "Cos! You said if Vtekdao left, we might have a chance. We'll just have to make him leave somehow. Dump something down the launch bay. Bodies! We could dump some bodies in on top of him!"

Cos looked up from his patient. "You can't go out there. None of us can. The Hagion revolution is not over. They'll be back. They want you, Rita, and they won't stop until they know you're dead."

Jesus. The way he said it I wondered if he shared the sentiment. I had to do *something*. Not only was my life at stake, so was my honor in the eyes of those I loved. I looked around the room at all the faces. They were not angry at me, Darwinia had said. Whether that was true or not didn't matter. We were all doomed if Vtekdao remained on the ship.

"What will happen if Vtekdao leaves? Will they drop their vendetta against me?"

"The revolution will end," Cos said. "Vtekdao will not be able to return to the ship; there is no power to do so. Vtekdao's orders will be remanded. You will be safe. Probably."

"Vtekdao's orders?" I knew it. "Vtekdao ordered my assassination?"

Cos sighed. "Seems likely."

I stared at the floor. That did it. I had decided.

I scanned the room for Jason, catching a glimpse of long toes peeking from beneath a white caftan. He sat on the floor, partially obscured by the watery walls of the central extraction booth. "Jason," I said, kneeling in front of him. He rested his head on drawn up knees. "I need your help."

He looked up, bluish depressions under his eyes, and nodded. "I made it. I didn't think I would."

"Everyone except Caylene and Ureyana made it."

"I know. I felt them...just *vanish*." His eyes glistened.

"A curse sometimes, to be of The One," I said, acknowledging his sorrow. "Jason, I have a plan. If we can get Vtekdao to leave, the revolution will be—"

"I know. Let's do it."

I smiled and pinched his stubbly chin and dropped his weapon in his pocket. "Thank you for believing in me."

"Now go see if Stella does."

"Stella? She'd never—"

"Ask her. I think you'll be surprised."

Stella, still clothed in battle fatigues, stood obediently at Cos' side, handing him instruments as he asked for them. Stella the surgical nurse. Stella the warrior. I never would have believed it possible. Her several brushes with death since transporting to this ship had brought out things in her I bet even *she* hadn't guessed were there. How ironic, now that things looked more hopeless for us than ever, that she had finally chosen life and discovered her function in the universe.

"I want to thank you for saving my life. Twice," I said softly to her.

"You would have done the same for me. Forget it."

Yes, I would have, but only if death were not her choice. "I need a volunteer for a nasty and dangerous mission."

"Worse than what we've already been through?"

"Maybe. Corpse detail, risking possible ambush. High pucker factor."

"Sounds treacherous. Who else you got?"

"Just Jason and me. We can do it, Sis."

She nodded. "Show me what to do, Sarg."

Was she joking or had her mind rescued her from this horrible ordeal by making her think she was really an enlisted soldier?

Jason stepped up beside me. *What difference does it make? You have her, don't you?*

Weapon in hand, I entered the raw disaster of Application, Stella and Jason close behind. The sanguine glow made the gore seem more arresting, the stench more blood-metallic than like pine cinders. Besides a few rows of jars containing dormant roach eggs, we three were the only living things there.

I picked my way through the tangle of severed limbs and torsos, crunching through the chitin fragments and slipping in black slime as I headed for the exit to the spiral. I stopped there, taking a deep breath, two decisions ping-ponging in my head: If there were Hagions out there, I'd withdraw and run like hell; if it was clear, I'd complete my mission as quickly as possible. I shoved my head through the wall and withdrew quickly, motioning with my hands to Jason and Stella. All was clear.

"Find some intact bodies and bring them out."

"What are *you* gonna do?" Stella asked, arms akimbo.

"What commanding officers are supposed to do. Cover our asses."

Stella and Jason rummaged through the butchery, pulling two complete but handless bodies up to the surface of the heap, and drug them through the wall.

I led them, glancing up and down the spiral for marauders, to the inner wall that concealed the launch bay running through the center of the ship. Pushing my hands through the wall, the fabric stretched like taffy, resisting as I spread my arms in an effort to pull a hole in the wall. At last the substance responded, dilating like a giant cervix. I caught myself as I teetered at the edge of the bottomless green tube. "God!" I took two short steps back, still holding the wall open. "Ok. Toss 'em in! Quickly, before it closes." The taffy wall strained to reclose around my hands.

They drug the corpses, leaving tell-tale black smears across the floor, and flung them down the shaft. I watched the corpses shrink to ants and wink out of existence. The orifice sucked closed.

Just as we turned to run back into Application, I heard the menacing click of Hagion hooves, growing closer, louder. The floor lurched sideways as something discharged from within the ship. *Vtekdao.* I fell, wrenching my wrists as I caught myself before my face hit. Jason fell beside me.

Scrambling to our feet, we dashed to the wall of Application. I frantically pounded the red dot and we smashed through the stew of dead Hagions, slipping, skating our way to Duty.

My caftan sticky and wet, I rushed to the outer wall, Jason and Stella sliding beside me, and touched the wall to transparency. A bright silver orb flashed from the left and sped towards Antarctica. "Vtekdao left! He's gone! It worked!"

Unexpectedly, the silver pod flared bright orange and exploded in a fiery spray of sparks. "Shit! He's blown up! Even better than I'd hoped!" I turned around, elated.

My spirits plunged rapidly.

Before me stood two roaches, black marbles leveled at my chest.

"The war's over. Your Honorable Altruist just committed suicide." I scraped forward on the weapon. Nothing happened. Again. The weapon was out of power.

A black smudge shot towards me, tearing into my upper arm

with burning coldness. I fell backwards, hitting my head on the window with a sickening clunk, the window rumbling in oscillation.

Screaming, Stella lunged at the roach. It fired into her; a red geyser gushed through the back of her padded vest, splattering her life towards Antarctica. Jason fired his weapon twice into the roaches as Stella fell twitching, blue eyes staring into infinity.

"No!" I heard myself scream, my voice a hollow and distant echo. My limbs tingled and became numb. A strange warmth poured into me.

Don't move! Don't talk! Jason screamed in my head. *You're dead. They have to think you're dead.*

In my peripheral vision I saw him blast the hands from the roaches. Hisses roared in my ears. Black spatters flecked my face, hung in my lashes. I closed my eyes. I was dead. I wanted to be dead. This ship would be my coffin and the two men I loved would be my pall bearers.

My breathing stopped, my head filling with buzzing and darkness.

There can be no light without the darkness. There can be no light....

CHAPTER 20

STRONG NUCLEAR FORCE

The ultimate authority is oneself.
—Qwiffian Handbook of Sapience

Standing before a jury of two hundred Hagions, hands bound in white cord, Jason Childress hung his head and cried. His tears ran, refreshing the dried splotches of blood—both Hagion and human—blemishing his white caftan. He lifted his face to the darkness of space pressing through the clear domed ceiling overhead, wet strands of hair caressing a pained expression. "Your Savior is dead." The ease with which he said that sent shudders of disgust and surprise through him.

Rita, dear Rita. He'd never told her how much he loved her, how much he *wanted* to love her. She was strong, freer than anyone he'd ever known, even though she carried her own prison around with her. She was trapped by her hatred for her father; it was an albatross she'd gladly hang on others who crossed her.

But it was not for Rita that he cried. "Let me help you. I offer the words of Hope in rebuilding what remains of your civilization."

Glaring yellow eyes with spinning pupils. Silence.

A Hagion stepped forward from the circle surrounding Jason, wadded, collapsed in a heap at Jason's feet, milky membranes sliding across still pupils with finality.

Another Hagion stepped forward beside its expired shipmate and aimed a black marble at Jason's chest. "Everything that happens is supposed to happen. It is the will of Hope."

"Do you hear me? You're dying! We *can* recover from this; the generators can be restarted. You have traveled fifteen billion light-years in search of your Benefactors. To give up now is not what Hope intended."

"We have no generators. We have no developing young. We have no Purpose. We have failed."

"No!" Jason raised his individually bound hands and beat the air, wincing as his fingers thumped painfully beneath the ligatures. The Hagions clicked backwards, widening the circle.

"You are *not* our Savior," another Hagion challenged from further out in the circle. "You do not *know* the words of Hope."

"I *am* your Savior *now*. I *do* hear the words of Hope, and I bring them to you." Jason closed his eyes, his mind spilling into fifteen other minds, becoming One with them.

"You must honor your potential. It is the will of Hope," he said calmly. "That you exist now is testimony to Hope's will. To choose non-existence through inaction is in violation of the will of Hope. This is truth." A strange warmth, a power that relaxed and straightened his aching body, suddenly took over. These words were true. He didn't know how he knew them, he just knew he'd always known them. He was of The One.

"How can we believe you, when we have lost so many to your aggression?"

The question was ludicrous. *Our* aggression? "And you are...?"

"Ngishkaok—First Flagellant to the Honorable Altruist."

Jason jerked to attention. Hadn't Ngishkaok been one of the Dissidents? What was he doing as Vtekdao's next-in-command? "Your Honorable Altruist committed suicide over Antarctica."

"It is Vtekdao who has done this contemptible thing. *Our* Honorable Altruist lives." As Ngishkaok said this, a Hagion from the back of the auditorium pushed through to the center and weakly approached Jason.

Jason looked down at the creature expectantly, just as its legs folded under it. "Savior," it said, chest heaving, "I am Shwength, the Honorable Altruist."

A formidable leader, indeed. Jason nodded to himself. He had lost track of the chain of command, and realized that with Tmait, then Vnoim gone, this must be Vtekdao's replacement. "You're sick. Let your Savior and your Benefactors help you, that you may fulfill The Purpose, and your own potentials."

"It cannot be. The generators—"

"We can fix your generators. Rita tried to tell you that before you ruthlessly attacked her, betrayed her."

"It matters not. Our kind is doomed," Shwength moaned.

"There will be no new generation." He recovered his footing and shouted out across the gathering, "Take zhan! Make an example of zhan—the last of zhaz kind on Lolbah, as we have become the last of our kind through zhaz treachery."

Several Hagions converged upon Jason and wrestled him to the floor. While five Hagions bound his ankles together, ten more stretched his arms at right angles to his head. With short bursts from a black marble, Shwength melted the cord, welding his wrists and ankles, burning cold, to the floor. Jason was pinned, helpless.

"You are wrong!" he screamed in desperation. "Don't do this! I am your Savior! I am the instrument of your salvation!" The tyranny of terror and fatigue threatened to crush him.

"You have nothing for us. You will die, human," Shwength said, weaving over him.

"Listen to me!" Jason spoke rapidly. "Once the generators are restored to operation, vivigenesis will resume.

"Look around you. Look at *yourself.* You are starving. Most of the fetuses in Application are dead or dying. Without the generators you cannot engage in Harvest." The circle of Hagions tightened around his prostrate body. His caftan clung to him, wet with sweat and urine. "What have you to lose by trusting us? How can anything we do possibly make your last breaths more miserable?"

Shwength's pupils rocked to a halt and reversed their spin as he swayed, frozen in place—*thinking.* The crowd shuffled and clicked uneasily.

Was this how it was meant to be? An astrophysicist living every space junkie's fantasy of contacting an alien civilization, unable to ever relate his experiences, his discoveries to the very people who had mocked him and oppressed his speculations.

He remembered the anomaly that had so obsessed him, that had ultimately brought him here. He had come in direct contact with it. He had wandered through it—a ship, of all things.

The inside of the ship was considerably smaller than the dimensions of the anomaly that penetrated thousands of miles of space over Antarctica. What kind of matter was this? Massive particles, surely; they would require so much energy no cyclotron existing would ever detect them. This "ship" was enough to slow a planet's rotation, yet did not crash to the surface.

Unseen, *dark*, energy congealed from the substrate of the All

That Is. Congealing in increments, *simulating* form and structure. *Simulating movement through space.* A sudden realization hit him, an understanding, destroyed just as suddenly by the absurdity of his situation.

The universe was indeed a bizarre place, a cruel and indifferent place. He relaxed in his restraints and began to laugh, softly at first, then out loud.

Laughing and crying. Crying and laughing. It was all an insane joke. All a complete waste of human effort and caring.

"Release zhan," Shwength suddenly ordered.

Hagions swarmed around him, freeing his hands, then legs. He stood uneasily on cold-numbed feet, shaking the blood back into his crumpled hands, weak with the irony of his new understanding. "You will enlist my help, allow the Benefactors to perform their most important of duties—restoring the generators?"

Shwength clicked up to him. "Agreed. The generators must be restored. The Holy Ones will survive and prosper. It is the will of Hope."

He sighed heavily, the fatigue, the trepidation leaving his body with his breath. That he was in no position to make demands did not stop him from playing his last card. "There's one more thing," he said softly. "Once the generators are operational, the Benefactors must be released to my custody."

Shwength's eyes bulged and he staggered backwards and collapsed in a light blue heap. "It cannot be! Without the Benefactors, The Purpose cannot be fulfilled! We...we cannot care for our young. We do not *know how*."

"You can't be serious! How can a species survive that can't—"

"J-Jason. It's true. Th-that's why Hagions need us...th-their B-Benefactors," Macro said from Jason's far left. From behind the central fountain, fifteen neohumans diffused into the crowd of Hagions.

Jason felt Macro's mind, then Doron's mind move into his own. His eyes filled with tears. They pleaded with him, made promises that would shock and grieve Rita, had he not vowed to reinforce her exclusion from The One. He didn't want to accept their proposition, but he knew he had no choice if everyone was to survive. It was right.

Everything, he now understood, had been prearranged by the colony, then by the Dissidents. And especially by Rita.

But she didn't know it. Rita must never know. She had been locked out of The One because her mission wasn't over. She couldn't know how important she still was.

The neohumans had their *own* Purpose, and Rita's anger with her past would be the catalyst the neohumans used to achieve it.

CHAPTER 21

OF THE ONE

*Not one property of reality is fundamental. All properties follow
rom the properties of other parts. The overall consistency
of their mutual interactions determines the structure and behavior
of the entire web of existence.*
—Qwiffian Handbook of Sapience

Voices. How could I be hearing voices? I opened my eyes to a ribbon of stars burning so brightly my eyes watered.

Cos' voice faded in and out. "...getting the visual... recalibrated."

The table on which I lay tilted sideways and I felt his warm hand on my jaw as he turned my head. I gagged. Something cold and tight pressed on my throat, preventing my head from turning freely. The nape of my neck tingled. I must be in surgery, yet again. I recalled the dull clunk I'd heard inside my head as I fell backwards into the window.

How many times could a person die without dreading resurrection?

Then I remembered Stella, her conviction and determination painted in red on the window, her dead eyes. Somehow, I knew her injuries were not repairable. I struggled to keep from crying. The tears won. The sound of my sobs made me even sadder and I cut loose with the wails of every loss I'd ever suffered.

"Rita, she made her choice. So did you," Cos answered my thoughts, still holding my jaw.

"Where's Jason? Is he...?"

"Jason's left. He's OK. Be still. I'm sorry there aren't enough molychines left to repair your arm as well. You'll have to heal on your own. As will I."

"I can't see."

"I know." He grunted. "This surgery ball's in my way—can't adjust your vision. Be patient."

"Did Jason...did he take care of Stella? Did anybody?"

"Stella's gone. She didn't die for nothing. She saved your life."

"Again," I whispered. Stella's last act would forever remain a mystery to me. How could someone who resented my very existence make the ultimate sacrifice for me?

"Because she needed to stand for something," Cos said. "She needed to make a difference."

"The horror of uselessness—never again," I whispered. I felt the cold liquid ball recede from my neck. A sharp pain pricked the back of my neck and Procedure flickered into view, replacing the lace of stars. We were alone. "Where is everybody?"

He looked down into my face. His face was thin, his black hair matted with sweat. "Cleaning up. Restoring the generators to working order."

"Then...then it's all over? We won?"

"Nobody *won*. Nearly two-thirds of the Hagions have died. The colony's diminished by two. And Stella."

"But the battle's over, right?" I propped myself up on my right elbow, hugging my sore left arm to my side.

"They believe Vtekdao is dead. They believe you are dead. There is no need for war." He grimaced, holding his right arm close as he sat on the edge of the exam table, his back to me. A reddish-brown stain spread across his right sleeve.

"My god, you're hurt." I sat up beside him and touched his sleeve, instantly withdrawing my hand. A hard bump protruded from his upper arm. "Shit, it's broken. Why haven't you done something about this?" The pain must be unbearable, especially for a sensitive Phaedran who had not known pain in his native form.

"No time. Not enough materials. Killers have low priority in triage, as you well know."

"Killers? You haven't—" Then I remembered. He'd blown away C'toikth's twin to save me. "But you had to! Our codes allow for killing when threatened with destruction."

"It just...feels...so wrong."

"Cos, dammit!" I'd said that phrase so many times it was a wonder he didn't think he'd been blessed with a new last name. "Why do you have such benevolent feelings for these...these *monsters*? They forced you into slavery! Not just recently, but fifteen billion years ago. You ran then. Why aren't you running now?"

"Running was not the solution. We were wrong. When Stella misbehaved, you endured her until she came around."

"What's this got to do with Stella? Don't change the subject. You have some explaining to—" It hit me so hard I nearly passed out. No. It couldn't be. Was it true? Is that why I'd been locked out of The One? "Cos, you can't be serious."

He shuddered a sigh. "I couldn't tell you. I didn't want you to know. I had to let you act on your own, decide for yourself what you would do."

"But lock me out—for that?"

"How would you have reconciled the knowledge? I know you. You would have gone berserk. I couldn't let that happen."

A chill etched through me. He was probably right. I wouldn't have been able to take knowing that his reason—*their* reason—for submitting to the Hagions went way deeper than their allegiance to me or the Qwiffian codes.

"This race is not the evil. Vtekdao is the evil." He sighed. "You were so brilliant, figuring it out for yourself that we were not from Phaedra, that we had created our planet—indeed this whole universe, that the corporeal form we took was not our original form. But you never went further. You never asked the obvious question: 'Who were we before we were Phaedran?'"

I stared into his pain-creased face, gazing beneath the surface, behind his Hershey-syrup eyes into hideous yellow orbs. I shivered as my stomach spasmed. *There can be no light without the darkness.*

All the pieces of this horrible puzzle were beginning to fall into place: the Hagions' use of the phrase "the Ancient Way," how Vtekdao knew I had killed my father, how the Dissidents had come to know of *QWF* and knew to enlist my help—all of it. Cosmigellan had locked me out of The One to keep me from being scanned, but had failed in that because of Jason.

For, the Hagions were of The One, only didn't know it. And until now, neither did I. "But why keep all of this from me? Why not confess that you hated Vtekdao as much as I did?"

"Your responses to Vtekdao would not have been genuine had you known."

"But...but—"

"A new order is underway. All because of you and your belief in yourself," he said. "We will rebuild this civilization piece by piece with a new template. Because of you it is now possible." He smiled, then winced, pressing his lips together as if to stifle a cry.

I forgot my confusion. "We've got to get your arm fixed."

"There will be no medical molychines available for several days. It is too late for me."

"Bullshit. Let me back into The One. I'll get help."

"Let me go, Rita. Nothing can be done."

"You think I'll settle for less than total victory after all we've been through? I opt for reunification. *Now*."

"But, you have Jason, why would you—"

"I love you, Cos. I need you with me, back inside my brain like before."

"The risk is too high. Reunification may disturb the phase-shift modulator. If that happens, you'll no longer be of this matter. You'll fall to Earth and die. We both will."

What a choice. If I didn't take the chance, I'd surely lose Cos; if I did, we could both die. It didn't take long to decide. Even with Jason in it, a life without Cos—my lover, my mentor—would not be worth living. "Let's do it."

"You are sure this is your choice? After all, it is you who takes the risk, not I."

"Yes. Yes!"

He nodded and reached beneath the exam table—that treasure trove of gadgets—and brought out a silver sphere. It looked like the same sphere the Hagions had used to vacuum him from me when I first came here. My mood brightened.

"Lie down."

I obliged him, protecting my sore left arm.

He placed the sphere, cold and heavy, on my forehead and pressed his palm flat against it, pushing as if to force it through my skull. The pain made me whine.

"When I'm in, hold the sphere to your head. Don't let go," he grunted.

I looked into his eyes, one way or another, for the last time. He cried out. His body shrank vertically and twisted into a thick rope of blackness, curling, spiraling, leaping into the sphere in a twirling coil.

I reached up quickly and held the sphere tightly against my head, waiting. My head filled with a pressure that threatened to expand my skull. I feared it would crack open, the contents gush out like pillow lava through an underwater fissure. Before I could scream, the room blinked out, supplanted by the star-flecked void. I felt my body falling, falling to Earth, falling to my death. Several seconds of terror possessed me before I realized that I was still breathing. Had I been converted to baryonic matter, separated from the ship in empty space, my lungs would have instantly evacuated. Once the panic subsided, I did indeed feel the exam table underneath me. Something else had happened: I had gone blind.

Cos! Cos, I can't see!

Consider that very fortunate. We have to get to Vtekdao's chambers, to the phase-shift initiator unit.

Our success was a tainted one. I sat up, squinting as if I could somehow conjure my surroundings from the slits between my eyelids. I thought for a second I could see the ghostly outline of the padded bench that ran along the wall. *No, I can't go tripping around on a ship I can't see. We need to get someone here to recalibrate the molychine.*

The device is permanently damaged. I can walk you through the ship. We have to get to the top level. Everyone will meet us there; we must be ready for them.

In the darkness I felt sixteen consciousnesses caress my mind. I had re-entered The One. A sudden sense of completion, liberation flooded through me. Their voices sang of fulfilled wishes. I gasped, understanding. *We're leaving? My god, we're really leaving?*

If I can remember how the phase-shift device works. The details of operation become a little cloudy after fifteen billion years.

I stood, laughing out loud, a welcome release from the ordeal of being a survivor. *Onward through the fog!*

Turn left. More...more...stop. Walk straight ahead. Slow down or you'll rebound off the wall instead of sliding through.

His precise directions guided me across an unseen floor, the black void and millions of stars groping at me from everywhere. I held my invisible hands out in front of me. But walking through empty space was too unsettling; I decided it was best if I continued on with my eyes closed.

I turned left after feeling my body move through the wall. The upward slope of the spiral walkway was a comforting sensation in the darkness. I walked close to the outside wall, ready for Cos' cue to enter Vtekdao's chambers, as I could feel alternating density fluctuations. For the community activity levels, density could be altered only by pressing the red dot, which I could not see. It struck me as peculiar how community levels could only be accessed by request, where the individual quarters on the Obligant and Ignorant levels, as well as Vtekdao's chambers, could be entered freely, even by accident, as I had discovered.

Open your eyes, I want to try something, Cos thought-voiced.

I backed up to the wall, steadying myself. I opened my eyes. I could see contours, the edge where the wall met the floor, though it was all quite dark, appearing very much like a cheap velvet painting. *How'd you do that?*

A feedback loop of a sort. You're seeing my mental interpretation of what your other senses are picking up, fed back to you and amplified.

How creative of you. I continued along the wall, knowing the soft echoes of my footsteps, the sensations of closeness to the wall, would help the images.

Here it is, Rita. Do you feel it?

I did. I turned and slipped through into the chambers of the Honorable Altruist—whoever it turned out to be if this civilization survived. The air was sticky with charcoal pine. I coughed. I had no chance to turn and run. A sharp pop burst to my left. Diving for the floor, scanning the obscurity for the outline of a Hagion, I could see only the ghostly images of Vtekdao's throne, the drape behind it. *I thought you said they think I'm dead! Why are they shooting at a dead person? I have no weapon to defend myself!*

In your right pocket! Jason put it there!

I dug for the cylinder and crawled along the floor, pulling myself along mostly with my right elbow, wanting to scream because of the pain in my left arm. *Where'd it go? I can't see it!*

Stay low. Follow the curvature of the floor, to your right. That's it. The phase-shift initiator is down this corridor. You have to get to it, calibrate the field intensity and coordinates before the colony arrives. You can do it, Rita.

I'd never been more scared in my life. The battles with the roaches, the mental games with Vtekdao, even Stella's death, were insignificant compared to crawling on my belly in pain, blind, weak from hunger and sleep deprivation, knowing a roach hid somewhere near and was waiting for the opportunity to blow a hole in me. It was enough to reduce me to a sobbing heap of self-pity.

But it didn't. One thing drove me on: I was so close to achieving my goal of recovering the colony back to Earth, the misery of my situation seemed trivial. I was convinced if I stayed close to the floor, the chance of being hit was slim. At least that's the way it had seemed during the battle in Application. Right now, it was the only consolation I had; I couldn't afford to scrutinize the logic too closely.

A pulsing buzz consumed the corridor.

What's that?

The phase-shift initiator in use. Rita, we're in trouble.

What do you mean? Cos, dammit!

Follow my instructions exactly. You'll need to get closer. Make no sound.

Getting closer wasn't what my mammalian soul had in mind. *OK. OK*, I thought more in reassurance to myself than in answer to Cos. I crawled, an inch at a time, my breathing threatening to betray my presence.

Closer. You'll have to be within inches before you can fire.

My god, Cos! It'll see me! It's armed, remember?

Zhe cannot see what it believes is dead. Zhe responds to sound and fires accordingly.

Suppressing grunts of pain, I crept closer. Less than a foot away, the milky outline of the roach winked between strange strobe-like pulses surrounding it. The pulse surged across my face, thrumming the hairs on my arms as I caught time-lapse glimpses of the roach's fingers moving rapidly over the keyboard on the wall.

What's it doing? What's that field all about?

Typing in a sequence. Zhe's protected from us inside the field. Bad for us: It's draining power we need.

The Hagion stopped and waited, the field still pulsing around it. I counted the cycles—two per second—without knowing why. I had been returned to The One, where I knew things without knowing how I knew them. Between the pulses, a shadow-lined finger pressed a final key on the wall.

Cos convulsed in horror.

I knew instantly why. *Goddamn him! Why would he do that? What's the fucking point?*

Ask yourself. You taught them individualism. You have to expect that when they stop acting as a unit, some may choose insanity.

What cities did he target? Where did he dump the molychines?

Rita, you must act now. Between the pulses. Fire between the pulses. Before zhe can send another bolus of molecular destruction to Earth.

I counted the pulses, became the rhythm, my own pulse syncopating with the ghostly light flashes.

Fire! Cos shouted in my head.

I scraped the barrel of the weapon. A shrill hiss severed the darkness. The pulsing light vanished. To my astonishment, nothing stood between me and the keyboard on the wall. *Where'd he go?*

Transported out. Get to the keyboard. Now.

I leapt to my feet, touching my hands to the keyboard; the keys had patterns in them like the ones in my quarters. *My* quarters, I laughed to myself. How had I learned to think of anything on this grotesque ship, except my friends, as *mine*?

I typed in the sequence as Cos recited it. It was only after keying in a mind-boggling 115 symbols that Cos informed me the colony couldn't be transported directly to the ranch. They'd be dropped in Antarctica.

Cos, dammit! They'll freeze to death! They're not dressed for a sub-zero climate.

"Not to worry," Jason's voice rang from behind me.

I jerked around in surprise. Just then Vtekdao's chambers filled with ghostly ripples. The colony had come. Ready to be released at last from the slavery they'd so readily submitted to. I touched them, entering each mind, my joy, my love, diffusing into each one.

Suddenly troubled, I withdrew my mental caresses. "Where are Macro and Doron?"

In the dark a ghostly silhouette reached up to my shoulder. "They've elected to stay," Jason said.

"No! What reason could they have—"

"They must. The Hagion race will die out if it is abandoned."

For an instant, I questioned why that was important,

immediately wanting to slap myself for thinking it. My disagreements with a few gave me no right to wish the extermination of the entire species. The misgivings I had over the loss of Macro were tempered with the knowledge that his staying, his assistance, would be the ultimate irony. Vtekdao had proclaimed Macro defective. How right it was that Macro should be so instrumental in preserving the Hagion race.

"You'll always be linked with Macro and Doron through The One. You won't lose them," Jason said softly.

Reaching into The One, feeling Macro's and Doron's happiness with their decision, I relaxed.

Rita, please complete the sequence, Cos insisted. *You'll have seven seconds to join the colony once the phase-shift initiator is activated.*

But why Antarctica? I know it's possible to set coordinates for the ranch; I was there twice.

Jason again touched my shoulder. "There isn't enough reserve power built up in the generators yet. It could take days," he explained. "I'm reasonably certain the coordinates you typed in will put us inside one of the structures at McMurdo base."

"*Reasonably* certain? Jason, that's not good enough."

"It'll have to be." Jason's ghostly outline left.

Per Cos' instructions, I finished the sequence at the keyboard. As my finger hovered over the last three keys, waiting for Cos' cue to activate transport, the darkness brightened to fuzzy gray. I looked around the room. The huddle of neohumans to my left was trimmed in a rainbow aura. I turned around.

Jason held his limp puppy in his arms as Linea poked a long instrument at the back of her head. Phoebe squirmed to life. I couldn't discern Jason's expression, but I felt him smile. He handed the puppy to Darwinia as he lifted the cover from the glass jar containing my cat, lifting the rigid little body out of her sleeping fluid. He held her upside down so the fluid drained from her lungs. Linea used the same tool on Shana. The cat choked and coughed, her lungs heaving for air. She yowled. I almost cried. She was OK, just as Cos had promised.

The group was gathered in a tight knot. I had an overwhelming urge to click my heels together, chanting, "There's no place like home." The horrible nightmare was over. Praise the Universe, it was finally over.

Pressing the last three keys, I turned to join the huddle. Just before I stepped down into the depression in which the colony stood, a loud pop exploded over my head. I froze.

The colony blinked out of existence before my very eyes.

CHAPTER 22

GRAND UNIFIED THEORY

What's right is what's left after everything else has gone wrong.
—Qwiffian Handbook of Sapience

There is nothing quite so heartbreaking as seeing everything you've worked so hard for, succeed...only to find you cannot be part of it. Like dying during childbirth.

Quite the bummer, as Stella would say. Stella. God, Stella, I wanted to slap you so many times for your hatred, and at other times hold you so close I could absorb your pain. Because, of the two of us, I was the stronger. Your last act, I now understand, proved that.

Through The One I learned that the colony had transported safely within the anteroom of a telescope dome down at McMurdo base, much to Jason's delight. I however, was trapped behind Vtekdao's throne, watching bolus after bolus of molychines blast down to Earth, their devastation released to Universe knew where by a single tenacious roach.

I had fired dozens of times into the pulsing field surrounding the Hagion. The frequency was too fast this time for me to penetrate it. Even if by some remote chance I made it back to Earth, there would be nothing left of human endeavor but powder and ruin.

As far as I was personally concerned, that wasn't the worst of it. If I didn't stop the roach soon, there wouldn't be enough power left to convert and transport me. I'd be stuck here for days, wired on lack of rest and food, while I waited for the generators to recharge.

Images of dissolved cities raced through my mind, transmitted to me through The One. Hundreds of cities had been affected as buildings, bridges, roads, machinery were reduced to granular piles. Most of humanity either stood scratching its collective ass in a feeble attempt to comprehend the wrath of their gods, or trampled and beat each other senseless in a doomsday frenzy.

A huge wave of determination suddenly swept through me. I

had to get to the roach. I had to keep trying until I simply *couldn't*— either from exhaustion or a direct hit from return fire. If I could get closer, just keep blasting at point-blank range until one burst made it through between the pulses of the protective field. . . .

I stood, hunched over, concealed by the drape. Slowly I stepped from behind it, crouching, moving silently towards the pulsing tube of energy. I aimed at the field, so close my knuckles burned with the pulses.

Suddenly, everything faded to black, the ghostly force field beating before me. The damn visual molychine had failed again. I fired repeatedly into nothingness as quickly as I could scrape my thumbnail up the cylinder.

Just as I rose we saw it in Cosmigellan's thoughts—a mere visual whisper—seconds before the blast from my weapon evaporated it into the infinite background of spacetime. All that remained was the hissing echo of its scream. The pulsing tube of energy faded. We couldn't believe what my eyes saw.

What happened?

Phased out of here again.

Dammit! I missed? I didn't kill it? Charged with the mania of desperation, I rushed to the control console. *Give me the sequence again! Quickly, before it comes back!*

It's not time, Rita.

What the fuck are you talking about? It's time! It's time!

You missed. You can't see zhan; I can. Wait for my cue, will you?

Not now with the lectures!

Zhe won't be back in this wherewhen until the next linear cycle. Zhe's out of phase.

Cos, dammit!

All right, all right. Don't get your tampon in a kink! We must wait twelve linear hours.

My god, why?

The generators are too weak. It could kill you to transport now. Besides, do you really want to leave now? The Hagion will be back; zhe will resume zhaz activities. Can you really leave now?

My blood ran cold, my skin becoming a sheet of goose-pimples. There was something predestined about everything that had happened since I'd been guided here. All at once, it made sense.

There was a reason I'd been left behind. A plan. And Cos, in his irritating wisdom, had arranged for me to play an integral part in its unfolding.

You bastard, I thought-voiced.

You misinterpret my intentions.

You knew.

It has to be this way. You are the solution.

The satisfaction of getting a good punch in at Cos would be denied me, now that he was safe inside my brain.

You need rest. You've been slipping into delta on occasion. If you don't stay alert, we could both dissolve into the substrate of The All That Is.

He was right. As long as I had to wait, I might as well try to rest some. I winced from the residual pain in my left upper arm as I lowered myself to the cold hard floor of the ship. There would be no risk in sleeping out here in the open like this. There was only one Hagion left that believed me to still be alive—to the others, I had died days ago alongside my sister.

I knew my sleep would be disturbed at best, filled with the replays of how I came to be in this place, fighting this impossible war, a war I could tell no country's government about, a war I had to fight on their behalf.

* * *

Twelve hours isn't very long. My body is rested but my mind has refused to shut down. The roach hasn't returned and I have a clear shot at the keyboard, can zap us out of here, avoiding a confrontation. I stand, squinting in the obscurity for outlines of the keyboard.

Of course, I know it is wrong to leave the ship with that last renegade roach on board sending his payloads of disaster to my planet. My return to Earth, to the ranch, to my quiet secluded life will be meaningless if I let the roach turn home base into rubble.

Less than a foot beside me, the eerie outline of the roach materializes in the darkness, its ability of remote transport a great advantage over me. He makes for the keyboard. Before he can press the first key to initiate the protective force field, I fire at the contours of his fingers. He screeches and hisses over the pop of my weapon. Knowing he plans to return fire, I lunge, my hands sinking into the soft upper chest. He falls backwards, taking me with him, crunching to the floor beneath my body.

"You will die, Savior! All of your kind will die!" His low voice is muffled, racked with hatred and pain. Instantly I know who the roach is. I should have figured it out earlier. I should have known he would deceive me yet again.

He squirms out from under me as I grab for him, sinking my fingernails into his brain, liquid spurting between my fingers as he scream-hisses. He pulls free, sliding beneath me, his cold rubber fingers gripping my ankle as hard granite teeth rake up my shin.

I scream, kicking like a roped pony, pushing down on his cushiony brain, fighting to dislodge him from my leg. He breaks free. I lunge in the dark after him, grabbing desperately for anything I can hold onto. My hands connect with a hard round knobby thing—a leg joint. I yank; the joint gives. He kicks furiously, screaming shrilly in my hold. Sharp hard hooves scrape up the inside of my arm, peeling a burning trench up to my elbow. I scream and let go, holding my arm to me, feeling the wetness soak through the caftan to my belly as the ghostly outline of the roach rights itself and turns to face me.

On my hands and knees, my shin burning, left arm throbbing with two injuries now, I follow the shadowy figure as it clicks slowly to the left. I have to stay between him and the control console. I lunge again. The roach hops sideways and I crash headlong into a solid wall.

He makes for the console. I stagger to my feet and rush him, sweeping my arms out in front of me in the dark. Falling to my knees I slide towards him and connect with his spindly legs, grabbing his ankles firmly and jerking forward. He falls backwards, crunching to the floor again, kicking and screaming in my grip. Before he can dig into me with his hooves again, I find the smallest part of his leg and jerk sideways. It snaps near the first joint. The roach scream-hisses and rips free, scrambling for the console in a crackling limp.

I propel myself at him again, meeting with his soft heaving chest. My hands move to his spindly neck as he struggles and gurgles, and I squeeze with every bit of energy I have left.

"You son-of-a-bitch!" I scream into his face. "Even your death was a lie! I should have known you'd stoop this low!" His chest heaves and wheezes under my wrists. "You set me up, you fucker. Never again." With no compunction at all, I feel my way up his face in the dark, avoiding the grinding boulder teeth, and slip my fingers over the bony ridges, burying them in his eye sockets. A hiss of protest shears through me as the slimy orbs squirt over my knuckles, popping from their cavities. Liquid flows from the emptied sockets as I reach down and crack, then rip the rubbery fingers from Vtekdao's remaining hand. His foul stench, his vileness is even more pronounced now, and I swallow a wad of saliva, fighting off nausea. The roach trembles violently in my hands, then goes limp. I release him, listening to him slump to the floor in a juicy crackle.

A peculiar kind of serenity settles over one who commits such an act. It is a feeling I'll carry with me all my days, because I need to remember, need to feel it again when the nightmares begin.

Do you understand why, now? Why you had to stay? You needed to purge the hatred you still have for your father by using it to destroy a whole race. I couldn't let you do that. Vtekdao is our only nemesis. Our argument was with zhan only.

His statements do not shock me. The pain throughout my body drums with every beat of my heart. *The sequence, Cos. Now!*

First, you must deactivate the molychines on Earth. You must.

I type in the keys as he dictates them, then key in the transport sequence again, running to the depression where the colony had stood half a day before. The shadow world fades to cold space. In an instant, my eyes sting with piercing white light as my bare feet touch cold cement.

All around me in an unfamiliar room stands the colony, all dressed in snow clothes. Jason pushes through the crowd and rushes to me, gently wrapping a heavy wool-lined coat around my aching body, kissing me passionately, pressing a furious erection against my all too prominent pubis. "Welcome back to the real world," he says.

* * *

W-we...w-will be l-leaving, now, Rita, Macro think-voices. *W-we w-will always b-be together. Of The One.*

Of The One, I answer, smiling at the big screen in the control room of the Cloud-Buster telescope. Delicate ripples dance on the

LILY SPLANE

screen where the Hagion ship still hangs invisibly overhead.

Even though I know Macro and Doron will be all right, happy in their new roles as teachers to their root species, I still can't keep a tear from running down my cheek.

Slowly, Macro. We can't deal with another earthslip from a hasty departure.

Sure, Doc. N-no problem. Kiss Rita f-for me. Often.

I'll do better than that. I'll marry her.

Looking into his face, I find seriousness where I expect to find jest. "Jason, I can't marry you," I say quickly, not thinking how it might hurt him.

"And why not? After what we've been through together, the trials of marriage will be a walk in the park. We've conquered a dictator, rescued a hybrid species, saved an ancient civilization. You think we can't deal with anything marriage can dish out?"

"Jason, I feel a great deal of affection for you. There is no doubt we will be good friends for a long time, but I can't *marry* you." Then I say with a sly smile, "I belong to the universe, and I am not an adulteress."

He laughs, tugging me around and leading me down two sets of stairs, through the anteroom to the outside.

There is no wind on this first day of Earth's escape with near destruction. The sun attempts to shine through the cloud cover—a salmon ball frozen in suspension at the horizon.

"And to think, none of it was real—real in the sense we understand it," Jason says, his breath ejecting white comets into the frigid air.

I take mental inventory of my injuries. The pain is very real for me. "Not real! What do you mean, not real?"

"That dark matter organized—had substance, form, occupied space—was strictly experiential for us. The ship congealed—'became' as we moved through it, from zero-point energy in the vacuum."

"You mean, it isn't there now?"

"Oh, it's there. Just not in a way we'd normally understand. Don't forget energy and mass are the same thing. My god, I should have seen it before. Someone should have seen it. Einstein tried to explain it using a fudge number he called the cosmological constant. His peers made him apologize for 'the greatest blunder' of his scientific life. But he was right. He knew."

My body catches fire. His ruminations are beyond me. For me, that's the most erotic thing in the universe. "Knew what? I don't understand."

"Dark matter *is* zero-point energy from the vacuum. And we have experienced it first hand."

I smile in the chilled air. "The universe is such a strange place. Everything fits together so nicely. Especially life. Just think: Without the Hagions, the Phaedrans wouldn't be here; without the Phaedrans, humans—intelligent life, the whole universe—would not exist.

Without darkness, there is no light, Cos thought-voices.

Jason smiles in response. "*We* are the means by which the universe experiences itself."

The stark whiteness of everything intensifies the cold and I shiver in Jason's embrace. His warmth is my only contact with humanity in the vast reaches of this beautiful unearthly place, reminding me that in my psyche lay the memories of unearthly experiences.

Even my own body bears the scars of alien battles, harbors the medical technology of surgical molychines, busy about their work in preventing the regrowth of crippling spinal arthritis.

"I knew someday I'd come here," I say.

Jason squeezes me gently, mindful of my injuries. "I always believed I'd return."

A menacing boom roars through the clouds, making the ground rumble in reply.

I know it is not thunder.

* * * THE END * * *

www.ingramcontent.com/pod-product-compliance
Lightning Source LLC
Chambersburg PA
CBHW050031180626
46810CB00002B/676